PUPPIES
ARE FOR
LIFE

Linda Phillips is in her early fifties and lives in Wiltshire. A former civil servant, she started writing six years ago, when her own two children flew the nest. *Puppies are for Life* is her first novel.

PUPPIES ARE FOR LIFE

Linda Phillips

FOURTH ESTATE • *London*

First published in Great Britain in 1998 by
Fourth Estate Limited
6 Salem Road
London W2 4BU

Copyright © 1998 by Linda Phillips

1 3 5 7 9 10 8 6 4 2

The right of Linda Phillips to be identified as the
author of this work has been asserted by her in
accordance with the Copyright, Designs and
Patents Act 1988.

A catalogue record for this book is available from
the British Library.

ISBN 1–85702–605–5

Typeset in Palatino by
Avon Dataset Ltd, Bidford on Avon B50 4JH

Printed and bound in Great Britain by
Clays Ltd, St Ives plc, Bungay, Suffolk

CHAPTER 1

After the first major row of their married lives Susannah and Paul Harding slunk separately to their bedroom and spent the night back to back.

In the morning they glared into their muesli bowls, cast agonised glances at their watches, and dashed out to their respective cars. She didn't remind *him* that he'd left his sandwiches in the fridge. And he didn't tell *her* about the mascara on her cheek.

But he did mutter something about seeing a doctor.

I do not need to see a doctor, she fumed silently as she scrubbed at her face in the office cloakroom later that morning. *All I need is an understanding husband*.

Then, much to the dismay of her friend Molly, who happened to be applying lipstick beside her, she burst into helpless tears.

'I thought everything was hunky dory these days,' said Molly, steering her red-eyed companion away from the row of chipped china sinks and along the concrete corridors of C & G Electronics in the direction of the canteen.

'Everything's fine,' Susannah tried to assure her

1

friend. 'It's just me, being very silly. Oh lord, what's Duffy doing there? I don't want him to see me like this.'

Mr Duffy, their boss, was hovering by the Flexi machine.

'Just checking up on us.' Molly grunted. 'Has to make sure we checked out *before* we powdered our noses.' She pushed through the doors of the canteen where a strong combination of boiled cabbage and chips assailed them, and quickly changed course for the salad bar.

'Things don't sound fine to me,' she said, picking up a tray.

'Well, they are,' Susannah insisted. She eyed limp brown lettuce leaves through the Perspex display unit, opted for grated carrot with watercress, and shuffled listlessly on. 'Buying the cottage was the best thing we ever did. It's been lovely decorating and settling in; wonderful to have no one to please but ourselves. We can watch what we like on the television, go for Sunday lunch at a pub. It's wonderful . . . only –' Her pale face clouded over.

'So what's the problem?' Molly prompted when they had paid up and threaded their way to a vacant table. Dumping her tray among the previous occupant's debris she settled her majestic figure on one of the chairs. 'No, don't tell me,' she said, raising her hands, 'let me guess. Er . . . the authentic gnarled old beams have got woodworm? Or the Aga's set fire to the thatch?'

Susannah flapped a hand at her friend, smiling a

little in spite of herself. 'Of course not! Would the surveyor have passed it if it had woodworm? And you know we didn't go for an Aga.'

'Oh, you know I'm only jealous.' Molly grinned, tossing her head, and then her face grew serious. 'Aren't you going to tell me what's really wrong, Sue?'

Susannah bit her lip. Could she tell Molly about the row? Would it help to get it out of her system? The scene had been replaying itself in her mind all through the night and most of the morning too. It was still so horribly vivid . . .

News at Ten had been blasting out its closing music when she'd wandered into the sitting room.

'There!' she'd said proudly, holding out the product of many hours' hard work. Her back ached; so did her head. It had all been worth it, though – because she could see now that she might actually make a success of this thing, given time. 'Well, Paul, do you like it? What do you honestly think?'

Paul yawned widely and stood up, unfolding himself from one of the chintz armchairs until his hair brushed the low beamed ceiling.

'What is it?' he asked, stretching and yawning again, and looking as though he wished he'd gone to bed hours ago.

'Well, you can see what it is. It's a teapot stand. Made out of mosaic tiles. I've just finished it.'

Paul blinked and looked more closely. 'Ah,' was his only comment.

'Is that all you have to say, *Ah*?' Susannah glared

3

first at her husband, then at the article in her hand. 'What's wrong with it then?'

'Um . . .' He scratched the back of his head and cast her a sideways glance. 'You *do* want an honest opinion?'

'Of course,' she replied, not meaning it, and something inside her went *phut*.

'Well,' he said, frowning, 'it's a bit – I don't know. What's the word – crude, maybe?'

'Crude? *Crude?* What do you mean, crude? This, I'll have you know, happens to be based on a Graeco-Roman design!'

'Is that so?' He stuck his hands in the pockets of his jeans, rocked back on his bony heels and treated her to one of his crooked, most supercilious little smiles. 'And did they actually have teapots in those days, do you think?'

'What? Who? Oh, you – aargh!' She snarled furiously, and flung it at his grinning head. It missed by inches and hit the wall, making a gash in the new magnolia silk-finish before bursting out of its wooden frame.

It was still lying in pieces on the carpet back at home, as shattered as her dreams.

No, Susannah decided, she couldn't tell Molly all that; it was somehow much too private. Ignoring her salad she leaned forward on her elbows.

'Actually,' she said, 'we had a bit of a barney last night, Paul and I.'

'You and –?' Molly's eyes grew round. 'Good heavens.'

'Yes. It's not like us, is it? Well, it wasn't exactly Paul's doing, really; more my fault, I suppose.'

'Never accept the blame for anything,' was Molly's prompt advice. 'Takes two to tango, remember.' She chewed thoughtfully on a bread roll, as though a picture of Paul doing a tango – all knotty knees and elbows – had temporarily taken her attention.

'Mmm . . .' Susannah was considering her friend's advice. She wished she could be assertive like Molly. And wasn't that just her problem? There had been few occasions in her life when she had held out for what she believed to be right. Normally she was placid and easy-going, doing herself down, deferring to others for the sake of a quiet life. She hated scenes; it was only when pushed to extremes that she was inclined to dig in her heels and say all manner of things that she wouldn't have dreamed of saying in the normal course of events.

One such incident came to mind right now – one that she had long since lived to regret, because parents were always right in the long run, weren't they? At eighteen she had defied her father and refused to re-sit a history A-level that she had badly failed. What was the point, she'd wanted to know? Taking after her mother, she was hopelessly non-academic; she would never achieve a pass. She might as well give up any idea she might have had about going to college.

Her father had been livid. A teacher at the boys'

part of the grammar school she attended, and struggling for excellence in all things so that he might one day make it to headmaster, it was hardly surprising that he did not take kindly to his daughter's new-found independence. But Susannah had stuck to her guns. She left school with her one A-level in Art and launched herself into the job market, landing – to her delight – a reasonably well-paid clerical job with a travel agent. Those were the days! Money in her purse. Clothes. The swinging sixties. And she had met Paul.

'Anyway –' Molly brought her back to the matter in hand – 'what was it that triggered off the row? That is, if it's not a state secret?'

'No-o, no, it's more – well – embarrassing.' Susannah hesitated while she picked open a minuscule paper napkin. 'I ended up *throwing* something at him, would you believe?'

Molly's next look was one of amazed admiration. 'Lord, what I would have given to see that! You, losing your cool for once, and the mighty Paul with his dignity in shreds.' She shook her head, chuckling.

'But *I* was the one who lost my dignity,' Susannah was quick to point out. She stared miserably at her plate. 'Paul remained his usual gentlemanly self. He just looked at me kind of stunned and walked away. Oh dear. I'm going to have to apologise this evening, I know I am, and I'm not looking forward to it one bit.'

'Don't do it then.' Molly grunted. 'I wouldn't.' She began to dig into a bowl of cold pasta, bringing fat rubbery twirls to her mouth in bundles of no less than six. 'I'm sure he must have asked for it. Men usually do.' She chewed quickly and gulped down a stream of Coke. 'But really, I can't imagine you two rowing. There can't be anything to row about. You've got everything you could possibly want in life: more money than you really need; a cottage most people would die for. *And* your kids are off your hands. What more do you want, Susannah – jam on your wodge of cake? Cream on top of the jam?'

'But – but material things aren't everything,' Susannah argued timidly. She stared at a distant window. 'Molly . . . haven't you ever wanted – well – personal fulfilment, I suppose is what I'm getting at? And – and recognition? Oh, not just for being a mother and a boring old pay-clerk, but for being good at something that *counts*? For doing something you've always wanted to do and –'

But then she noticed the lines of discontent that had gathered round Molly's lips, and was suffused with guilt. Molly was struggling to bring up three growing children on a pittance in a council house, she hadn't had a holiday in years and there was no man in her life at all. How could she be expected to understand?

'Oh –' Susannah ran a hand through her short hair – 'you don't want to hear about my petty little problems, Molly. Let's talk about something else.'

'They weren't petty little problems just now. I thought the world had come to an end.'

'But things get on top of me at times, just like they do with anyone. Oh, I don't know, Moll. Perhaps all the decorating's taken it out of me.'

'Perhaps you should take another holiday,' Molly couldn't help adding with more than a touch of sarcasm. The Hardings had only recently returned from a Lake District weekend in a plush hotel. They were always bombing off somewhere for 'a little treat'.

Susannah pushed away her plate with an air of resignation. 'OK, fair enough. So I'm a spoilt bitch. I've got a wonderful life and I should be grateful for it. Let's just say I'm going through some sort of mid-life crisis and leave it at that.' She stood up and tucked her bag under her arm. 'Look, I don't know about you, Molly, but I must get back to the office. I need all the Flexi I can muster for that funeral I'm going to tomorrow.'

She began to hurry away, but wasn't quick enough to avoid hearing Molly mutter to herself: 'Mid-life crisis my giddy aunt!' Her tone implied that life for most people was a whole series of crises – real ones. And that Susannah didn't know she was born.

Not a single red light. Not one tail-back of traffic. Susannah's Peugeot hummed homeward that evening on virtual auto-pilot, leaving her too much time to think. Time to think about uncomfortable things like whether Molly was right about not apologising: should she apologise to Paul, or he to her? He *had* practically asked to have something thrown at him, after all.

The gears clashed from fifth to second as she changed down for the Sainsbury's roundabout. Why should she be the one to climb down? Where had his support been when she needed it? All he had done was belittle her efforts. But then, wasn't that what he had always done?

Her thoughts flew back to their early days together, when Simon was just a toddler and Katy no more than an infant. Paul had risen hardly any distance up the civil service ladder by then and they'd had to watch every penny he earned.

Mothers who went out to work had still been the exception rather than the rule in those days, and Susannah had never been exceptional. What could she do anyway? Jobs for the less than well qualified had been scarce and not extravagantly paid. Anything she earned would have been swallowed up in childcare costs.

She had tried to help out at home as best she could. There were the children's clothes she'd run up from market remnants and tried to sell; the teddy bears she'd made with bells in their ears one Christmas; the rag dolls that it had been hard to get Katy to part with; lampshades; envelopes – everything you could think of.

But Paul had pooh-poohed the lot.

'Don't give up the day-job,' he'd once told her,

eyeing her almost-stagnant production line of headless bodies . . .

Susannah's knuckles whitened on the steering wheel. Maybe he'd meant it as a joke, but it had hurt then and it hurt now.

It had hurt last night when he'd joked about the teapot stand, which was why she had suddenly exploded. Resentment had been building up for years. Oh, she'd give anything to wipe that superior expression from his face, have him look up to *her* for a change, with pride and – and respect. But she couldn't see that happening in a million years. Unless she had some success.

Success. In Paul's book that meant making money. So that was the answer, wasn't it? She would have to make some money, even though they were no longer greatly in need of it. It was the only measure of success that Paul and the rest of the world recognised.

And it wasn't all pie in the sky, when you thought about it. Other women had done it before – made fortunes by making things – especially in the eighties. You could hardly pick up a magazine at one time without reading how so-and-so had begun by mixing pots of cream or make-up in their kitchen, or printing lengths of cloth in the spare room, and they'd ended up running empires. So why shouldn't she do something similar? Of course it would mean having to suck up to that nauseating Reg Watts in the craft shop once more, but nothing ventured nothing gained, as the saying goes. Yes, that's what she would do: she would hurry home right now, collect one of the other teapot stands . . . and sell it!

CHAPTER 2

Harvey Webb prised himself from the warm leather interior of his Mercedes, set his face against the wind, and threw the door shut behind him. The discreet 'clunk' of the lock usually pleased him inordinately, only right now it hardly registered; his mind was on other things. How infuriating that he'd forgotten to get Julia something for her birthday in town!

He'd already bought her the main present – a garnet and pearl bracelet – but she liked to have lots of little things to unwrap. And the last thing he wanted right now was to disappoint Julia.

Oh, if only he had thought of it sooner. He could have scooped up armfuls of suitable tat in Bath, but all that talk with Jerry and Adam had put it right out of his head.

Or maybe too much lager had, he conceded, looking up and down the deserted village street, although to tell the truth he always seemed to be forgetting things lately. It wasn't as if he had much to think about either. Bugger all, in fact. But these days it seemed that the more time he had to think –

and the less he had to think *about* – the more forgetful he became. That was what redundancy did for you.

Turning up the collar of his trenchcoat he began to pick his way across the sodden grass verge in search of somewhere that might sell gifts, but all he could see ahead of him was a knitting wool shop with ugly yellow film stuck over its window and a bakery that had sold its last crumb. Unless . . . yes, he was sure he remembered correctly: across the green there was a craft shop of sorts. He'd spotted it the day he and Julia had moved into the Old Dairy and she'd sent him out to find milk.

And was that the biggest mistake they'd ever made, he wondered for the hundredth time as he pushed on the plate-glass door of Heyford Handy Crafts: moving out to a village, when all they'd ever known was the town?

'It's so, so pretty here,' Julia had said when she'd first set eyes on the place, dancing up and down the narrow streets in unsuitably high heels, and he couldn't help but admit that it was. Then. Hard to resist in mid-summer was the chocolate-box setting of Upper Heyford with its big round duck pond, its fourteenth-century church, its thatched public house and matching cottages – all grouped pleasingly round the obligatory patch of green.

But it wasn't so pretty now. Harvey shivered. No, not in November. Gone were all the flowers that had spilled freely from countless basket arrangements; gone were the tables outside the Golden

Fleece. The trees were naked, the grass clogged with leaves. It looked downright dismal under heavy grey skies, and he sighed, longing for spring to come round, as he elbowed his way into the shop.

Reg Watts leaned forward on his heavy arms and leered at Susannah on the other side of the counter.

'Well, Mrs Harding,' he said above the jangle of the old-fashioned bell, 'what have you brought me this time? Dried flowers? Corn dollies? Or something I can actually sell?'

'You did manage to sell some of my flower arrangements, Reg,' Susannah replied with icy politeness. She glanced in the newcomer's direction, annoyed at the untimely intrusion. This was the last thing she wanted: an audience to witness her battle with Reg Watts.

The man, she noticed, had strolled to the far corner of the shop and was pretending to examine china mugs. But somehow she just *knew* he was listening to every word.

'Yes, I know I sold a *few* of your things,' Reg moaned, taking a mangled handkerchief from his pocket and arranging it in a pad. Judging by his nasal twang he had a very bad cold indeed. 'But everyone's doing dried flowers these days,' he went on, elaborately wiping his nose. 'They're all going to classes to find out how it's done. The only thing they come in here for is to pick up ideas. No, there isn't much call in these parts . . . Have you tried hawking them round the shops in Bath?'

The stranger had picked up a glass paperweight and was holding it up to the light. Or was he using it as an excuse, and really studying Susannah?

'Coals to Newcastle,' she snapped. 'Every other shop in Bath seems to be stacked to the eaves with dried flower arrangements. But I didn't come to talk about those, Reg. Take a look at this.'

Under Reg's cynical gaze she pulled back layers of tissue from the parcel she had placed on his counter. 'Now, you don't have anything like *this* in your shop, do you?'

'Hmm.' Reg reached out reluctantly to grasp the item with both hands. He tipped his head backwards to view it from under his glasses, then ducked his head forward again to peer at it over the top. Susannah wondered why he bothered to wear the things when they so obviously didn't help.

'No,' was the ultimate verdict. 'No, I don't stock anything like this. And do you know why?' Reg beamed at his victim triumphantly. 'Because there isn't any call for the likes of this either.'

Susannah gritted her teeth. 'But how do you know there isn't going to be a demand for something,' she persisted, 'if you never actually display it?'

She glanced round the shop, avoiding the stranger's eye. It was crammed with useless junk. In all honesty there was no room for more, and her teapot stand would be lost among the chaos. The world was full of hopeful artists, potters, and makers of useless knick-knacks. What chance did she stand? Then she saw the stranger's hand reach out towards a rag doll.

'Display it?' Reg was muttering. 'Well, I don't know about that. The thing is –' He twirled the stand in one hand. 'Well, what I mean to say is . . . what exactly is it?'

'It's a teapot stand, of course! Or any kind of pot stand for that matter. *Anyone* can see that.'

Susannah whipped round in amazement; Reg's only other customer had come up behind her and stolen her very words. She found the man smiling disarmingly above her head – and rewarded him with a hostile stare. Oh, how she already hated him for his suave, easy-going confidence. Clearly nobody had ever made *him* feel small, insignificant, and utterly, utterly useless. It was going to take more than a frozen expression from her to knock him off his perch.

'Harvey Webb,' he told her, nodding at her agreeably and reaching across to pick up the stand for a closer look. He turned it over in his hands while Susannah cringed. She now wanted nothing more than to throw the thing in the bin, forget the whole project, give up the idea of doing Something and being Someone. Criticism from Paul was bad enough; criticism from the rest of the world was unbearable.

'This is really rather nice,' Harvey murmured eventually, his thumbs sweeping the mosaic surface in obvious appreciation. In silence he studied the frame. 'You made the whole thing yourself?' he asked, slanting Susannah a glance.

'Yes!' she hissed back, taking them all by surprise, and she snatched the piece from his hand. There was one thing worse than criticism, she decided, and that was male condescension. Arrogant sod. At least Paul had been honest. 'Yes,' she went on, lisping childishly, 'I made it all by my little self. Now isn't that just amazing? And Daddy didn't help me at all.'

The two men gawped at her as she thrust the stand back in a carrier bag.

'Now,' she said, her voice normal again as she dusted off her hands, 'if you'll both excuse me, gentlemen, I'll take up no more of your time. I'll just run along home and amuse myself some more.'

She pulled open the door, stumbled over the threshold, and let the door clang closed behind her. Reg and Harvey were left still gaping, their eyebrows raised in bewilderment at the swinging 'Closed' sign.

Outside on the pavement Susannah ducked her head into the wind and headed blindly down the street, feeling hot-cheeked, light-headed and unreal. She wiped her forehead with a shaking hand. What had got into her lately? She had never behaved like that before in her entire life. Well, not often. She could take a lot of 'aggro', but sometimes something would snap and she would go hurtling over the edge. She wished she hadn't made an exhibition of herself just then, though.

'Hey!' a voice said behind her, 'you forgot to pick this up.'

She stopped. Harvey what's-his-name hadn't actually followed her, had he? Not after the things she'd said? But he had. And he was holding out her black leather handbag with SWH stamped on the flap in gold. She had forgotten she had put it on the counter.

'Thank you,' she murmured, taking it sheepishly from his outstretched hand, and expecting him to go straight back to the shop. But he didn't. Somehow he had managed to position himself ahead of her so that he was standing in her path, and she realised for the first time how stomach-churningly good-looking he was, in a Richard Gere-ish kind of way. He stood looking directly at her, his hands now stuffed into the pockets of his trenchcoat for warmth, an infectious smile twitching at the corners of his lips.

Time kicked its heels while she eyed him back belligerently, but eventually she felt that one of them had to say something, so nodding at the doll he carried tucked under his arm with its felt feet sticking out, she said, 'I hope Reg doesn't take you for a shoplifter. Hadn't you better go back?'

'What?' He looked vaguely at the shop, then at the upturned doll. 'Oh, it's all right, don't worry. I chucked a plastic card at him on my way out. I'll go back and settle up properly when we've had our cup of tea.'

'Our –?' She looked at the hand on her arm – a moderately large hand with broad, straight fingers.

'Well, *I* could certainly do with one.' His eyes roved over her face. 'And I rather think you could too.'

There was no question of refusing; he didn't give her a chance. He hustled her down a cul-de-sac before she could even begin to think what was happening. And in no time at all they were sitting opposite each other in the Copper Kettle with the doll propped against a sugar bowl as chaperone.

'Not as comfortable as I'd hoped,' he remarked, grimacing as he tried to settle himself on his chair. 'One of those places that looks better from the out-side than it actually is, I'm afraid. I haven't sat on one of these horrible things since my Sunday school days.'

As he bent to examine the cane seat she saw that his hair grew thick and strong down the back of his head and was hardly streaked with grey at all. Paul's was entirely grey and it didn't grow right from the forehead like it used to either. There ought to be a way, she mused silently, of telling a man's age by the amount his hair had receded. Like the rings on the trunk of a tree. A decade per half-inch perhaps? But that wouldn't work; it would make this man young enough to be her son, which he was patently far from being.

'Oh dear,' he said, coming up a little flushed, 'I suppose that dates me horribly, doesn't it, talking about cane seats in Sunday schools?' It was as if he'd read her mind. 'In this day and age it's probably pre-formed plastic, if they have them at all. I mean, I don't know . . . do kids still go to Sunday school these days?'

Susannah hesitated. She didn't want to sit drinking tea with a perfect stranger, making polite conversation about chairs and Sunday schools, of all things. And he hadn't even asked her if she'd wanted to come; just assumed she'd be delighted to have his company. She firmed her lips and stuck her jaw out a little, making up her mind to answer him only in monosyllables. But he was a difficult sort of person to dislike and she relented almost immediately.

'Mine went to Sunday school for a while –' she told him, smiling faintly in spite of herself – 'until they learned to vote with their feet, that is. But – that's going back quite a few years now. I don't know what goes on these days either. Anyway, if it's any comfort to you, I remember having chairs like this at Sunday school too. So there; that dates me as well.'

And don't you dare come out with any pat little 'Oh, surely you're not that old' nonsense, she silently warned him. But he didn't and she felt disappointed. Nor did he pick up on the mention of children, from which she deduced that he didn't have any of his own or he would have leaped at the chance to talk about them, which was a shame because he looked as if he would have made a nice dad.

But now he seemed to be gazing about him and wondering what to say next. No doubt he was already regretting having brought her here and couldn't wait to get away again.

'Ugly little trollop, isn't she?' he came out with in the end, the laughter lines round his mouth deepening good-humouredly. 'Our friend here, I mean –' he inclined his head in the direction of the doll and added in a stage whisper – 'not the waitress.'

Susannah glanced at the elderly waitress shuffling from table to table and allowed herself another small smile, then she smoothed creases from the doll's dress with hands that she didn't know what to do with. She suddenly felt warmer than she had all day. This man was turning out to be quite a charmer. But – she pulled herself up sharply – didn't she know better by now than to put trust in charming men?

'Why did you choose this doll,' she wondered out loud, 'if you really think she's awful?'

'Well –' he watched Susannah's deft fingers tweak the doll's clothes into better shape – 'there was another one sitting beside her, dressed in a creamy lacy underthing and a coat of green – um –'

'Velvet.'

'Is that what it was? Yes, I suppose so. Well, I'd have preferred that one if it had been up to me. Much more tasteful, I thought. But I knew Julia wouldn't agree with me. She never does. She's more a frills and ribbons type, you see.'

'Uh-huh. Julia being your . . . daughter?'

'Wife.'

They leaned back to accommodate the arrival of the tea things.

'So,' Susannah said lightly, happy to leave the stirring and pouring to him since the tea had been his idea and he seemed to want to take charge, 'you don't think much of Lucy-Ann, I take it?'

'Lucy-Ann?' Glancing up from his teabag dunking his eyes followed Susannah's back to the doll. 'Oh lord. You don't mean to tell me . . . not more of your handiwork, surely?'

'I made them both, Mr – er –'

'Webb,' he had to remind her, 'Harvey Webb.'

'– and I made them different to appeal to all tastes. Not that it made a scrap of difference,' she added bitterly.

'Sorry?' He looked puzzled.

She drew a long breath, wishing she'd not made the comment. Now she would have to explain. 'They've travelled the length and breadth of the country with me over the years, those dolls, moving from shop to shop on sale or return. Just about anywhere my husband's work has taken us, they've gone too. Yes –' she sighed, putting down her cup – 'Paul's spectacular promotions have taken us all around the country – abroad as well on two occasions – while my sad little failures have trailed along behind us.' She forced a grin. 'Congratulations, Mr Webb –'

'Harvey.'

'– *you* are the first mug ever to actually buy one.' And, she thought, surprised at herself, you're the first person I've ever told this to.

He appraised her gravely – as gravely as a face like his would allow. 'I think,' he said after a pause, 'I'm beginning to see why you were a bit touchy back there. But they're beautifully made, those dolls. And so is the Roman teapot stand. I meant what I said about that.'

Inadvertently – or not, she couldn't be sure – he had covered one of her hands with his as he spoke, and holding her eyes with his own he went on, 'I think, Mrs Harding, you're one hell of a talented lady. And don't let anyone tell you you're not.'

She gazed back at him with obvious pity. Men were so utterly transparent it was unbelievable. Did he really think she was going to fall for this stupid malarkey? Any minute now he would conjure up a huge shipping order that he was sure he'd be able to get for her: a thousand teapot stands, he would reckon, for someone he just happened to know in the business. In return, of course, for . . . well, really, he must be desperate, the dirty old so-and-so!

Frustration that had only been lightly tamped down since its last eruption swept her to the edge again. She slid her hand from beneath his, grabbed hold of her bag and stood up.

'And you, Mr Webb,' she replied as coolly as her wavering voice would allow, 'are one hell of a patronising bastard.'

23

CHAPTER 3

The flowers shivered in their cellophane as Paul walked past. He stopped and looked down at them, arrested by a flash of remorse. He had only come to the service station for petrol and perhaps the evening paper, but should he buy flowers for Sue?

''Scuse me,' a young woman in a green coat rasped in his ear as she attempted to dance her way around him. She might as well have bawled, 'Get out of the flaming way!', her tone was so full of irritation.

Paul stood his ground for a moment, blocking the woman's path and treating her to a hostile stare before politely holding open the door for her. Women these days! What on earth was the matter with them? Bolshie. Aggressive. They'd stab you in the back as soon as look at you.

And what was the matter with Sue? What did she think she was playing at? She'd damn nearly killed him last night. If that mosaic thingy had caught him on the head, goodness knows what might have happened. He was certainly seeing a side of her just lately that he'd never seen before, and he didn't like it one bit.

When had things begun to change? When Katy went to live in London, he supposed. But at first it had all seemed for the better. Susannah didn't appear to be one of those women who pined over an empty nest – unless she was doing her best to hide it. But he didn't think that was the case. And they had both thought it a good idea to go for the cottage too; so it couldn't be that.

No, everything had been great to begin with. If retirement was going to be like this, he'd thought, then let them chuck him out of his job tomorrow! One of these pushy power-hungry young women could bash their brains out in his place, and the best of British luck to her.

Next thing he knew, Susannah had wanted to set up a work room for herself. Fair enough, he'd said, a hobby would be nice for her. He had helped her organise the room and not batted an eyelid at the cost of stocking it with materials. Meanness had never been one of his failings, and he'd quite enjoyed the project. But what he hadn't bargained for was the amount of time she ended up spending in the room when it was finished.

At first it had been the odd hour or so. Then he would find her, in the middle of TV programmes, stealing out of the room for what he thought was going to be a trip to the fridge for an apple, or a brief visit to the loo, and not coming back for hours. He even woke up a couple of times in the night to find the bed stone cold beside him.

And then she started making excuses for things like not going out for a walk with him, or to the pub for a drink. She would always have 'something to do in her work room'.

Gradually, day by day, he was losing her.

'Oh, er, number four,' Paul muttered to the forecourt attendant. Taken abruptly from his wool-gathering he began ferreting for his wallet while a queue built up behind him. At last, anxious to be out of the place and alone again with his thoughts, he threw down two twenty-pound notes, though by the time the assistant had checked the notes for forgery and slowly counted out a handful of small silver change he realised it would have been quicker to use his credit card.

But at last he was free to go – except that some-one was blocking his way.

''Scuse *me.*'

Paul found himself glaring into angry blue eyes again. The woman in the green coat, having helped herself to a free read of one of the magazines on display, had dropped it back on the shelf and made for the exit at precisely the same moment that Paul reached it.

He sighed, pulled the door open and let her pass through ahead of him.

'Women!' he snarled. Not only had he received no thanks whatever for his chivalry, he had been rewarded with a two-finger sign.

The flowers were still shivering in their cellophane as he stomped past them. But Paul had made up his mind. Susannah would not be getting a bunch. She simply didn't deserve it.

Black. Something black. It had to be something black.

Susannah yanked the hangers along the rail, setting her teeth on edge. Black suited her mood just fine. What a shambles she'd made of things that afternoon! If she'd kept a cool head she might at least have had the satisfaction of selling one of her dolls: cause for celebration indeed. Even Paul would have been forced to concede that. As it was, Harvey Webb, if he had any sense, would probably have marched Lucy-Ann straight back to her shelf in the shop, demanding the return of his credit card. He might have been genuine, too. He might have been a useful contact. He might even have bought her teapot stand, had she not flown off the handle.

But now she had really burned her boats. She would never be able to face Reg again, and the likelihood of finding other suitable outlets was pretty remote. Of course there were plenty of likely shops in the area, but she knew from experience that very few would show any interest in her work; and it would take her for ever to get round to them all. She simply didn't have time. She would try as soon as she had a spare moment, of course – but her most immediate priority had to be her Uncle Bert's funeral.

Her father had phoned her late one evening with news of the death, his voice revealing shock, for all its bluster, because his brother had been two years his junior.

'Bert's next-door neighbour,' Frank May had thundered down the line, 'a Mrs Wardle – ever met her? Well, she thought you might like to go to the funeral. Apparently you always sent Bert a card at Christmas. Can't think why,' he'd added with a sniff of contempt, because he'd never had much regard for Bert himself.

'He taught me to play Canasta,' Susannah had tried to explain, remembering how her uncle had sat opposite her at his little card table for hours at a time, sucking placidly on his pipe while the more boisterous members of the family cavorted around them. That was how she had always thought of him, if she'd thought of him at all: as something of a loner; a bit of an odd-ball whom nobody under-stood, except maybe herself. Perhaps she took after him, she mused, lifting a black satin party dress from the wardrobe rail.

Of course, black satin was entirely unsuitable for a funeral, even supposing she could still get into the dress, which was doubtful, but it had long been one of her favourites and she couldn't help holding it against herself, recalling happier days. Days when she had been content with her lot and this madness about wanting fulfilment hadn't seized her. What had happened to change things? Was Paul right? Should she really see a doctor?

She turned her head from the mirror to listen to a sound outside. As if conjured up by her thoughts, Paul's car had squeaked to a halt on the drive. And that was him coming into the cottage. Now he'd stopped on his way through the kitchen – no doubt to look at the day's mail – and silence fell once more.

Susannah pretended absorption in her task, dreading the coming confrontation. Another battle, she thought wearily, because she no longer felt inclined to apologise. And the likelihood of Paul suddenly seeing the light and showing under-standing towards her was very remote indeed.

Eventually – after what seemed like decades – Paul creaked up the steep little staircase to their room in search of her. She didn't have to look round to know that he had come into the room and was standing at the foot of the bed, his jaw tense and truculent as he slowly pulled off his tie.

But suddenly he was behind her, much closer than she had imagined, his hand coming up to knead the back of her neck.

'Susie,' he sighed into her hair, 'I'd forgotten all about your old Uncle Bert. And I'm sorry. No wonder you've been so uptight. It must have been a bit much, coming on top of the kids flying the nest and us selling up the old family home.' He turned her round to face him, his hand still mas-saging imagined knots at the top of her spine. 'There've been too many changes in a short space of time,' he told her, smiling down at her indulgently. 'I think perhaps I should have been surprised if you *hadn't* blown your top. Don't you?'

She swallowed her amazement and gazed back at him; he had actually managed to come up with a solution that let them both off the hook without either of them having to admit they were in the wrong.

Did he really believe his own reasoning, though? His expression revealed nothing, it seldom did, but she thought not. The problem was still obvious to them both, and they really ought to discuss it. But when it came to relationships it was typical of Paul to sweep difficult issues under the carpet.

He couldn't help being that way: he had been brought up by a single aunt, his parents having been killed in a London air-raid towards the end of the war, and he had had only narrow experience of relationships. His views on parenthood and families were consequently based on ideals, and he couldn't bring himself to admit that they might fall short in any way.

'Paul, I –' she began, but he put a finger to her lips.

'Don't let's waste any more time, analysing,' he said, turning away. 'It's all over. Finished. Forget it.'

'OK.' She caved in. She hadn't the energy to pursue the matter right then.

'Well, what do you think of this for the funeral?' she asked, snatching at a hanger and swinging a pleated skirt around on it. 'I've a jacket that matches, somewhere.'

'It's fine. Perfect. I like it.' The relief in his voice was obvious: they were back on an even keel. He flashed her his most wicked grin, which prompted her to throw the garment aside in disgust.

'It looks like my old school uniform,' she said.

'I know; I remember it from your old photographs.' He squeezed her bottom. 'Perhaps that's why I like it.'

'Cradle-snatcher pervert,' she murmured, knowing he was nothing of the sort. She nestled against his chest. She hated not being friends as much as he did and wondered again why she had rocked the marital boat. Held tight in the circle of his arms, the temptation to forget her crazy ideas was immense; life would be so much easier if she could do that. Could she?

Paul unbuttoned his shirt and drew her closely against him so that she could feel his erection against her navel. For a moment she tensed and almost prevented him from taking things any further, but then she remembered that they could make love when and wherever they fancied without fear of interruption, or the possible embarrassment of their offspring. It had taken them a while to adjust to this new-found freedom, but when they had got used to the idea they had made love joyfully and with abandon in just about every room in the house.

'Would you like me to come with you tomorrow?' Paul asked, unclipping the fastening on her bra. 'Drive us both up to London?'

'To the funeral?' Her head jerked up, leaving the tickly nest of chest hair and the comforting smell of his skin. For Paul to make such an offer was a penance indeed. 'But why? You hardly even knew my uncle.'

'Neither did you,' he tossed back at her, then he quickly compressed his lips. But he was too late; he'd given the game away. Using Uncle Bert as an excuse for his wife's odd behaviour didn't wash.

Desire flew out of the window.

'You'll hate the funeral, you know you will,' she said, pulling away from his arms. 'It's not your kind of thing. Thanks all the same, Paul, but I'll go on my own as planned.'

CHAPTER 4

Julia crawled across the mattress to her own side of the bed, her buttocks wobbling invitingly. Leaning out to retrieve her nightdress, she was careful to take her time; Harvey would get a good long – and hopefully stimulating – view. But it was no good and they both knew it, although there was nothing he would have liked more than to oblige her.

'I'm sorry.' He sighed, staring helplessly. Oh to feel normal again!

'It's OK,' she said, and collapsed into the pillows.

'But it's your birthday . . .'

'I said it's OK. It can't be helped. Forget it.'

'But we always do something special on our birthdays.'

'Well, we'll have to do something else that's special, that's all.'

'Oh, I'm getting o-o-old,' he said, dragging the last word out into a long self-pitying moan. 'Correction, I *am* old.'

'You're only as old as you feel, Harvey.'

'Right now I feel a hundred.'

Julia knelt up beside him and began pulling the

sparse folds of shiny blue satin over her shaggy, highlighted hair. She wriggled, shaking the bed as she eased the garment over her breasts. Harvey looked on morosely as he watched them bounce, rubber-like, back into place. Nothing.

'Look,' she said, sliding under the quilt, 'this is only a temporary thing. It's like – well – missing periods, you know? You get a shock in your life, a bit of bad news, and the next thing you know your body's all up the creek. Women are used to this sort of thing. Well, *I* am anyway; you know what my cycle's like.'

Harvey did know. He had had to learn to live with it.

'It's this being pensioned off that's done it,' Julia went on. 'But we'll get over it soon. You'll see.'

'Made redundant,' he corrected through clench-ed teeth. 'Don't make it sound even worse than it already is. And it's nothing whatever like missed bloody periods! For heaven's sake, girl –' he thumped the mattress with his fists – 'don't you hear what I'm telling you? I'm old. I'm old! They were right, weren't they? They were right all along.'

'Who were? What?' Julia lay back on one elbow and considered getting up. It was probably too early for her yoga class, but anything was better than lying here listening to Harvey in one of his moods. She glanced at the clock on the bedside table, spotted a stack of cotton wool pads and a bottle of nail varnish remover among the debris, and began to take off 'Burnished Bronze'.

'Everybody was right,' Harvey went on. 'All those kind, well-meaning souls who told us we would regret it.'

'Regret –?' The word had caught Julia's attention.

'I mean,' Harvey amended hastily, wrinkling his nose as the acetone hit him, '*you* must be regretting it. Marrying me. You've still got your life ahead of you. And all those things they said about finding it difficult with such a big age gap between us are beginning to make sense. There you are, in the prime of your life. And here am I –' he looked down at the mound of his body under the covers – 'a clapped-out husk.'

Julia regarded her husband gravely for a second. Until recently he had not been so – so – negative. Yes, that was the word to describe him these days. She had never seen him like this in all the time she had known him. On the contrary, he had always been so positive, so alive, and vital, and – what did they call it? – motivated. The way she liked him to be. She scarcely fancied him like this. Actually she'd gone off sex a bit herself just lately, so perhaps that had something to do with it . . .

But these thoughts disturbed her a little so she dismissed them.

'Oh, you're being silly, Harvey,' she scolded. 'Just because you aren't in the mood for once doesn't mean anything at all. Talk about making mountains out of molehills!'

Harvey kept his next thoughts to himself. He couldn't tell Julia that this morning's fiasco was the culmination of days of going off it. There had been times when he had had to exercise his imagination even more vigorously than his body, just to see him through. Up until now it had worked well enough. But this time it hadn't worked at all.

'I tell you,' she said, throwing back the quilt to deal with her toes, 'you weren't like this when you were working. You were full of energy all the time, not lying around moaning and feeling sorry for yourself.'

She's right, he thought, pulling the bedding back to cover the parts of him that offended right now. And that was a first, too. When did Julia last let drop a pearl of wisdom from her full, pouting lips? Must have been some time before he met her.

Annoyed with himself for his lack of charity – especially as it was her birthday – he put out his hand. 'Sorry,' he said, stroking the warm roundness of her left arm and finding that the feel of it under his finger-tips only brought home to him more vividly her enviable youth. 'I don't mean to be a pain. I'll take you to Partridges for dinner tonight. OK?'

'Lovely,' she said, bending to kiss him and letting her breasts swing forward near his face. Perhaps there's still a chance, she thought, flicking her tongue out to find his. But she quickly pulled away from him and left the bed; she could see by his eyes that he had slipped further from her than ever.

Frankly relieved that she'd gone, Harvey watched her snatch underwear from an open drawer and waggle her way around the bedroom in search of other bits of clothing. Then she disappeared into the bathroom and turned the shower on full gush. Never mind that she switched off *The Time, The Place* en route without asking him whether he wanted to watch it or not; he did, as it happened. And never mind that she activated a country and western cassette in the hi-fi system without asking him whether he wanted that either. He didn't. At least she had gone.

Without too much effort he managed to reach the remote control where she had tossed it, and retrieved the programme; it would at least stop him thinking. But as luck would have it what did he find? A group of po-faced people banging on about how they had had to face redundancy.

'Terrific,' he muttered, and was about to zap it to kingdom come when one of the speakers caught his attention. In spite of himself he was soon straining to cut out Julia's sing-along with Tammy Wynette in the shower, and to concentrate on the tragedies of life.

Well, what should he do with the rest of his own, he wondered as the presenter signed off rapidly and the closing music began to clash with the Tammy/Julia duet. Open a restaurant with his redundancy money like that twit on the box? At least, having loaned thousands in the past for similar ventures, he knew all the pitfalls one had to avoid. That chap he'd just been watching hadn't a clue: he was obviously grossly under-funded and going to come a cropper.

How about back-packing round the world? Even though he had all but forgotten how to put one foot in front of the other. No, better to sell the car – perish the thought – and sail round. He stared at the ceiling. He really must do *something*.

A cloud of 'Obsession' announced Julia's return to the bedroom and unaccustomed jealousy licked through him. Julia had always found plenty to keep her occupied. Since leaving the bank where she had worked as his secretary she had, at various stages, taken up 'hairdressing in the home', sold underwear on the party plan, and taught aerobics, aromatherapy, yoga and more recently, reflexology. She was qualified in none of these things, it had to be said, and would have looked blank if anyone had suggested she ought to be. But she always got by, and no doubt she always would.

Harvey had often wondered whether the typing certificates that had got her the bank job were genuine.

In the early days, when she had first tripped into his office each morning trailing a blanket of power-ful perfume and oozing sex, he had hardly cared whether she could type or not. She had pepped up his life no end at a time when it had begun to go stale because all his friends seemed suddenly to be married and unavailable.

He found her fascinating and different, like no

other woman he knew. The fact that her lip would curl in a snarl if he dared to ask her to type something, or that his letters came back as mis-spelt missives set crookedly on the page, seemed somehow irrelevant. She would bat her long lashes at him, rendering futile any complaint, and make him feel horribly wrong for daring to be critical. He felt the need to protect her; to do things for her, when she was supposed to be looking after him! Before long he was in love and wondering how it had happened.

Re-discovering Lucy-Ann lying on the carpet Julia picked her up and sat her on the shelf where a crowd of other dolls and stuffed animals jostled for space.

'She's lovely, isn't she?' she said, standing back with her head on one side. She smiled at Harvey where he lay spread out on the bed with his arms behind his head, and blew him another thank you kiss.

But Harvey knew it was the bracelet he had tucked inside the doll's bloomers that had gone down best. It sparkled on Julia's wrist as she dressed herself in a red stretchy body-suit and tight black jeans. He sighed. How much longer would she stay with him? Until his money ran out? He'd never felt absolutely sure of her; now he was even less certain. And she was so damned difficult to talk to. She kept her thoughts to herself – presumably in the belief that she had nothing worthy to say to a man of his superior intelligence. So he'd given up asking for her opinion, and if he were suddenly to defer to her after all these years he felt he would take a dive in her estimation.

He opened his eyes slowly. Julia had pulled on cream high-heeled boots and a matching leather jacket with fur lining. Her lips were an identical red to the body-suit, and her skin sported a false tan. Leaning towards him for a final kiss she gazed into his worried face.

'You know, Harvey,' she said in her earnest, oddly motherly way, 'you really should find yourself something to do.'

The garnet and pearl bracelet clashed against the steering wheel as Julia started the engine. She clucked her tongue and secured the clasp. Really, she thought, Harvey should not have spent so much money. He might not get another job. He kept saying he would, but it wasn't going to be that easy. She was more aware of the situation than he gave her credit for.

Huh! When did he give her credit for anything? He wouldn't even discuss things with her – kept his own counsel about anything important on the assumption that she wasn't clever enough to understand.

And she didn't need to be given things like this, either, beautiful though they were. But he went on doing it year after year as if this was the only way he could hang on to her. It was annoying and some-how degrading; as if she could be bought. She loved him for himself, but he never seemed to believe it.

Her eyes fell on the pile of books in the passenger foot-well. He wouldn't believe her capable of doing GCSEs either. Actually she could hardly believe it herself. Her tutor was constantly having to assure her that she really had it in her. Fancy! Dumb old Julia doing exams! Harvey would laugh his socks off if he knew.

But he wouldn't know... yet. Wait until she passed and had certificates to prove it. Then he would have to laugh on the other side of his face.

She had thought the game was up when he was made redundant. How could she continue to keep her studying secret? But the past few weeks had shown how easy it was to pull the wool over his eyes, even with him being at home all day. He had simply assumed that she was out of the house so much because she had taken on more hairdressing; more yoga classes. He hadn't objected at all. Presumably he felt he could hardly do that since what she earned would be their only income for a while.

Until recently she had wrestled with her assignments at home or in the college library, but of course home was out of the question now, and she had taken to going to the public library because it was eight miles nearer than the college and there were so many things to fit in to her day. This was undoubtedly risky but it couldn't be helped. She just had to keep her fingers crossed that Harvey didn't walk in one day and find her there. She would die if that were to happen. She would. She would die.

CHAPTER 5

'Another corned beef sandwich?'

Uncle Bert's elderly next-door neighbour advanced across the carpet with a mountainous plate in her hands. 'Plenty more in the fridge, Mr May. Another three plates at least.' Mrs Wardle looked sadly about her. 'I didn't know how many people to make them for, you see.'

Frank May, latterly headmaster of the Harold Vincent Comprehensive School, Middlesex, waved away the plate in a lordly manner. He also declined a chocolate finger and a lemon-flavoured cup-cake.

'I suppose Bert didn't keep any beer?' he asked, getting up on a sudden hope. Tall, solidly built, and with a shiny pink dome of a head, he dominated the dingy front room of his brother's terraced house. And, looking at him, it was difficult for Susannah to believe that her father lived permanently in the Dordogne. No amount of time in the sun seemed to turn his English ruddiness to a decent tan.

'Beer?' Mrs Wardle's hat quivered as she looked round at her laden trays. She had made quantities of tea in large brown earthenware pots. 'Well, I can't say I would know about beer,' she said stiffly, 'but I'll go and have a look in the scullery.'

Susannah felt obliged to help herself to another sandwich since there were so many about to go to waste, but her stomach protested after the first bite. She doubted whether she could manage to force down any more of the margarined monstrosities.

'Family all right?' Frank asked. They hadn't had much chance to talk at the funeral.

'Oh, we're all very well, I'm glad to say.' Susannah put down a thick crust. 'Katy's having a whale of a time in a flat with some friends – not far from here, as a matter of fact. I might look in on her later if I have time.

'And Simon's still doing well at the estate agent's in Bristol. He and Natalie are getting on fine, though of course we'd still love them to get married. Justin is adorable – it's hard to believe he's ten months old already. As for Paul – well, he was going to come with me today but he found he had a meeting . . .'

Her voice trailed away and she looked down at her uncomfortably high black shoes. She didn't like having to tell a white lie about Paul, and now she was going to have to ask after her wretched stepmother.

'And Jan?' she forced out. 'She decided not to come with you?'

'She's – er – fine, thank you. Fine. But Bert was nothing to her, really – she only met him once or twice – so there didn't seem much point in her coming all this way.'

'You surprise me. It's not like Jan to miss an opportunity to go round the London stores.'

'Oh, how lovely to live abroad!' Mrs Wardle broke in. She had come back into the room empty-handed, having apparently forgotten why she'd left it. 'I think it's a wonderful idea. All that sea, sun and fresh air.'

'We're miles from the sea,' Frank said abruptly, and he turned to look round the room in a dismissive manner that made Susannah feel even more awkward than she had before.

Mrs Wardle, it was true, was not the kind of woman her father would suffer gladly. She was niceness personified: one of those people who smile constantly and too closely into your face and can't do enough to please you. No, definitely not his type; but that didn't excuse his behaviour.

'Er –' Susannah thought quickly – 'it was really very good of you to organise the funeral and everything, Mrs Wardle. I hope it wasn't too much trouble.'

'Only too happy to do it, my dear. Not that there was much to be done. Bert had arranged everything years ago with the Co-op, you see. So very thoughtful of him, wasn't it? But that was his way. Just like the vicar said.'

'Yes . . .' Susannah frowned as she recalled the brief eulogy. Words had streamed easily enough from the vicar's lips, but what they had boiled down to was that Bert had been a nobody who had made no mark on the world – a fact that Susannah found profoundly disturbing in her current frame of mind. She had yet to make a mark of her own.

Frank coughed noisily, anxious to draw things to a close.

'Well –' he barked a laugh with no trace of humour in it – 'can't hang around here all day eating and drinking, can we? We – er – ahem – ought to get down to business.'

Susannah and Mrs Wardle looked blank.

'The will, of course, the will,' he was finally compelled to explain. 'Now I know the poor old s— I mean poor old Bert's only just been seen on his way, so to speak, but none of us has the time for life's little niceties, do we? I've got a flight to catch, and Susannah's got a train, so . . . well, where have you put it, Mrs Wardle?'

'Put what?' The woman flushed to find attention suddenly upon her.

'The will.' Frank visibly seethed. 'My brother Albert's will. He must have left one with you.'

But no amount of prompting could make Mrs Wardle recall a will. Or a solicitor. Or anything relevant. So Frank allocated them each a room and told them they must search it. Thoroughly.

'Da-ad! You can't!' Susannah hissed, tugging at his sleeve.

'What? Why not? What else d'you expect me to do?'

She jerked her head in the direction of Mrs

Wardle. 'It can wait, I'm sure,' she declared loudly, and her father went off in a huff. She didn't know what on earth he was doing upstairs; all she knew was that she was left to clear up the tea things.

Eventually she went to watch him turning out boxes and tipping drawers on to her uncle's bed.

Bert had apparently collected silver paper and brown paper bags; bus tickets and bottle tops; string, candles and match books; books on fishing and fell-walking, and birds, and railways and trees.

'Dad, this is really awful of you . . .'

Frank caught her expression and had the decency to show a little shame – if a slight deepening of his skin could be attributed to that emotion.

'I don't like having to do this, Susie, any more than you like standing there watching me. But this house is going to have to be disposed of, and the sooner I find the will the better. Someone must be named as executor. And it can't be left through the winter with pipes freezing up and everything. There'll be bills to sort out too: the gas, the electricity . . . it can't all just be left.'

She looked up from a pile of old newspapers that had come to light. They went way back – one of them even mentioned food rationing. 'But what makes you think Uncle Bert left the house to you?' she asked.

'I didn't say that's what I thought, did I?'

'No. But . . . you do think so, don't you?'

Frank grunted as he dragged a shoe box from under the bed. 'Who else do you think he could

47

have left it to? You? Since you were such great pen-pals?'

Susannah gritted her teeth at the little jibe. Dad would be out of her hair in an hour or so. Just put up with him for a bit longer, she told herself, and you needn't see him again for – oh, ages.

'Of course he won't have left it to me,' she said. 'But I wouldn't go building your hopes if I were you. It can't be worth much, can it? Haringey isn't exactly the up and coming area of London, you know. Anyway –' she moved to peer over his shoulder as he blew grey dust off the lid of the box – 'you've got loads of money, Dad. I don't know what you're getting worked up about.'

'Why do children always assume that their parents are made of money? And I'm not getting worked up. If anyone's getting worked up it's you two hysterical women. Anyone would have thought I was trying to rob Bert's grave.'

'He hasn't got a grave; he was cremated. And it's *not* us making a fuss,' she insisted, 'it's you.'

'What's got into you all of a sudden?' Frank growled as the lid flew off. It wasn't like Susannah to stand up to him like this.

'Nothing. Nothing.' Did everyone think she was behaving oddly? 'Well, it looks like you've turned up trumps. That's a will if ever I saw one.'

Frank didn't need to be told. He'd already smoothed out the folds. 'Christ!' he muttered.

'What? Tell me.'

He thrust the document towards her.

'Who the hell's this Dora Saxby?' she said when she'd studied the interesting part. She could scarcely keep amusement from her voice: her father hadn't benefited at all.

'A woman he used to see.' Frank's watery pink eyes looked bleakly into the distant past. He put a finger in his ear, as he often did when upset about something, and absently raked it around. 'I thought he'd given her up. She was married, you see. Perhaps he didn't give her up after all. I lost track.'

'A woman? I never knew.' Susannah grinned. It was the best news she'd had all day. At least her Uncle Bert had lived a little. An image came to her mind. 'There was an old dear at the back of the chapel today. I thought she'd got left behind by mistake. But I suppose it could have been her.' She looked down at the will again and couldn't resist rubbing salt into her father's wound. 'Did you see I'm to have five hundred pounds and the card table? Perhaps I'll spend the money on air tickets for the family so we can all fly out to see you and Jan in your lovely romantic farmhouse. You must have finished all the renovations by now, surely? When would you like us to come?'

But they both knew she was only bluffing; Susannah would not voluntarily spend *any* amount of time in Jan's company. Jan – a teacher at the same school as her father – had never been forgiven for befriending him and eventually taking her mother's place. Even though her mother had been dead for several years by the time Frank and Jan married and Susannah then eighteen, she hadn't been able to understand how her father could be so disloyal as to go after another woman. She still couldn't.

The phone rang and rang in the empty cottage. Simon put down his receiver in disgust. Where had his mother got to? She hadn't been at work – the guy who'd picked up the phone there had no idea where she was – and she wasn't at home. But he badly needed her advice. He had no idea what he was going to do.

Reluctant to leave the comparative warmth of the phone booth, even though it smelled disgustingly of urine, he slumped against the Perspex wall. But his eyes fell on the baby buggy outside and he knew he ought to get moving. He would in a minute, he promised himself; right now he felt safe from the world.

Justin would be OK out there for a while. He was protected from the cutting wind by his plastic bubble and was fast asleep with three fingers in his mouth, blissfully unaware of his mother's defection.

Simon made a fist and thumped the side of the booth. How could Natalie do this to her own child? How could she do it to *him*? Spurred by anger, he rolled out of the kiosk, grabbed the buggy, and set off down the street, hunched in his anorak and hoping no one would recognise him.

'You aren't normal!' he'd flung at Natalie two

days previously as she'd struggled out of their flat with a suitcase in one hand and a typewriter in the other.

'Not all women are born mothers,' she'd growled back. 'I didn't want him. And it was your fault we had him in the first place. So you can jolly well look after him.'

She humped her things down the stairs.

'Oh, don't keep dragging all that up!' he groaned. 'It wasn't my fault the wretched thing burst.'

'They test them to destruction, you know. Blow them up on machines. You just handled it wrongly.'

'Well, there's no point going over it again. It happened and we have to live with it. You should be thinking of Justin, not your stupid career.'

Simon couldn't understand it. Justin was so cute and smart and lovable; a great kid. Nobody could not like him. How could his own mother be so set against him?

He had glared into the car that came to pick Natalie up. That friend of hers – Lara – had something to do with it, he was sure; she'd been putting all sorts of ideas into Natalie's head, bit by bit. Feminist ideas. Ideas about independence and dedicating oneself to one's career.

Of course, Simon acknowledged, jerking the buggy up a high kerb, feminism was nothing new to Natalie – she'd been brought up on it, after all – but she hadn't pursued it so avidly before. Not until Lara had come on the scene. And everything had gone downhill from then on.

Losing his job had been the last straw.

'Well, at least you can look after the baby now,' Natalie had told him when he'd come home and broken the news. That was all the sympathy he'd got. 'It'll save me having to keep ferrying him around all the child-minders. *And* it'll save the expense.'

'But – but what are we going to live on? Your salary's hardly enough.' Teachers were notoriously poorly paid, and Natalie was at the bottom of the scale.

But she seemed to have worked things out already – as though she had been planning it all for months.

'I –' she cast him a wary glance before looking away again – 'I think I'll move in with Lara for a while. That should work out a lot cheaper.'

Simon blinked. And blinked again. 'But what about me and Justin? There won't be room for us – and I wouldn't want to live with Lara if you paid me. We can't go on living here either, with nothing coming in.' He shook his head as though he had an insect in his ear. 'Nat, none of this makes sense.'

'Oh . . .' She flapped him aside with one hand. 'Go and move in with your parents. They'll be delighted to have you, I'm sure.'

Had there been sarcasm in her tone? Simon reached the door of the flat that he must vacate at the end of the week. What had she been suggesting? That they wouldn't welcome him with open arms? Well, they would; and they would love to see more of their grandchild.

Not that he could contemplate such a thing, of course. How would that make him look? A grown man, with responsibilities, running home to Mummy?

Not if he could help it.

'Grief!' Harvey muttered to himself when he finally got out of bed. His sleep-swollen eyes fell on the debris on Julia's dressing table and followed a trail of jumble to the bathroom. He hadn't noticed how untidy Julia was all the years he had been out working. Or if he had noticed it hadn't bothered him. It was only now, stuck with it for most of the day, day after day, that it was really beginning to get to him.

Heaving himself from the bed he picked up a pair of red panties, two flimsy blouses, and a heap of wet towels. He dropped the clothes in a white wicker Ali Baba and hung the towels on a heated rail. He cleaned out the shower, tidied up the line of toiletries that ran almost the entire length of the bath tub, and then made the bed.

And he didn't stop there. Fired by – well – he wasn't sure what had brought on this aberration, he went on to clean the whole house. And when it was all in order and fit to be photographed for *Homes and Gardens*, he had a late lunch sandwich and a long, hot shower. Then he sat down at the piano in the lounge.

Mozart, he thought, his hands stiff and unco-operative; that's what I need. Something to make me feel human again.

But he discovered that what he could hear in his head could no longer be reproduced by his fingers. Not surprising, since he hadn't played for years. It didn't matter though; there was no one around to listen. So he went on playing, stumbling over the cold keys and repeating his many mistakes, his thoughts drifting about with the music.

Was this real life, he asked himself: cleaning the house and strumming out tunes? Was this what soldiers dreamed of in the trenches when they were miles away at war? Did they really yearn only for their homes, for their loved ones safely about them, and all this crashing, unmitigated ordinariness? And when they were safe and sound at home did they yearn for excitement again, wishing they were back in the thick of it?

Harvey dropped the lid with a jangle and covered his eyes with his hands. Being out in the thick of things didn't seem to be the answer either: caught up in the world of business, making money, dashing about in pursuit of an absorbing career. No. All that really gave you was an excuse for not addressing the big, burning question; you could simply tell yourself you hadn't the time to think about it.

But now he had all the time in the world. The question stood before him, and nothing would make it go away. The ultimate riddle – a riddle he couldn't begin to discuss with his nearest and dearest because she wouldn't have the remotest idea what he was on about – was beginning to drive him crazy: *what the hell was this life all about?*

But a loud thundering at the front door prevented him having to come up with an answer just then.

'Yes?' he demanded, his eyes sweeping the small band of workmen he found propping up the porch.

'Mr Webb? We've come early,' their spokesman told him with a grin. 'Now 's not often that happens, is it? We saw yer car on the drive, so we knew someone must be in, and we thought – well, you ain't likely to object, are yer, mate?'

'Object? To what?' But Harvey had spotted a blue van with writing on the side and it began to trigger his memory.

'Object to us getting on with it,' the ring-leader said. 'Make a start, kind of thing. Get the gear into the house and have another look-see. Know what I mean? Then tomorrow we can get down to things bright 'n early.'

'Oh.' Harvey's face fell. 'The bathroom. Of course.'

Some time ago Julia had decided they must have the guest bathroom refitted, and he had absently agreed. At the time, when quotations and so forth had been bandied about, he hadn't taken much notice except for the final cost. He had nodded at colour charts and samples and hadn't thought he would be much affected by the actual work; he'd certainly never dreamed he'd be part of the surroundings when it happened. Now he realised his privacy was about to be invaded, when all he wanted was to be left alone with his misery and the great mystery of life.

'I suppose you'd better come in,' he said, holding the door a little wider, and he watched in dismay as the work-party shambled past him in paint-splattered boots. Within minutes every room in the house seemed to be cluttered with copper piping, a shiny new bathroom suite stuck all over with impossible tape, ladders in three different sizes – what would they need those for? – and a stack of filthy tools. All Harvey's work of the past four hours had gone to a ball of chalk.

But the boxes of tiles Julia had selected for the walls were too much to stomach.

'Oh no,' he said, taking one between his fingers as though it stank, 'definitely, absolutely, and most decidedly not. This lot can go straight back where they came from.'

And then he had an idea.

CHAPTER 6

The green hold-all with tan leather trim bumped against Frank's thigh as he walked towards the boarding gate. It bulged so much with goodies for Jan and himself that it made him tilt as though drunk. His arm muscles were strained and he was panting heavily. He was getting too old for globe-trotting, he decided. But at least this was the only luggage he had to worry about. He wouldn't have to hang about the airport waiting for suitcases to be disgorged; he could get straight off home to Jan.

Lord, what a wasted trip! And how was he going to break the news? It was the last thing Jan would be expecting to hear from him. They had both been so sure of Bert's money. For five short days they had blissfully assumed that all their problems were over. And now they were back to square one. Back to the nightmare that had begun almost as soon as they had left England and was still going strong.

Frank sighed as the crowd slowed to a crawl. No amount of goodies would ease the pain for his wife. Poor Jan. She had always been such a help to him – even before Rose died. A kind-hearted colleague whom he'd respected and grown to love. She didn't deserve all this.

He handed over his boarding pass, tender warmth flooding his hard old heart. Dear Jan. What would he have done without her?

Simon sat in his car, staring up at the converted house. On the outskirts of Bristol and less than a mile from the one he and Natalie had lived in, it looked almost identical: Edwardian, three floors under a grey slate roof; run-down and generally uncared for.

He bounded up the path.

'I told you not to come here,' were Natalie's first words. She looked furtively over her shoulder and Simon was well aware of Lara hovering in the background. But he wasn't going to be deflected.

'I've gone to a lot of trouble finding someone to keep an eye on Justin –'

'You really shouldn't have bothered.'

'The least you can do is listen to me. Come outside for a walk.' He began to pull her across the threshold and she frowned under her straight blonde fringe. Clearly Simon was determined; there was little point in arguing. 'My shoes –' She stumbled into them and let him lead her outside, but in the street she rounded on him.

'You know this is utterly pointless.'

'No it isn't. Listen to me. First of all, you can't just walk out on me like this. It isn't fair. I can't help it if I've been laid off.' *Let go* was how it had been put to him. As if they were doing him a favour!

'I haven't walked out on you, Simon. Not permanently, anyway.'

'What? Well, what's this all about then? I really don't understand. We should be facing our problems together, not split up like this.'

'We need some time on our own. Some space to think things through. Face it, Simon. Things hadn't been going right, had they? Not since...' She looked down the street. Words seemed to have become too painful for her. It was as if she couldn't bear to talk about Justin and the way his coming into their lives had changed things. Unlike Simon she had never been able to accept the unplanned pregnancy, and when Justin finally arrived had regarded the bundle in her arms as one might an unexploded bomb. Nurses had attributed her fits of weeping to the baby blues, but although they had subsided, little else had improved since then.

Natalie turned to Simon, biting her lip, her anorak flaring in the wind behind her. 'You can claim benefits, you know. And you could get a room somewhere. Oh, you've got a brain in your head, haven't you? I'm sure you'll manage all right.'

Simon snorted in incredulity. That she could wash her hands of him he could maybe come to terms with, but to be parted willingly from her child... well, it still boggled the mind.

'Oh, Natalie...' He groaned. He stepped towards

her, his eyes moist, his hands slipping inside her coat.

'No, Simon.' Her voice was cold. 'Don't. And don't come to Lara's flat again. She's not happy about it. Phone me at work if you must, and we'll meet up, somewhere, sometime. You can bring Justin with you, if you like,' she added grudgingly, and with that she ducked into a path that led to the back of the house and disappeared from view.

Simon was left on the pavement with a heavy heart – and a fearful one. Bring Justin with you *if you like*? And *Lara* isn't happy? This Lara obviously meant more to Natalie than anyone else did. He spent the rest of the evening wondering why.

'Got rid of him already?' Lara smiled approvingly. 'It didn't take you long.'

'Yes.' Natalie's smile was less strong. Pleasing Lara brought a glow of pleasure . . . but it was hardly enough to banish her doubts. She wasn't sure about the course she was taking, in spite of her bravado in front of Simon. Was she really a wicked mother? Or was Lara right about leaving Justin with Si? It didn't seem right to have to support a man, but . . . oh, she didn't know. She was tired of thinking about it all. So horribly, desperately tired. And it made life that much easier, falling in with Lara.

But heaven knew what Simon's parents would think of her when they found out what was going on. They would certainly not approve, neither would they understand. Hell. She really didn't want to fall in their estimation – any more, that is, than her inept handling of Justin must have lowered her already. Oh, she'd noticed how Susannah looked at her, as if she was doing everything wrong. Not that she said anything of course – never interfered. She could just feel it.

Really, the Hardings were much better parents than her own; she quite liked them. They had been good to her and Simon, giving them money and helping out. She wouldn't want them upset.

Oh, but she really couldn't think about them either. She had too much else to consider. And all she wanted to do, really, was sleep.

Susannah's saw made comforting *phwitt-phwitt, phwitt-phwitt* noises as she cut up lengths of wood in her work room – or studio as she had recently begun to refer to it. It was dark outside at the moment but, during the day, light slanted through a sky-light as well as from a window at one end of the room overlooking the garden, making it not only a practical place in which to work but a pleasant one. In the centre was a large wooden table with a pair of stools pushed under it, and beneath the window was a work bench and a deep square sink. Her materials were neatly ranged on shelves.

Not for her the chaotic methods of the stereo-typical artist; Susannah had to have everything in perfect order before she could create – and that included the whole cottage. If a bed was unmade or a cup unwashed it had to be dealt with first.

Susannah loved the room, her pleasure in it only slightly marred by a sense of guilt. Paul had wanted to convert this single-storey extension, which the previous owners had used as a play room, into a dining room and she had had to battle it out with him.

'Where will we entertain?' he'd argued, looking round at what space was available and finding it seriously lacking. Cottages were all very well, he had begun to realise, but unless you could afford three knocked into one they were a bit claustrophobic.

'Oh, there's enough room for a table in the alcove in the lounge,' Susannah had pointed out with a wave of one hand. She had no patience for serving up elaborate meals, and dinner parties bored her rigid.

'Hardly ideal.' Paul wrinkled his beakish nose at the idea. He'd recognised, though, the determination in his wife's eye and had eventually decided to back down.

Now, coming in from a meeting that he'd told her – over the phone when she got back from the funeral – that he wished he'd chaired himself because then it would have taken up only half the time, his face registered that same frowning displeasure.

'You're early,' Susannah said, removing a length of moulded wood from the Workmate and barely glancing up at him.

'It's gone seven o'clock.' He stood impatiently

watching her, his briefcase still at his side.

'Your dinner's in the microwave,' she went on. 'I've eaten mine already.'

'Oh.' His shoulders drooped as he nodded his head in unwilling acceptance of the fact, but he hung about for a bit longer, shifting from one foot to the other as though hoping circumstances might change: Susannah might drop what she was doing and decide she should head for the kitchen. She might mix him a gin and tonic, or give him a welcome-home kiss. She might stand on her head and do cartwheels . . . He went upstairs to get changed.

And returned less than ten minutes later wearing a polo shirt and sweater that set Susannah's teeth on edge; Paul had about as much colour sense as a cat.

By now he was carrying his dinner plate in a cloth with one hand and a glass, knife and fork in the other. He arranged them neatly on a corner of the table before hooking one of the stools with his ankle and parking himself on top of it.

'You don't have to eat in here,' Susannah told him with a little laugh. But the words had a chilly rasp to them.

'What do you want me to do?' he tossed back at her. 'Drop sauce on the living-room carpet, or sit in the kitchen on my own?'

'No –' she shrugged carelessly – 'I just thought that, what with all the sawdust in here and everything . . .'

'Tastes like sawdust anyway,' he grunted, cautiously licking the fork. 'A bit more isn't going to make much difference.'

He ate in silence for a while, pausing between mouthfuls to watch her, his head cocked on one side.

'So what's it going to be this time?' he finally got around to asking.

Susannah tightened the vice a little. 'A coffee table – eventually.' She glanced up to find him sawing at a chunk of lasagne with apparent difficulty.

The problem seemed to be one of those dried-up corners, she noted with dismay, where the pasta pokes up through the sauce and turns to indestructible cardboard in the oven. Stainless steel cutlery was no match for it – the saw she held in her hand might be more suitable – but he managed to spear it at last and surveyed it with resignation. It sat solidly on the prongs of the fork, steaming gently, and looking about as palatable as layers of loft lagging.

And if she was meant to feel guilty about the quality of the meal that evening, she did. Pulling something from the freezer and re-heating it simply wasn't good enough, she reminded herself, even if you had made it earlier yourself. Guilt could only be kept entirely at bay by starting a meal from scratch and creating a sink-full of dirty pots. Then you had proof that you cared.

'What's wrong with the table we've got?' Paul

wanted to know, ploughing manfully through the meal.

'Nothing. Nothing at all. This isn't for us anyway.' She hesitated before going on. 'It's going to have its top done in mosaics.'

'Oh.'

Their eyes met.

'Bringing out the big guns now, are we?' He was trying to make a joke of it and not succeeding. 'I mean, if you threw something that size at me . . .'

Damn! She'd splintered the wood. 'That could always be arranged,' she growled.

He grinned at her crookedly. Then suddenly pushing the plate to one side he went over to where she was working.

'Here, hadn't I better do that?' He jerked back the sleeves of his sweater to reveal the hairy backs of his wrists.

It was some seconds before she realised what he was about. 'What? No, no, of course not,' she protested. But she was practically having to elbow him out of the way. Or was he elbowing her? A ridiculous little scuffle ensued during which she grew increasingly cross. 'Look, I did do woodwork at evening class, you know.'

'Yes, I know you did, but –' he shook his head with a kind of shudder – 'I can hardly bear to watch you. You've made a right little cock-up there, haven't you?'

'It's nothing I can't put right. And if you hadn't

sat there, chewing – a-and putting me off – I'd be almost finished by now.'

'That's right, blame me.' He shrugged and folded his arms. 'You just carry on and make a pig's ear of it; I'll enjoy the laugh. It just doesn't seem right, though, somehow.'

'What doesn't?' She straightened up to glare at him. 'The fact that a woman can be perfectly capable of carpentry? Really, Paul, you must try to move with the times. You sound like you've just stepped out of the Ark.'

'Well, I can't help that. I was brought up to believe certain things. In my day girls got pastry sets for Christmas and boys were given tools. You knew where you were. If someone's since decided to move the goal posts, why should I have to change my views?'

'Because, dear husband, you're going to look like some kind of dinosaur if you don't.'

Susannah stood poised with a pencil in her hand. It really was difficult to concentrate with Paul hanging round. Usually he watched television or strolled down to the pub when she was involved with the chores or whatever. Why had he chosen her to be his source of entertainment tonight?

'You know,' she went on, while Paul 'helpfully' held her ruler in the wrong place, 'you've had it too easy all these years. You haven't had to adapt. What would you have done if I'd been a fully fledged career woman? The sort you hear about these days. You know: educated up to the eyeballs; smart, good-looking top executives; nannied children etc., etc. I don't think you could have coped.'

'I really don't see why not. On the contrary, I would have liked it very much.'

'Well, of all the bloody nerve!' Susannah threw down the pencil.

'What?'

'How can you say that? You know perfectly well you wouldn't have been able to hack it for one moment. What would you have done when your career clashed with your wife's? When you needed to take up a post in – in Timbuktu, say, and she had to be in London?'

'We'd have worked out something.'

'Cloud cuckoo land,' Susannah muttered.

'You ought to have gone to college, Sue. You still could, you know, if you wanted. I wouldn't stand in your way.'

'I see.' She nodded grimly. 'So you really do think you'd have preferred a professional wife. You no longer think I'm good enough. You can't go bragging to your pals at work about your wife who's doing such-and-such a clever course at so-and-so college and who's going to walk off in a few years' time with some spiffing sort of degree. All you can talk about is my wife who's only a pay clerk and mucks about making these god-awful coffee tables.'

'Susannah,' he said wearily, 'this is not what I'm saying at all. Nothing could be further from my mind. What's actually bothering me at the moment, if you really want to know, is that I feel you slipping away from me, and I don't know why. You're remote. You're preoccupied. We don't do things together any more. I'm beginning to wonder whether you stayed with me because of the children all these years and now you'd like to go.' He stared out through the window at the night. 'I don't understand what's happening to us.'

Susannah melted towards him. It must have taken a lot to admit his insecurity – Paul, who normally exuded nothing but inner strength; a core of solid rock running through him that could never be shaken.

'Paul, I –' But the phone began to ring. Tutting with exasperation, she snatched the receiver off the wall.

The voice on the line was not immediately recognisable; it was thin, high, and tearful.

'H-hello?' it said haltingly, then there was a long, drawn-out sniff. 'It's me. I'm at the station. Can you come and get me?' Then the caller cut off.

'Don't tell me,' Paul said as Susannah looked blankly surprised. 'That was one of the children . . . Simon?'

'No.' Susannah's thoughts had gone winging in a different direction: sickness, death, disaster! But she managed a grim little smile. 'When did Simon ever phone us?'

'Not since he discovered it cost money. So it was Katy, then, was it?'

'Well, how many children have we got? Yes, it

was our dear Katy. She wants me to pick her up at the station.' Susannah frowned as she moved towards the door. 'She sounded very upset. I wish, now, that I'd had time to pay her a visit after the funeral. I was a bit rushed, though, in the end. What do you think's the matter?'

'No idea. Boyfriend trouble, I shouldn't wonder. But I'll go.' He'd already reached for an old gardening jacket behind the door, eager to have something to do. 'You'd better make up the bed, hadn't you? I doubt whether she'll be going back to London tonight.'

'The bed . . . yes, of course. I suppose you're right.'

The guest room had been the last one they'd decorated in the eight months since moving in, and there had been little point in making up the bed before it was needed. Actually, Susannah thought, it seemed a shame to take the new, co-ordinated sheets out of their packets. But Katy might need them so she would have to.

She sighed. She had so wanted to get on with her new project; this additional interruption was most annoying. But she instantly admonished herself for her selfishness. What kind of mother was she, to put new sheets and her own needs before a daughter who sounded as if she was in trouble?

After leaving school Katy had spent a year at secretarial college and had lived at home until she was twenty while she gained work experience with an assortment of local companies. When London beckoned with its better opportunities and higher salaries she had set herself up with a good job there, sharing a bedsit with a college friend, and leaving her parents feeling slightly nervous for her safety but with their blessing.

They needn't have worried. Katy had fallen on her feet. When months passed with barely a backward glance or a visit from her they had decided it was time to look to their own future, hence the purchase of the cottage. So, Susannah now wondered, what could have gone wrong?

Casting a last lingering look at her splintered wood, she went upstairs.

Paul scanned the small group of people waiting outside the station. There was Katy all right; she'd abandoned her luggage and was running full-tilt towards him, her arms stretched out for a hug. Nice to know someone loved him. And she didn't look ill or anything, which was a relief. Her 'problem' was probably nothing at all. An incident blown up into a crisis, if he knew his little Kate. It would all be over by bed-time. And then perhaps life in the cottage would feel a bit more normal for a few days – if she was going to stay that long. She would probably stay the weekend, anyway. And her mother could hardly ignore *her*.

CHAPTER 7

When the bed was made Susannah stood back to look at the room. Everything in it was new, not just the sheets. Out had gone all the dilapidated furniture they had made do with over the years, and in its place was pine. The carpet and curtains were new too, and it all looked very inviting.

Giving the neat row of scatter cushions a final tweak, she switched on the two pleated table lamps and ran downstairs; already there was the unmistakable throb of Paul's car outside on the drive, and the slam, bang, boof! of closing doors meant he'd successfully accomplished his task. He had brought Katy home.

Susannah reached the lounge just as Paul came staggering in with a huge blue suitcase weighing down one hand and a ghetto blaster in the other. He was followed by their daughter carrying – nothing at all. Except a tiny handbag in quilted leather that dangled from her shoulder by a chain.

'Wow!' she said over her mother's shoulder after the briefest of dutiful kisses. 'Is it finished now?'

Her big brown eyes, made larger than life by the none-too-discreet application of eyeliner, began taking in her surroundings. She'd seen the cottage a couple of months after they moved in, when they were just starting work, but hadn't been back since they'd transformed it.

But Susannah found it impossible to answer right then; she could only stare at Katy's new hair-do. It had been bleached blonde from its normal, beautiful red-gold, and most of it had been cut off – except for one odd strand, which for some reason had been left to run down over her left cheek. Parts of it caught on her lashes as she blinked, though she seemed not to notice the inconvenience.

Susannah caught Paul's eye and saw him shrug; then he gave her a quick shake of the head. So he had no idea why they were being honoured with this visit either. What had they talked about in the car, for heaven's sake? Trust him to leave all the awkward questioning to her.

'Yes, it's all finished,' Susannah said, spreading her arms wide and trying not to stare at the disastrous hair. 'What do you think of it, Katy? Do you like it?'

Katy made considering noises in her throat. 'It's much smaller than I remember.'

Susannah and Paul exchanged glances again. So far, everyone who'd seen the cottage had raved about its cosiness and its charm; they weren't accustomed to it being criticised.

'It's certainly smaller than Windy Ridge,'

Susannah had to concede, 'but you know we bought it with a view to retirement.'

'But that won't be for ages yet!' Katy shot her father an alarmed glance.

'You don't have to be old these days,' Paul told her. 'People are being thrown out of our place at a rate of knots.'

'But that won't happen to you yet, will it?' Now it was Susannah's turn to look fearful.

'Who knows what will happen?' Paul picked up the suitcase because it was blocking the sitting room. 'I'll take this little lot upstairs.'

'You've bought a new three-piece suite,' Katy declared as her father struggled out of the room. 'What was wrong with the old one?'

'What was *wrong* with it?' Susannah laughed outright. 'What was *right* with it, more like. After you and Simon had used it as a bouncy castle it was never the same again.'

She looked at Katy who had sat down stiffly on the chintz two-seater and was gazing thoughtfully round at the pale peach carpet. Anyone seeing her would have thought she had come home to discover a new set of parents instead of just different furniture.

'Come and look at the spare room,' she said brightly to cover her disappointment. Why wasn't Katy falling in love with the place like everyone else?

Katy rose to her feet and trudged up the stairs in ugly lace-up ankle boots that looked almost identical to a pair Susannah remembered being forced to wear as a child. She had loathed those boots almost as much as the thick brown stockings that went with them. Come to think of it, Katy's skin-tight leggings strongly resembled those awful stockings too. Ugh!

'You saw our room when you were here before,' Susannah reminded her at the top of the stairs. 'But you haven't seen this one done up. This is the guest room.' Pushing open the door with a flourish she saw that the suitcase now dominated the bed and the ghetto blaster was perched on top of the smart pine dresser. It didn't look quite the same.

'Oh,' Katy said from the door. She slowly stepped in, her eyes drawn to the bed. 'You've got a new bed too!' she gasped. 'What have you done with my old one?'

'Katy –' Susannah picked up a doll from the window-sill and fiddled with its hat. She had dressed it to tone in with its surroundings, but Katy appeared not to have noticed it. Turning round she found a recumbent Katy – boots and all – testing the bed fully clothed. 'Katy –' she began again; but how could she explain to her daughter that this was not exactly her room? Nor was it her home any more, not really. Well, of course it would always be home to her in a sense. And yet . . . it wasn't.

'We – er –' she thought quickly – 'we decided we ought to put in a double, since this is really a guest room, you know. I mean, when you're here a single would be fine, but when Simon and Natalie come to stay – and little Justin, of course – it makes sense to –'

'But this one's hard as a rock. Mine was nice and soft. It had a hole that fitted me, too. Right in the middle of the mattress.'

'Well, now it's gone to the tip.' Susannah sat the doll down with a bump. 'This mattress will be much better for you,' she added, struggling for a more sympathetic tone. After all, she reminded herself, Katy had definitely sounded upset about something over the phone. 'Soft beds are bad for your back. And anyway you'll not notice it just for a few days.'

Katy slanted a look at her mother. 'I've come for much longer than that.'

'Oh . . . really? How – how come you've got time off right now? I thought you were saving your days for Christmas.'

Katy swung herself off the bed. 'I've lost my job,' she said flatly, beginning to pull drawers from the dresser to see what was inside. There was nothing in them; only a woody piney smell that began to permeate the tiny room.

'Lost your –' Words failed Susannah for a moment. Then she hurried over to where Katy was standing. No wonder she'd shown no enthusiasm about the cottage, with news like this on her mind. 'Oh, Katy I'm so sorry! But how?' She could see the girl's reflection in the cheval mirror and sensed that tears were close in spite of her attempt at nonchalance.

I –' Katy swallowed – 'I can't do the work any more; they've given me the sack. I've got two months' pay to come – and – and – oh, Mum, I don't know what to do!'

Susannah saw her own distraught face reflected back at her as Katy turned and buried herself in her arms. When her daughter finally came up for air she ventured another question.

'But why can't you do the work, Katy?' She took the opportunity of brushing aside the hair lock. 'You were managing very well. I thought they liked you. They made you secretary to the Head of Department, didn't they?'

Katy nodded and sniffed and mopped her eyes with a tissue. 'I thought he was so nice at first but he turned out to be nothing but a slave-driver.' She snorted with disgust. 'He had me working all hours and I didn't get a penny extra money for doing it. But if you complain you're done for, you know; they just get shot of you for some reason or other and find someone else.

'Do you know, there were forty-three applicants for that poxy little job? I was over the moon when they picked me. But now –' her tears welled up afresh – 'I've got RSI!'

'Oh good God!' Susannah whispered, her stomach taking a turn. This was her worst night-mare realised: that a child of hers should contract some deadly disease. How on earth would she cope? She found herself sitting on the edge of the bed, not knowing how she had got there, or what

76

to say. 'But what is it, this RSI?' she managed eventually. 'I don't think I've ever heard of it.'

'Where have you been all your life?' Paul said suddenly from the door. 'It's what typists and chicken factory workers get these days –' He went over to Katy and hugged her for the second time that evening. 'Isn't it, my precious love?'

Katy nodded and allowed herself to be comforted by her father's long, strong arms. He was like a cuddly bear in his thick woolly sweater and she sighed with a surge of relief.

'Repetitive Strain Injury,' Paul went on over his daughter's head, for Susannah's benefit. 'I was watching a programme about it the other night. If you perform the same movement with your hands over and over again . . .'

But Susannah was nodding dumbly; she now recalled hearing about it. You got pains in the hands and arms after a while. Some people got it really badly and were crippled for the rest of their lives: they couldn't even lift their arms to do their own hair. And they would never be able to work again.

'A lot of doctors,' Paul was saying, 'don't even believe it exists, let alone trouble themselves to try and sort out a cure. I believe I read about a case in the paper recently where someone successfully sued for compensation. I'll look into the possibilities tomorrow.'

Katy cast him a look of gratitude: at least he wasn't taking the attitude that she was swinging the lead, like some people did. 'I can't do anything much with them,' she said holding out her hands. 'And they hurt like flaming hell. Do you think I could have a hot water bottle, Mum? Oh, and I'll need you to unpack my case . . .'

'Of course Mum'll make you a hot water bottle, won't you dear?' Paul was still clinging to his daughter as though she had been away for ten years instead of only a matter of months. He let her go at last and followed Susannah downstairs.

'Well, this is a turn-up for the books, isn't it?' he said, rubbing his hands together as they went into the kitchen. 'Fancy getting our Katy back! Now you won't be bored any more.'

Susannah turned and stared at him for a moment, before going over to the sink. She began to run water on to the sad remains of lasagne she found there and went to wipe spills from the microwave.

'How long is this RSI business going to last?' she asked, Paul trailing her round the kitchen. She stopped to throw a startled look at the ceiling as loud thumping came down through the beams: Katy had managed to plug in the ghetto blaster.

'No idea,' he replied. 'I expect she's hungry, don't you? What have you got to give her?'

'Oh, I don't know.' She suddenly felt extraordinarily tired.

'Well, I must say you seem really pleased to see your own daughter. Couldn't you make more of an effort? She needs your support, poor kid, not the cold shoulder you've been giving her.'

'Oh, I haven't! Have I? I didn't mean to. It's just that ... look, there's some ham for your sandwiches tomorrow...'

'Give it to her, I don't mind. *I* don't begrudge my daughter anything in her time of dire need, even if some would. Not when the whole world must seem to have turned against her the minute she's set foot in it. Poor kid.' He watched Susannah take bread from the bread bin. 'I don't understand what's the matter with you, Sue. You're her mother, for heaven's sake.'

'She's a young woman now, Paul, not a child. Do you realise I'd had two babies by the time I was her age?'

That seemed to throw him a little. 'God,' he muttered, 'were we crazy?'

'Just normal for those times. You got married, scraped as much of a home together as you could for a year or so, and then got down to filling it. Just think if we'd waited until I was older, we'd still have little ones hanging around.'

'Hmm,' he said, still thoughtful. 'I don't mind our young Justin, of course, but little ones at our age ...'

'Well, that's the way it would be if I had been your career-type,' she pointed out. 'Career women are putting off having babies until it's practically too late to bear them. Over forty they are, in some cases. Here, the hot water bottle's ready.'

'Hmm,' he said again.

It lay between them on the work top – a dingy

flop-eared apology for a rabbit that Susannah had taken from the bottom of the medicine cupboard. It bore a label forbidding anyone to throw it away, on pain of death.

Paul finally picked it up and held it out to her. 'I think it would look better if *you* took it up. Don't you?'

Jan was in celebratory mood. She had opened a bottle of Côtes de Bergerac, prepared a crisply roasted duck, and made the farmhouse kitchen as cosy as possible – given the difficult circumstances – with candles and a huge fire. Now all that was needed was for Frank to loosen up a little after his journey, and they could have a memorable evening. But, having demolished the food and drunk two-thirds of the wine, Frank was still withdrawn and barely communicative.

She observed him across the table with the detachment that even a short separation can bring. Something was definitely wrong. Of course he was no spring chicken – nor was she – but the trip back from England seemed to have drained him far more than it ought to have done.

She reached out to the block of mature English Cheddar that now sat between them and cut herself another piece from its corner. 'Absolutely delicious,' she pronounced, popping crumbs of it into her mouth. With her cheeks sucked in and her eyes half-closed, she looked to be in seventh heaven.

'Mmm,' Frank said absently, toying with a crust of bread. It would have been more than his life was worth to have failed in the minor duties he had been given for the trip, and he congratulated himself on having at least managed to remember the block of cheese, the jar of ploughman's pickle, the slab of fruit and nut chocolate, the eighty tea bags, and the three tubes of Jan's favourite moisturising cream from Boots.

'Have another piece,' Jan urged, so that she, too, could help herself again without appearing greedy. 'And,' she ventured to add, 'tell me when you think the money will be sorted out.'

So far they hadn't talked much about the funeral or its implications; Frank had stripped off for a shower the minute he got in and she had been busy with the meal. But still Frank wouldn't be drawn.

'I suppose,' Jan pressed on, 'it'll take ages, won't it, having to sell Bert's grotty old house before we can do anything else? Or did you get the solicitor to agree to hurry it all along? Couldn't it be sold by auction, perhaps? Or –'

Frank swallowed down more of the wine while his wife prattled away, hardly aware of its subtle flavour; tonight he desired only numbness. Eventually, realising that even another bottle wouldn't be sufficient to achieve that, he raised his travel-tired eyes to hers and told her as gently as he could that they could expect nothing from his brother Bert.

'Oh, but . . . surely . . . ?' Jan suddenly lost her

appetite and let fall her piece of cheese.

Fingering a locket that hung perpetually round her neck, her gaze wandered past Frank's left shoulder and pierced the gloom. In the light of the wavering candle-flame her closely shorn head appeared gaunt, her neck thin and scrawny, and her eye sockets deeply shadowed. Only her eyes shone through like glittering marbles.

'Well, who *is* going to get Bert's house? Susannah? Not that I'd begrudge it her really. You know I hold nothing against her, even though she's never taken to me . . .'

'No, well, it's not Susannah; it's some old flame of his.'

Jan giggled her relief. 'Now I know you're teasing me. For a minute I thought –'

'No! No I'm not, Jan. Honestly. I only wish I were.'

And Jan could see from his face that he was telling her the truth. 'But –' Her gaze wandered over his shoulder again. She could just about make out the tarpaulin that stretched from one side of the farmhouse to the other. It concealed a door-less, window-less construction yawning open to the winter sky. 'I never knew Bert had an old flame. The wily old devil.'

'Not so much of the "old". Don't forget he was younger than me.'

'Yes, but he always seemed so much older, somehow, on the few occasions I met him.' She sat back in her chair, her hands slapping down on the table. 'Well, this is a turn-up for the books, I must say. What are we going to do now?'

'I'm sorry, Jan, really I am.' Frank ran a hand over his face and looked glummer than ever. 'Why don't you go ahead and say it: it's all my own stupid fault? I should have been nicer to Bert while he was alive. Brotherly love and all that. Then we'd be out of this dreadful mess.'

Jan let out a sigh. 'I never wanted to be married to a hypocrite, Frank. At least you're always honest about your feelings.'

'Yes, and just look where it's got us: well and truly in the mire.'

It wasn't in Jan's nature to be down-hearted for long. 'Actually,' she pointed out, 'apart from your air fare for the trip, we're no worse off than we were a week ago.'

'We're not a jot better off, though, either.'

'But at least we've got each other.'

Frank managed a smile at last. Dear old Jan. He should have known she would hold nothing against him.

He looked at the remaining goodies, unpacked in delighted haste and still scattered across the table. It had been a horrendously expensive shopping trip, all in all, but well, what the hell . . .

'Fancy a bit of this chocolate, love? Or a good old cup of tea?'

'Dad!' Susannah recognised her father's breathing over the phone before he actually spoke. 'What's

the matter? Are you still here – in England, I mean?'
She imagined him stuck at the airport, the victim of
some sort of strike, and desperate for a bed for the
night – although he would have to be really
desperate to consider coming to Wiltshire for one.

'No, I'm home. Sorry if I woke you up, I know
it's very late.'

Jan had crashed out on the bed after the meal,
but tired though Frank was he'd not been able to
sleep. Must have been the cheese. Or the chocolate.

'It's OK.' Susannah yawned widely. 'But what is
it?'

'Well, I've been thinking.' Thought of nothing
else for God knows how long. 'There must be some
way of contesting that wretched will. The whole
thing's totally unjust.'

Susannah sank into a depression at her father's
words. Somehow she knew she was about to be
involved.

'Well,' Frank went on, 'it's absolutely hopeless,
me trying to do anything from here. I can hardly
spend hours on the phone running up bills. And
letter-writing's too long-winded by half. I want this
all sorted out. And quickly. Look –' his tone became
soft and conciliatory – 'you'd better pop over and
have a word with that solicitor chappie of Bert's;
see if you can make him see sense.'

Susannah felt hysteria close at hand. He made it
sound as though she had only to run across
the road and knock on the nearest door; forget the
hassle of catching trains or the miles of M4 and

the tortuous drag round the M25.

'Pop over – ?' she heard herself echo.

'Well – you'll need to make an appointment first,' he added as though she were fresh out of school.

'But Dad –'

'I'd come myself if I could . . . but it might be a fruitless exercise. All that way for nothing . . .'

'Precisely. That's exactly what it would be: for nothing. A total waste of time. And –' she shook her head at her father's audacity – 'I don't know how you can think of pursuing it anyway. If Uncle Bert wanted this Saxby woman to have the house, then who are you to deny him?'

'I – it's the principle of the thing. I'm family and she isn't. I've no doubt she's nothing but a fortune-hunter, and Bert was a sucker if ever there was one. She's conned him into leaving it to her. I know she has.'

'And then bumped him off, I suppose? Oh, Dad! I've got enough on my plate right now, without running about on fool's errands. How am I supposed to find the time?'

But Frank May was not to be troubled with practicalities. He had given his daughter her orders. And he expected to be obeyed.

CHAPTER 8

Katy hooked aside the odd lock of her hair and peered at the bedside clock. She rolled on to her back with a groan. Her parents had gone to work hours ago; the old plumbing had creaked and gurgled at some ungodly hour and thoroughly woken her up. But she had managed to go back to sleep again.

She supposed she ought to get up. But what for? The day – or what was left of it – stretched endlessly ahead. Absolutely hours of it and nothing at all to do. She hated winter.

Her eyes travelled round the room. It was quite pretty, if you liked that sort of thing, and better now that she had arranged some of her own belongings around it. Andrea had promised to come down with the rest of her stuff as soon as she could; then it would look more like home.

Home? Huh! This place didn't feel like home. And what a reception she'd had! Dad had been all right – still treated her like she was six, of course, but she was used to that – but Mum, well, you couldn't exactly say she had been overjoyed.

Well, that made two of them. Because *she* wasn't

happy about it either. She didn't want to be here. Who, given the choice, would want to live with their parents? But what else could she do? Live in a cardboard box? Walk the streets like some girls did?

No, she had had to come home, like it or not. She'd had no other choice.

Susannah slumped down at her desk without bothering to take her coat off and dared Molly, with a long dark look, to say anything. But Molly was not that easily put off.

'What's up with you?' she chirped. She was one of those people who were at their best early on in the day, and the smell of wet shoes, damp coats and dusty files was not enough to daunt her. She treated Susannah to a cheery grin.

'You look knackered,' she said, unwrapping her first Kit-Kat of the day. 'Surely you can't have been decorating again?'

'No,' Susannah roused herself sufficiently to reply. 'We've finished that. Just don't ask.' But then she immediately began to tell Molly how her father was breathing down her neck about the will, and about Katy coming home with her problematic hands.

'That's tough,' Molly said when Susannah was through. 'You can get RSI from playing the piano, you know. And the violin. Well, anything that uses a lot of fingering, I suppose. Poor kid.'

'Heaven knows how soon she'll recover... I suppose she *will* recover?'

I –' Molly searched her memory to remember all that she'd heard on the subject – 'I don't really know much about it. Is she seeing a doctor?'

'She saw one in London. He gave her an injection which worked for a while. Obviously it wasn't a cure. She's going to make an appointment with our GP. Lord, but I'm exhausted.'

Susannah hid her mouth as she yawned, and when the yawn subsided her eyes focused on Andy from the computer room. He was threading his way among the work stations at the far end of the office carrying a stack of bar-marked documents – BMDs – similar to National Lottery tickets but A4-sized.

'Looks like bad news for someone,' she said, beginning to unbutton her coat.

Molly twisted her pudding-shaped body to observe Andy for herself. 'You're right,' she agreed. 'Rejections for some poor sods. I hope none of them are ours.'

'Me too,' was Susannah's fervent reply.

She unlocked her drawer, ran a comb through her hair, checked her lipstick in a piece of old mirror, and slammed the drawer shut again. Then she picked up a Biro and clicked the button on it, full of good intentions – until she found Andy beside her.

'Oh no,' she groaned dramatically, and buried her head in her hands.

'Sorry,' Andy mumbled. 'The machine wouldn't read these. We don't know why.' He dumped a pile of the documents on the desk at her elbow. 'Maybe there's a flaw in the paper, or something.'

Susannah riffled the pages in horror. 'But – but – it's *got* to have read this batch!' she protested. 'This is the shift-workers' overtime! If they don't get the money in their banks this week they'll lynch me.'

Andy shrugged. 'If you'd put them in earlier, you'd have time to do them again. As it is . . .'

But taking a day off for the funeral had put her week out of kilter. That was her official excuse, anyway. The fact was that she had lost interest in the job of late, and mistakes were the result.

'What am I going to do?' she wailed to Molly when Andy had sauntered away.

'The usual: make manual payments this week to keep the punters happy; put new bar-marked forms in next week so their records look OK. Oh, and recover the manual payment next week too, because the new bar-marks will pay it again.'

'I know. I know. I know.' It wasn't the first time they had had to tie themselves in knots trying to beat the system.

'I'll give you a hand if you like.'

'You're a treasure.' Susannah sighed deeply. 'I hate this rotten job.'

'Don't we all,' came the stock reply.

'Right,' Susannah announced when she returned from the stationery cupboard. 'Manual payment forms for Accounts.' She slapped them down on her desk, split them in half, and pushed a pile across to Molly.

Molly reached out and examined one. 'I suppose you realise Duffy has to sign these?'

'Grief, he doesn't, does he?' Susannah's depression increased. She could picture the humiliating scene with her superior. He would fix her with one of his dark, withering looks before firing a barrage of questions at her, all cleverly designed to make her appear a bigger fool than she already felt.

'My,' Molly was saying, 'but they're going to love having to make out all these cheques in Accounts. But never mind. Are these the shift-workers' claims? OK, we'll soon zip through them. Erm –' she strummed her lower lip – 'where are your workings-out?'

'Ah.' Susannah looked up over her IN tray; she had just come up against the same snag. 'I – er – don't actually have any, Moll.'

'What do you mean, you don't have any? You must have reckoned up how many hours they've done. Why aren't they down on the sheets?'

'Well –' Susannah tried to look innocent. 'I never do put them down. I tot them all up on the calculator and bar-mark it straight away. It – er – saves a whole lot of time.'

'I see.' Molly was trying her hardest to stay calm. 'But what happens when you get a query?'

'Well . . . that only happens for the odd few, and I just work those out all over again.'

'Oh, you do, do you? Great. So this isn't simply a question of a quick estimate of what they're owed, is it?'

'Well –' Susannah wriggled on her chair – 'no.'

'This is going to take all day.'

'Oh, I don't think – hey, wait a minute! Are we stupid? All we need do is take the info from the duff bar-marks!'

'The bar-marks!' Molly clapped a hand to her head. 'Why didn't I think of that? So, dear Susannah, where have you put them?'

Susannah looked about her. 'Damn. I gave them all back to –'

'Andy.'

'Andy!' Susannah shrieked and made a dash for the door.

'Sorry,' Andy said when she found him. 'I've just put them all in the shredder.'

'So why do you do it?' Molly said when the task was done and Susannah came back from Accounts. 'I've always wanted to know.'

'Do what? Make extra work for us both? Well, I think that's a bit unfair, Molly. I don't have control over the pathetic reading machine.'

'No, this, I mean, *this*. This wonderful, stimulating job.'

Susannah looked vaguely at the wall above Molly's head; her mind was still with the forms she had dumped in Accounts. Should she confide in Molly that she had authorised them herself?

Mr Duffy had not been in his room when she'd needed his signature, and she'd not wanted to waste more time waiting for him to show up. So

91

she had closeted herself in the ladies and quickly worked her way through them, scribbling her own name at the bottom of each. 'Harding' didn't bear much resemblance to 'Duffy', it was true, but she hoped no one would notice. She was sometimes authorised to substitute for him, after all, so it was unlikely to be queried.

But Molly was still waiting for an answer. 'Why *do* you put yourself through this aggro?'

Susannah had had enough for one day. She had started to clear her desk to make things easier for the cleaners who were supposed to perform miracles in the night but somehow managed not to find dust and balls of fluff.

She paused in the middle of scraping pens, pencils, and rulers back into the drawer. 'What else can I do? I never qualified for a decent job.'

'But that doesn't matter, does it? You don't have to do anything really. You could sit at home all day doing . . . I don't know . . . whatever turns you on, as the saying goes. I mean, you really don't need the money, do you?'

'Oh Molly –' Susannah looked at her friend uncertainly. Had something of what she'd wanted to tell her the other day filtered through after all? Could she confide her true aspirations? Or would Molly laugh at her?

'Let's just say that work keeps me out of mischief,' she said, getting up and reaching for her coat. 'And what on earth would I do without you to talk to all day? I'd go stark, staring bonkers.

'Thanks for helping me out, Molly; I'll do the same for you some time.'

'You're not going home already?' Molly looked at her watch in mock horror. 'I suppose you realise you're leaving in core time, Mrs Harding?'

'I do. And I don't give a damn.' Susannah grinned, wrinkling her nose. 'Sometimes I like to live dangerously.'

The trolley trundled up and down the aisles as fast as Julia could push it. She snatched at items as she passed them, her irritation increasing with every pause.

New pan-scourer... fabric softener... bleach. Toilet rolls ... panty-liners – must be needing those soon ... bubble bath ... Oh, but she shouldn't be doing this!

Shopping was Harvey's job now. She simply didn't have time. What a waste of a morning. She should be down at the library reading *The Go-Between*.

But Harvey was hopeless at shopping, probably because, having three big sisters to spoil him, he had never learned how to do it. He would load the car to the gunnels with all sorts of useless things that she wasn't sure they could afford at the moment: with wines – all carefully chosen, judging by the length of time he'd been gone – or with cream cakes that they weren't supposed to be eating because of their waist-lines, or with jars of black olives that would last them till kingdom come.

Nothing you could make a decent meal with.

Last week she had found a tin of snails with Champagne in one of the kitchen cupboards. Snails, of all things. Every time she opened the cupboard and saw it, she felt she wanted to be sick.

Cold meat? Bacon? Cheese? Can't be bothered to stand in that queue.

Eggs . . . salt . . . cooking oil . . .

They'd had some odd concoctions lately, thanks to Harvey: curry with tagliatelle; pork chops with black bean sauce; tea without milk; ditto Weetabix. They seemed always to be out of milk. A joke, considering they lived in what was once a dairy!

You'd think a man with Harvey's brains could do better. Surely *anyone* should be able to keep house? How had he made it to area manager, for heaven's sake? But there's clever and there's clever, her mother was wont to say.

Julia was beginning to see what she meant.

When Susannah got in from work Katy was wandering down the stairs, wrapped in a pink spotted dressing-gown with coffee stains down the front. Her face was bare of make-up and she looked ten years younger than her age. She also looked as though she had just woken up.

Susannah checked her watch with raised eyebrows and hung her coat on one of the hooks in the lobby.

'Cup of tea?' Katy enquired, following her mother into the kitchen.

'Oh, Katy, that would be lovely!' Susannah quickly changed a tut of annoyance into a grateful sigh; she had been about to remonstrate with her daughter for doing nothing about the heap of laundry. She could see it still sitting in a damp tangle inside the washing machine, and it would have been nice to come home just once to find it hanging up and beginning to dry. But evidently that hadn't entered Katy's head.

Oh for a five-minute sit-down, Susannah thought; then she might be able to face the washing, clean around a bit, and get the dinner started. Any thought of exercising her creative powers in the studio later that evening lay on an impossibly distant horizon. Perhaps she would feel better after a cup of tea . . .

But when she looked up from the jumble of washing, Katy hadn't moved from the doorway. She had her arms crossed over her chest and her hands tucked into her armpits.

'I can't lift the kettle,' she said helplessly, and Susannah felt suitably shamed.

'Sorry, love, I forgot,' she sighed. 'I suppose they're no better today?'

'No. 'Fraid not.' Katy wandered over to the work-room door and pushed it ajar with her foot. 'What's in here? I don't remember this.'

'It's my studio.' Susannah spun round and hurried after her, anxious to defend her domain. 'Don't you remember? It was full of all our junk while we were sorting ourselves out. That's why you don't recognise it.'

'Oh, yes.' Katy sniffed. 'There's still some junk by the looks of it. What's all that stuff up there?'

Susannah swallowed. To the uninitiated it might not look much. 'Well –' she ran a hand through her hair – 'those pretty little coloured things on the top shelf are called smalti and the others lower down are called tesserae. And that stuff over there is for making mortar.'

'Grief, Mum, whatever are you up to now?'

'What? Oh . . . nothing. I'm just having a go at mosaics.'

'Oh.' Katy nodded. 'Mosaics.' She had at least heard of such a thing.

Perhaps she might even be interested.

'Look –' Susannah darted into the room and took one of her teapot stands down from a shelf. 'I've started by making these. I figured that if I could manage something like this then I could tackle bigger things later on. Because the principle's much the same, you see. There are several methods of going about it; I'm not sure whether I'm doing it right, really, but . . . trial and error, I suppose. I'm having a go at a coffee table now. That design over there –'

'Have you sold anything yet?'

'What? No . . . no. I haven't sold anything yet.' Susannah's jaw tightened. Katy was no different from Paul. 'Give me a chance! I've only recently got started. Now if I had a bit more time . . .'

'Kettle's boiled,' Katy called over her shoulder. She was already back in the kitchen, trying to get the lid off the biscuit tin using only the heels of her hands. It flew off with a clang and she stuck her nose inside. 'Oh, Mum, there's nothing in it!'

'Of course there's nothing in it.' Susannah ran over to the kettle. 'I haven't bought biscuits since the day you left home.'

'Have you got any chocolate cake, then? Or my favourite cornflake crunchy stuff?'

'Katy, for heaven's sake. When have I had *time*?'

'Oh, but you could make some cakes, couldn't you? And you must have something nice somewhere.' She began to search through the cupboards. 'I'm absolutely starving.'

'But –' Susannah shook her head in exasperation – 'you must have made yourself some lunch, didn't you? Or – or breakfast?'

'I had a bowl of that rabbit food you and Dad like. I couldn't find Shreddies anywhere.'

'Well, we don't eat –' But Susannah gave up then; the phone was ringing insistently and she still hadn't brewed the tea.

'Hello,' she snapped, tucking the cordless receiver under her chin. It was almost bound to be Paul, checking up on things as usual. He phoned most afternoons to make sure she was home safely – or to check that she was chained to the cooker, perhaps?

With her hands free she managed to pour water on the teabags while frowning at Katy across the room. Katy was flapping her hands at her and mouthing that she was going upstairs to have a bath. Oh, for a lovely hot bath!

'Hello?' Susannah said again when the caller still didn't speak. The aerial had been making hissing noises.

'Oh, hello,' came the smooth reply, and Susannah pressed her ear closer to the phone. It was a man, but she couldn't place the voice.

'This is – er – the mug who bought Lucy-Ann,' the voice explained, and her shocked 'Oh!' came out more like a strangled 'Aargh!'

Her thoughts had been so far from the likes of Harvey whatever-his-name-was that she was completely thrown. Moreover, he had actually bought her doll! Was he about to demand his money back?

'I hope you don't mind my phoning you like this,' he went on, 'but – well you *are* in the book, as you know . . . under H,' he added good-humouredly, to cushion her obvious surprise.

'Yes . . . yes, we *are* in the book,' she found herself echoing stupidly. She and Paul had been impressed at having got in the directory so soon. But what on earth was all this about? She wandered back into the work room for no particular reason, and slid on to one of the stools.

'Do you phone everyone in the book?' she asked, wincing at her damn-fool question. She leaned her elbows on the table and one of her fingers found its way to her mouth. She bit down on it hard so that it hurt.

'Um . . . no,' he answered cautiously. 'I only phone people I know.'

'But you don't know me. Not really.'

'Oh, I don't know about that . . . We had tea together. We talked. And I bought your doll. Isn't that enough to be going on with?'

'Well . . . yes, I suppose it is.' Susannah closed her eyes. If she didn't manage to come out with something intelligent soon she would kill herself. 'Er – how is Lucy-Ann? Did your wife like her after all?'

'Very much so. She certainly did.'

'And – and was it a special birthday? One of the dreaded Os?'

'Not particularly special.' A slight pause. 'She was thirty-three this time.'

And make of that what you will, Susannah thought, her eyebrows rising a little. Quite an age gap.

'Yes,' he went on, 'she was my secretary at the bank, you see. A few years ago now. I was branch manager at the time.'

'Oh.' Susannah picked up a pencil which she twirled around her fingers as she listened. She visualised a blonde sitting on her boss's knee, giggling. High heels, split skirt, and a blouse that strained its buttons. A gold-digger if ever there was one.

'Which bank are you with?'

'I'm . . . not actually with the bank any more.' Something like a spit hissed through the receiver.

'You know how it is these days: they decided they couldn't afford to keep me on. I've been given the golden handshake a little earlier than I ever dreamed.'

'There's a lot of that around,' she said. And could it really happen to Paul? 'Will you be able to get another job, d'you think?'

'Hardly likely at my age. I'm keeping my old contacts, though, just in case; an ear to the ground, so to speak. Anyway, I didn't call you to whine down the phone about my troubles. I want to come and see you.'

The pencil leaped out of her hand. She hunched over the phone and massaged her temples. 'I can't think why,' she said, literally curling in on herself with embarrassment. 'I – I wasn't exactly civil to you the other day, was I?'

'Weren't you?' he lied glibly. 'I can't say I noticed. But I've been told I have a thick skin.'

Suddenly something inside Susannah clicked. Recalling their meeting had brought back something he'd said; and she wondered how it had failed to impress itself on her at the time. 'You knew the pot stand was Roman, didn't you?' she blurted out. 'A Roman design, I mean.'

'Well, of course I knew what it was! Any fool ought to have been able to recognise that much.'

But not my smart-arse husband, she thought.

'And that's what I wanted to come and see you about, your mosaic stuff. I'd like to see what you're doing. If I may.'

'Really?' Susannah gulped down her surprise, her eyes swivelling to the coffee-table design she had pinned on the wall. This man was genuinely interested? She simply had to be dreaming.

'You – you're very welcome, of course,' she said, 'but I'm afraid there's not much for you to see at the moment. I – I'm actually between commissions.' She stuck her tongue in her cheek and chewed it.

'Nevertheless,' he insisted, 'I imagine you have a studio?'

'I – yes, yes I do. Here. Here, at home. Right here.' She was nodding like a puppet now.

'So you could give me some idea about . . . it's Turnpike Cottage, isn't it? That's what it says in the book. So I could drop in . . . when? Sometime, let's say, on Monday, perhaps?'

'Well . . . yes. You could come . . . yes!' She stopped nodding and forced her tumbling thoughts to sort themselves out. 'Could you come at about half past four, do you think? I'll try to be here by then.'

'Four-thirty on Monday it is, then. Fine. I'm very much looking forward to it.'

Susannah ignored the buzzing tone with which he left her. Her head was up by the ceiling and her feet were somewhere above the ground. Her heart hammered frantically against her rib cage, because he had made it sound as though he wanted to commission something. But what on earth had she done that she could show him? The answer was: precious little.

She simply must get down to some work. But when?

It was several seconds before she realised that Katy was watching her from the door. How long she'd been standing there Susannah had no idea, but a light of suspicion lingered in the girl's watchful gaze.

'Mum,' she said thoughtfully, 'I can't turn the bath taps on.'

CHAPTER 9

Susannah sat beside Paul on the train to Paddington, glad that neither of them had to commute every day. Nothing could be more depressing than this daily slog to work and back, she decided, her eyes roving the rows of men and women huddled in winter overcoats, and watching rain as it spattered against the windows because it was still dark outside and there was nothing else to look at. In comparison to these people she felt almost as if she were on holiday, even if she was going on her father's pointless errand to the solicitors.

Paul, the *Telegraph* held up in front of him, appeared oblivious to the passengers and the weather. And to his wife.

He wasn't usually petty, but Susannah wondered whether he was a little put out at having to 'slum it' in second class: being on official business he was entitled to first-class travel, and he had downgraded because of her.

Normally he drove to his office in Swindon, but today he was going for a JAR.

'For a what?' Katy had asked, when her mother

had told her where they were going, and why. 'It's a long way to go to a pub.'

'It's not the sort of jar you're thinking of. It means: Job Appraisal Review; having a chat with the boss.'

'Oh.' Katy quickly retreated. Anything that went on in offices, she didn't want to know about right now.

And neither do I, thought Susannah, emitting a gentle sigh but nevertheless picturing the piles of work waiting for her back on her desk. Now, if she could spend all day doing mosaics . . . She hadn't yet told Paul about Harvey Webb coming round to look at her studio. What would he make of it? Maybe she wouldn't tell him at all – unless something concrete came out of it. Oh, she should be getting on with it, though, not sitting here going to London. At this rate there would be nothing for Harvey to see.

The train had drawn into Reading.

'I don't know how long I'll be,' Paul muttered out of the side of his mouth. 'We'd better make our separate ways home. If we don't end up on the same train, you can have the car. I'll get a taxi from the station.'

'OK,' she agreed, vaguely disappointed. She'd been half-expecting him to suggest meeting for lunch. She could murder a lunch somewhere nice . . . Covent Garden, perhaps? She hadn't been there for years. They'd often strolled through it when they first met – only then it had been the real

McCoy, selling fresh fruit and vegetables; not what it was today.

Perhaps Paul hadn't suggested lunch because he planned to meet up with some of his old colleagues. Perhaps he had other meetings; other things to do. He hadn't been very forthcoming, actually; in fact he'd been unusually preoccupied . . .

After the briefest of goodbyes they parted on the concourse at Paddington.

Surely, she thought, watching him striding away from her, he couldn't be worried about what his boss would be saying to him later? Normally he earned high praise. No, he could have nothing to worry about.

Paul found himself bending over Wesley Morris's secretary – and admiring her marvellous breasts – with little recollection of how he had got there. His journey from the escalator at Paddington to the department's building off Tottenham Court Road had passed in a blur.

Susannah had dominated his thoughts. Katy's home-coming hadn't improved her mood, and he'd been so sure it would. If anything it had made her worse. Well, OK, maybe she was worried about Katy – weren't they both? But what a way to show it! Shunning the girl, pretending nothing had happened, that it would simply go away – that was no way to deal with the problem.

And then there was the matter of his interview. He had heard Susannah tell Katy that he was going to London for his annual JAR. He hadn't bothered to put her right. He had carried on stepping into his trousers, nearly ripping the stitches in his annoyance with her. If she had so little interest in him these days that she couldn't recall that he'd had his JAR two weeks ago – well! He wasn't going to remind her.

Not that he could have told her much about his meeting today. Wesley Morris had been vague over the phone. But he had a pretty good idea what it would be about, and could have confided his worries to her. Then she could have helped him prepare himself for the worst; told him everything would be all right. Comforted him. Hell, that was what wives were *for*.

As it was, he must face things alone. Feeling worried. And insecure. Because this, surely, was it. What else could it be but his marching orders? Sorry, mate – more staff cuts to be looked for, more savings. Sod off, thanks a lot, goodbye.

It couldn't have come at a worse time either. They were going to have to support Katy again. They had overspent on the cottage. Bought a new car. Booked up a fortnight's skiing in February. Of course he would get a nice lump sum ... but a drastically reduced income. Supposing they lived till they were ninety? You can't live off a lump sum for ever.

But he must stop all this day-dreaming and concentrate on the coming interview. Keep his mind on one problem at a time ... and try not to stare at

Wesley's secretary: she was giving him the strangest of looks.

'Go right in,' she told him from under her lashes. 'He's expecting you any minute now.'

Paul's gut twisted as he opened the door. He may have been on good terms with Wesley for many years but that wouldn't make the next half hour any easier.

'Bad trip?' Wesley asked, smiling thinly from behind his desk. 'You're looking a bit frazzled, Paul, to say the least.'

'No, no,' Paul lied, taking the proffered seat. 'I'm fine. Never better. How about you?' He leaned forward, squinting. 'What on earth have you got in your hand?'

'A tennis ball,' came the swift explanation. 'You squeeze it like this, you see, over and over again, and it's – er – meant to be terribly good for you.'

Paul nodded knowingly. 'So that's the latest, is it?'

Wesley was always on to some gimmick or other. One week it might be buckets and buckets of water, because he'd heard that you should drink umpteen pints every day; another it might be a bunch of seaweed stuck up your nose supposedly to increase your sex drive. If Wesley thought there might be something in it, he would do it.

'And how is this moth-eaten, hairless sphere that looks like something you whipped off your dog going to do the least bit of good?' Paul asked.

'Well, it builds up your bones ... or your

muscles . . . or something.' Wesley ransacked his memory, still squeezing for all he was worth. 'Or is it supposed to relieve stress? You've got me there, Paul. Can't remember. Just know it's doing me good.'

'Obviously not as an *aide-mémoire*,' Paul murmured. He straightened his face and his tie. His stomach gave another warning wrench. In a moment he would know his fate. 'I suppose you *do* remember why you sent for me?' he asked, propping his left ankle on the opposite knee.

'Ah.' Wesley's eyes slid sideways to the window, and a second later came back to the ball. Giving it a final crush, he placed it in a pin tray, then leaned back in his chair to face Paul.

What he was thinking about right then was anybody's guess. His expression gave nothing away.

'Frank, this must stop. Right now.'

'What? What must? I'm not doing anything.' Except raking around in his ear.

Jan clicked her tongue; shook her head. 'You know very well what I mean.'

Frank put down his cup of coffee. 'I'm sitting here minding my own business.'

'And worrying yourself half to death. You don't fool me, Frank May. I've known you far too long.'

'Yes.' Frank sighed. 'I know. I can't help it. I know that daughter of mine too. She'll have been to the solicitor's by now, and she'll not have handled things properly.'

'Now, Frank, that's most unfair. Susannah will do her best.'

'But it won't be anywhere near good enough. She'll allow herself to be fobbed off. She'll agree with everything he says.'

' "He" might be a woman.'

'The girl never had any spine. No spunk – not like you or me – no nerve.'

'You can hardly expect her to take after me. I'm not her natural mother.'

'No.'

'She's like Rose, from what I can gather. And I wouldn't have said *she* had no spine. She knew how to get what she wanted, didn't she? And so does Susannah, when pressed. There are more ways of skinning a cat, as they say.'

'Can't say I've heard that expression ... but you're right, of course. And maybe that's what I'm afraid of. Susannah will get what she wants all right, which is for me not to get Bert's house. And she'll get it in her own quiet way by doing sod – absolutely nothing: simply going through the motions with the solicitor, and not really pushing my case.'

'But I can't see the solicitor "going through the motions",' Jan said. 'Wouldn't it be in his interests to have someone contest the will? Wouldn't that give him more work and more fees, in the long run? He should take up your case like a shot.'

In silence they contemplated the mysteries of the law, but could come to no firm conclusions.

'Oh, I don't know,' Frank groaned. 'This is awful. I want to be there! Why didn't I go and sort it out for myself?'

Jan finished sewing a button and broke the thread. 'That letter from the builder hasn't helped much, has it?' She closed her sewing box with a snap. 'Fra-ank . . .' she said after a while.

Frank looked up, alerted by his wife's change in tone.

'Frank, perhaps another trip to England is called for after all. Not just for you, but for me as well.' Her eyes gleamed with excitement and sudden hope, while Frank's narrowed shrewdly as he studied her. He saw plans almost written there in ink. 'Are you thinking,' he said slowly, 'what I think you're thinking? Because –' he struggled with himself – 'I'm not sure I can do what you want me to.'

'What, admit that we made a mistake?' Jan took Frank's coffee and tipped it down the sink. 'Have all those know-alls who said we'd regret it proved right? Well, maybe your ego will suffer slightly in the beginning. But who cares if we look like silly fools? In the long run it will be worth it, won't it? Come on, Frank, shift your body, get weaving. There's a heap of work to be done.'

Natalie was two steps from Simon before she even noticed him. She had emerged from the school entrance carrying a basket, apparently oblivious to other staff members leaving with her. Now she plodded down the steps, taking her time. She stopped at the sight of his trainers, looked stricken, and glanced around her. It was as if she were seeking escape.

'You shouldn't have come here!' she hissed from the back of her throat. 'I thought I said you were to phone.'

'What's the matter? Do we stink or something? Are you ashamed of us?'

Her eyes drifted down to the buggy. 'And you shouldn't give Justin those lollipops. He's far too young for things like that. What if he swallows the sticks?'

'As if you really cared,' Simon sneered, then found to his dismay that Justin was calmly offering his mother the sticky red sweet, presumably so she could take a lick at it. Anyone watching would have thought he'd only been parted from her for a minute, and that she was the most wonderful mother in the world.

What a joke. Instead of bending down to his level and saying, 'Yum yum, thank you,' like any well-adjusted adult would have done, Natalie ignored him.

She shifted her basket to the other hand. 'Well, have you found yourself somewhere to live yet?'

'No. We might have to sleep in the car.'

She knew he didn't mean it. 'The sensible thing would be to sell that, wouldn't it?'

'Not until I have to.' Simon kicked the wheels of the buggy. 'How will I shift my gear from the flat without a car? Not that I've anywhere to shift it.

I'm having a problem, if you must know, finding somewhere to rent. Everyone's charging the earth. Or they don't want to know about kids. So I thought –' he cleared his throat – 'I'd go to my parents' like you suggested. Just for a while, of course. Until I can sort something better.'

Natalie nodded slowly but refrained from passing comment, much to Simon's relief.

'So why don't you come over this weekend to see us? Before Justin forgets who you are?'

There was fat chance of that, Simon thought bitterly; Justin was lolling out of his buggy now, grinning hugely, gurgling for all he was worth, and trying to attract Natalie's attention. Little traitor. Why couldn't he grizzle and whine at her, the way he'd been carrying on all day?

'I might come, if I can make it,' she said. 'But I might not. What . . . what have you told your parents?'

'About us? I haven't told them anything yet. I'll think of something when the time comes. Don't worry. I won't blacken your name. I won't, honestly.'

'Thanks.'

'Not that you give a damn.'

'Oh, but I do. Your parents are OK. I wouldn't want them to think me . . . because I'm not. Not really. I'm not! Anyway –' she lifted the basket to chest-level, looking worried and confused. 'Must go . . . got tons . . . see you soon, I expect.'

'Yeah. See you soon. You will come, though?'

But she'd stirred herself to a half-hearted jog and was already some way down the street. She really couldn't wait to get away from him, it seemed.

'You will come, won't you?' he yelled after her. But somehow he wouldn't bet on it.

'So how was it? Your JAR. Was it all right?' Susannah slumped down in the seat Paul had saved her, in case she happened to be on the same train.

'About as pleasant as your trip to the gynaecologist,' he said loudly, and slung his briefcase into the rack.

'What?' She laughed incredulously, embarrassed because the train was still waiting to pull out and in the lull many an idle ear must have picked up on the conversation. 'But I haven't been to see a gynaecologist! What in the world makes you think I have?'

'What makes *you* think I went for a JAR?' he countered.

'But –' she thought frantically – 'you said . . . oh, no, you went for that recently, didn't you? Sorry, I must have got confused.' She glared at a woman across the aisle who smiled sympathetically back at her. 'Well, what have you been doing in London? I don't think you ever said.'

'What I told you was that I was seeing Wesley Morris.'

'Yes, I know, I know. But what about?'

'About work . . . and – and staff. And so on.'

Susannah waited dutifully to learn more, but nothing came. All this fuss, she thought crossly, and he had nothing to tell her!

'And the solicitor?' he asked eventually. 'What did he say? You see *I* remember these things.'

'Oh, him? Not a lot.' If Paul wanted to be bloody-minded and not tell her anything, then she wouldn't say anything either. Two could play at that game.

She pulled a magazine from beneath the flap of her bag where she'd secured it, thumbed it open and pretended to read.

CHAPTER 10

Straightening up from his weekly inspection of the windscreen fluid container on Saturday morning, Paul was surprised to discover his son pulling up on the drive behind him. He lifted his head slowly to the growl of a noisy exhaust.

'Didn't know you were coming, Simon,' was his guarded response as the lad uncurled from the vehicle like a spring. 'Perhaps your mother forgot to mention it.'

'No.' Simon slammed the door of his hatchback and gave a breezy grin. 'She isn't expecting me either. I thought I'd surprise you if you were in. And I've brought a key in case you were out.' He went over to his father, shoved his hands in his jeans pockets, and stood rocking on the outer edges of his trainers. 'How's it going, then – the new car?'

'Fine. I'm very pleased with it.'

Simon slid into the driver's seat, fiddled with each of the controls and jiggled through all the gears, his eyes taking on the far-away gleam that men tend to get in their dealings with brand new cars. His dad was lucky to have all this: super car, nice home, uncomplicated wife, and of course employment; all the things he'd taken for granted that he would have too.

'Where's Natalie?' Paul asked, poking his head through the open window. 'Haven't you brought her with you today?'

'Oh . . . no.' Simon opened the glove box. 'She might be over later. Christ!' He suddenly slapped his forehead. 'I forgot all about Justin!' Leaping from the car he rushed over to his own less-than-satisfactory model where he found the child was still asleep.

Justin was strapped safely into his padded seat with his chin doubled up under his rosebud mouth and his striped bobble hat half-covering his eyes. His limbs jerked as Simon released the seat from its moorings but he settled again almost immediately.

Susannah emerged from the kitchen at that point, her eyes focused affectionately on her grandson.

'For heaven's sake! Bring him in out of the cold,' she said in an exaggerated whisper, and began rubbing her upper arms at the sudden change in temperature. She had been peeling potatoes in the kitchen when she spotted the new arrivals.

'Just admiring the new car, Mum. No, let me take him in; he's quite a weight. Oh, but could you bring in the nappy bag, d'you think? It's in the back of the car. It's not locked.' He smiled mischievously. 'Justin was making some fiendish noises before he dropped off. He was going sort of cross-eyed, too.'

'Oh dear. No Natalie?' Susannah lifted out the nappy bag and glanced around as though expecting her son's girlfriend to materialise from behind a bush.

'No, no Natalie.' Simon dumped both baby and chair on the nearest kitchen work top as if they were so much shopping. 'Mmm, chocolate cake! Smells good. A lot better than Justin does, anyway. When's it going to be ready?'

'Not for ages yet. It needs butter icing and chocolate and . . . look, Simon –' Susannah gripped his elbow to prevent him taking off into the cottage – 'Simon, I can see it might be necessary to bring Justin's cot with you in case he needs a proper nap – obviously he's getting too big for the carry-cot now – but did you really have to bring that cat?'

On lifting the hatch she had come face to face with a complacent black kitten dozing behind the bars of a wicker basket. Its white paws were tucked under its chest and it had a crooked black smudge on its nose.

'Gazza,' Simon yelped. 'I forgot about him too.' He rushed out on his long legs and was back a moment later. 'It's a good job you reminded me, Mum, or he might have had an accident too. Oh, don't worry, he's properly house-trained now. He really is quite good.'

'I'll bet.' Watching as he bent to release the cat, Susannah spared a thought for her brand new furniture, even if Simon hadn't. 'But –' she began.

'Well, well, look what the cat brought in,' a voice

said behind them. They turned to find Katy in her pink dressing-gown.

'That's a nice way to greet your brother,' Simon said. 'And what are you doing here, sister dear?'

Katy pouted. 'Staying for a while,' she muttered, then put a hand out to the cat. 'Oh, let me hold him. Please! He's so lovely!'

'Staying?' Simon's eyebrows lifted as he queried this statement with his mother.

'She's got problems with her hands. From typing,' Susannah explained, whipping the cake from the oven and slamming the door with a thud. 'She can't work for a while.'

'Oh, really?' Something like contempt flickered across Simon's face. 'How long's "a while" going to be?'

'As long as a piece of string,' Katy growled. Then her expression became animated. 'Have you got any string, Mum? Cats like to chase after it, don't they?'

'Yes, he'd like that,' Simon agreed. 'And he's terrific with a ball; that's why we called him Gazza. Just wait till you see him in action. Where's my old table-tennis set, Mum? There's bound to be an old ping-pong ball or two in there.'

'I bet Mum's thrown it out,' Katy told him.

'Oh, Mum, you haven't, have you?'

Susannah ran a hand through her hair. Ping-pong balls? String? The cake to finish and nappies to change? She didn't know where to start. 'Heavens, I don't know,' she said, but she was

118

actually thinking: *my son will be twenty-four next birthday; my daughter twenty-one. Yet here they are, playing round my feet with a kitten like they were still in nursery school. Where did I go wrong?*

Then she remembered what she had been going to say several minutes before.

'Simon,' she said, addressing the top of his head again, 'why have you brought all that stuff in the car with you – the buggy, the hold-all and the bath?'

But at that point Justin woke up. And he didn't like where he was. Simon scooped him from his chair and carried him into the sitting room.

'Look, Justin,' he told the distraught child, 'this is Nana and Grandpa's house. Don't you remember? It's all nice and decorated now. Isn't it lovely and cosy?' He stood looking about him. 'It's not as big as I remember it,' he told his mother. 'Did you bring the nappy bag through?'

'Yes, I did.' She dumped the bag on the floor and folded her arms. First Katy did nothing but criticise, and now Simon. 'And this place is plenty big enough for the two of us, I'll have you know. Your father and I are delighted with it. When the time comes and we've only got our pensions to live on, you'll both see how sensible it was for us to move.'

'OK, OK, all right, Mum.' But Simon was not paying much attention. He suddenly stood back from the baby and the nappy-changing business he'd embarked on, wearing a look of distaste. He shot his mother a glance. 'I don't suppose . . . ?'

Susannah knelt down to take over the messy

task. 'And you haven't said why Natalie's not here,' she said, lifting Justin's lower half with a deft tweak of the ankles. She whisked the disposable away and memories came flooding back with the first squirt of pink baby lotion. Somehow, though, nappy-changing wasn't quite the same when the child wasn't your own. She was relieved when the job was over and she could address the other end with baby talk.

'Who's a lovely clean boy now?' she cooed, putting her face only inches from the child's. Justin had seen his Nana in Bristol less than a fortnight ago but now he stared back at her as though she were an alien. Not one smile of recognition. Not a flicker of a reward for what she had just done for him. Ah, well.

'Can I have him now?' Katy asked, the kitten having escaped her. It had taken refuge under the television and now, perhaps inspired by the nappy-changing business, had decided to wash itself; it had one tiny leg poised delicately in the air. Katy took Justin over to the window, to 'see if Grandpa's finished working on the car yet'.

'Simon,' Susannah tried again, 'you still haven't told us why Natalie hasn't come with you. Is she all right? Is she not well?'

'She's fine. Fine. Just busy. She . . . may be over later.'

'And –' Susannah shook her head as she tried to fill in by guess-work what Simon seemed reluctant to tell – 'why have you come to see us on your own? How long do you intend to be here?'

'Thanks, Mum,' he grunted. 'You make me feel really welcome.'

'Oh, Simon, I didn't mean – it's just that – well, I do need to know how many to cook for, and if you were thinking of spending the night here there's nowhere for you to sleep at the moment, as you can see. You know you're always perfectly welcome, but –'

'Am I?' Simon stuck his jaw out as he looked around the room, and his eyes fell on his sister. Katy had beaten him to it. 'Look, I can sleep on this sofa here. No problem. I don't suppose it makes up into a bed, does it? No? Well, anyway, it's not very long, I know, but I'll manage.'

'And Natalie – if she comes over? Does she sleep standing up?'

'Now if I put all the cushions on the floor . . .' He looked about him again, pretending not to have heard. 'What happened to that nice big sofa we had in Windy Ridge? That one was really huge. And it was much more comfortable than this.'

'It wasn't really, you know. It was old and worn and the springs had gone to pot. It would never have fitted in this room anyway. We took it to the tip and –' Susannah snapped her lips together. What was she doing? Why should she have to explain her purchases when it was nobody's business but hers and Paul's? She wouldn't dream of criticising the awful bedsit that Katy had been sharing with her friend, or Natalie and Simon's scruffy rented flat.

Natalie had the weirdest of tastes, in Susannah's opinion: hideous blankets adorned the most uncomfortable seats in Christendom, and there was a peculiar arrangement of what looked suspiciously like covered orange boxes that they used for storing their clothes. She and Paul had never passed comment, though. Not within earshot anyway.

'What do you think they've done with all the money we gave them?' Susannah had whispered to Paul after their first visit to see the couple in the home they'd been setting up together.

'Lord only knows,' he muttered as they drove off down the road. 'They're taking this recycling thing a bit far, aren't they? Do you think they realise what a fire hazard it all is? Knock one of those smelly candles over and the whole place would go up in flames.' He gave a derisive snort. 'Do the environment no end of good, that would. I only hope Simon's had the sense to get them properly insured.'

'Oh, don't say things like that,' Susannah said with a shiver. 'And to hell with the insurance; what about the baby, when it arrives? Perhaps we should give them each a smoke alarm for their birthdays.'

Paul had glumly agreed with her. He was pretty fed up. He hadn't liked the idea of Simon and Natalie living together, even if it was the way things were done these days. Particularly when there was a baby involved. And of course that was another thing he didn't like: the fact that they had started a family so soon.

'Look, Simon,' Susannah said now, one hand on her hip, the other clamped to the top of her head as if afraid it would blow off, 'even if you sleep in here –' and she wasn't very happy at the thought of her beautiful new sitting room being turned into a doss-house – 'even if you sleep in here, where do you think you're going to put Justin? Cots take up an awful lot of space; there simply isn't room for one. Not that I would want a cot in here for long anyway.'

'You can't have my room,' Katy put in quickly, 'I've slept in the only sheets. And there wouldn't be room for Justin and me together either, if that's what you were about to suggest.'

Susannah felt two pairs of eyes on her, as if she could magically expand the cottage to accommodate them all. Or were they expecting her to –? 'Oh, no,' she said. 'Most definitely not. Your father and I are much too old to have a baby in our room.'

'What's age got to do with it?'

'Oh, be reasonable, Katy. Can you honestly see your father and I getting up in the middle of the night to see to a baby? No, no. Much as we love him, of course . . .'

'He's very good, you know,' Simon said.

'But we'd be nervous wrecks within days. And how long is this going to be for, Simon? You know, you still haven't said.'

'I don't really know yet.' Simon met her eyes, looked away again, and began to busy himself with stripping the sofa and fireside chairs of their beautifully upholstered, pristine cushions. Lining them up on the floor, he was trying them out for size when his father wandered in from the garden.

'He's going to sleep on them,' Susannah explained.

'What – now?'

'Don't be silly, Paul. Tonight. And maybe tomorrow night. And . . . I don't know how many nights after that. Simon was about to tell us, weren't you, Si?'

But Simon had gone into the kitchen to look around. When he pushed open the door to the studio his face lit up. 'But this is great! I'd forgotten about this. It was a play room once, wasn't it? And there's even an electric radiator. If we push that old table out of the way and tidy up some of the mess, it'll be a perfect room for Justin!'

'Yes,' Susannah heard herself say from a long way off, 'absolutely perfect. Now why didn't I think of that? But you never did tell me, Simon, why you had to bring the cat with you too. Just what is this all about?'

Simon waved his hands at them all, a sickly grin on his face. 'OK, OK, I can see it's big confession time. Let's go and sit down and I'll tell you all about it.'

The sitting room was crowded with all four of them seated, Justin and Gazza taking centre stage on the oval patterned rug.

'We've split up,' Simon told them bluntly. 'Oh, it's only a temporary thing. Temporary until I can get a job, that is.'

The room fell strangely silent. But not for long.

'Another job?' Paul said. 'What – can't you manage on the one you've already got?' He had never been in favour of Simon going into the estate agency business straight from sixth-form. Bad enough that he had showed no inclination to go to university – and that was Susannah's fault. She had a dread of being a pushy parent and had half-convinced Paul that it was better for the children to make up their own minds about what they wanted to do – with disastrous, in Paul's opinion, results.

But an estate agency! And that was before the property market took a dive. Things were bound to be hard right now.

Simon shook his head. *Another* job? Stupid Dad, his expression was clearly saying.

'Well, a lot of people are moonlighting these days,' Paul defended himself.

'And jolly good luck to them!' was Simon's bitter reply. 'I can't find even one job, let alone two.'

'I don't believe I'm hearing this,' Susannah said from her chair. 'First Katy. Now you. Oh, I know the circumstances are different, but heavens, even so . . . both of you!' As well as Harvey Webb.

Unemployment. It was as though a plague had crept into the house. They had been hearing about it for a long time now – people had succumbed to it in droves – but so far it hadn't afflicted them.

'That's rotten luck, son,' Paul said eventually, and Simon couldn't bear to look at his father; he was sure to have an 'I told you so' expression on his face. And if he hadn't, then that was somehow worse, because he deserved it. If only he'd listened to his father . . .

'Oh, Simon, I'm so sorry,' Susannah said. She shook her head and looked bleakly down at her hands. What could one say at times like this? Especially since there was little or no chance of Simon getting a similar job elsewhere. And what else could he do that would pay him well enough to help support a small family?

'We can't afford to rent the flat any longer,' Simon went on, 'not on Natalie's money alone. Oh, I know I can claim benefit or something, but – well – we were finding things a bit tight as it was. Even though we could save on a childminder with me at home, it's not going to be anything like enough to make much difference. So we thought about it long and hard, and in the end we decided there was only one thing for it. We would have to go our separate ways for a while and pull in our horns and save. So Natalie's gone to stay with a friend.'

'And I suppose the friend couldn't take you all?'

'No, she hasn't the room.' Simon cast an agonised glance around at his family. 'You see, I really didn't have much choice. And it makes sense for me to have Justin with Natalie still in work; I'm the one who's going to be stuck at home all day, at least until I can find a job.'

'And the cat?' Susannah couldn't help asking. 'I suppose Natalie's friend wasn't willing to take on the cat?'

'Oh, she would have done,' Simon reassured her. 'Only she's allergic to them.'

'But Simon –' Susannah spread her hands – 'we're not geared up to a cat here. They like to have their freedom. Windy Ridge was fine for old Tammy before she snuffed it, but how will this one come and go? We can't keep opening the door to let it in and out. We can't even have a window open for it at this time of year.'

'Oh, Mum,' Katy said, 'don't make such a fuss. Dad can always make a cat flap in the back door.'

'Yes – I suppose that's a possibility. . .'

'You must be joking,' Paul cut in. 'That door's the original one; you won't catch me making holes in it. Nor in the front one,' he added quickly, seeing Katy about to suggest it.

Simon put his hands over his ears. 'All right, all right. You don't have to make a song and dance about it. Gazza's quite used to using a dirt tray. I've brought all that stuff with me.'

'And where do you propose to put a dirt tray?' Susannah wanted to know. 'In my kitchen, I suppose, where I'll be putting my foot in it every five minutes.'

'Oh, Mum, don't be like this!' Simon sent his mother the pleading look that had got him sweets and biscuits when he was half the size he was now. 'What could I do but bring him with me? Kittens are like puppies, you know; they're not just for Christmas. You wouldn't like me to take him for a drive along the M4 and forget to bring him back, would you?'

'Don't be silly, Simon.' Susannah shuddered in horror. His little-boy look had only worked in part. A large portion of her was filled with an overwhelming resentment: resentment that he'd taken it entirely for granted that he could dump all this on her without so much as a 'Do you mind?'.

Simon sat back on the sofa, his face grim and sulky, as if he couldn't fathom why his parents were making such a fuss over a small kitten when he had a mountain of problems a mile high on his shoulders. He stood up, banging his head on a beam and not improving his expression. 'Talking of dirt trays,' he muttered, rubbing a growing lump, 'I'd better go and set it up before Gazza needs to use it.'

'I think he's left it a bit too late for that,' Katy said with a giggle when he had gone.

Susannah followed her gaze. The kitten had taken itself off to a corner of the room where a large rubber plant stood in a ceramic pot. There, perched over a hole he'd just dug, Gazza blinked blithely back at them.

CHAPTER 11

'That was really yummy,' Katy pronounced next day, having crammed the last crumbs of chocolate cake into her mouth. She licked her fingers one by one and wiped them on her dressing-gown. 'Can you make another one, Mum?'

'If I can find the time.' Susannah sighed, tipping a laundry basket out on to the kitchen table and wondering how she was going to get so much stuff dry on a foul wet Sunday in November.

Where on earth had it all come from, she had wondered earlier, finding sleeves and trouser-legs cascading over the edge of the bathroom storage stool so that the lid would no longer lie down to make a seat. Then she had realised: Katy and Simon must have brought some washing with them. Dear souls.

'Tell them to do it themselves,' was Paul's suggestion when he found her clucking over it. But she knew *that* would never work. She had tried that in the past, and had thought better of it when she came home one day to find Katy's favourite blouse – and absolutely nothing else – enjoying a long leisurely programme in a machine full of sudsy water. Another time she had opened the door of the airing cupboard to discover Simon's soggy contribution draped all over her dry things.

'Aren't you going to get dressed today?' Susannah asked Katy now as she began to make a row of unmatched socks on the clothes horse.

Katy had pulled the colour supplement towards her when she finished her slice of cake, and was absorbed in it. 'Mmm, I will later,' she said, not looking up.

'And aren't you going to have something proper for breakfast today? Chocolate cake is hardly suitable. Why don't you have some toast? And an egg?' Susannah tried not to stare at the hollows at the base of Katy's pale little neck. She had hardly an ounce of fat on her, and if Susannah hadn't witnessed how quickly the cake was disappearing, she might have seriously considered the possibility of her daughter being anorexic. Or bulimic. Or both.

'Heavens,' she went on, receiving no response, 'I dread to think what you've been feeding yourself on while you've been living away from home. What did you and Andrea use to do about food?'

'Oh –' Katy looked vague – 'we used to manage all right. Chips, and – and pizzas and things. *You* know.'

'Well, that doesn't seem very – oh, Paul, what are you doing back so early?'

'We haven't got to the pub yet,' Paul said, fishing

in the depths of a carrier bag. 'I thought I'd get you this.'

'What is it?' she asked, finding her hand suddenly weighed down by a cold and solid lump.

'Beef,' he proudly informed her. 'I thought Katy needed fattening up, and she used to love her Sunday roast. Well, I knew you didn't stock this kind of thing any more, so Simon and I popped over to Sainsbury's to get it for you. They're open on Sundays, you know.'

Susannah wished they were not.

'How awfully jolly kind of you,' she said. 'But Simon doesn't eat meat now, he was telling me only yesterday. He and Natalie –'

'Oh, I'll make do with vegetables, Mum. So long as there are plenty of them.'

'Right.' Paul looked pleased that everything was settled. 'Well, we'll be off then. Ready, Si? Back about half past one.'

'Well, that was really delicious,' Paul said, throwing his napkin aside. 'It was well worth waiting for.'

Everyone agreed with him – especially Gazza who'd had a share – even though the meal hadn't made it on to the table until the early part of the evening.

'Well. I'm glad you all enjoyed it,' Susannah said. 'Now you won't mind washing up.'

'Just stick it in the dishwasher,' Simon told her, yawning, and stretching.

'What dishwasher?'

'Uh? Where's it gone?'

'It wouldn't fit in this kitchen. Anyway, with only two of us here it hardly seemed worth keeping it.' Susannah ignored their stares. Anyone would have thought she'd sold her own grandmother. She got up from the table and went into the studio; she simply *had* to get on with her work.

'Oh, you're not messing about in here, are you?' Paul complained later when the washing-up was finally finished. She had had to turn a deaf ear to the shrieks and arguments that had ensued.

'I am *not* messing about,' she said through clenched teeth.

'Well, whatever you like to call it . . . you can do it any old time. You don't want to be stuck in here on your own. The family's all together again and we're going to watch a video. Aren't you going to join us?'

Suppressing a 'huff' of exasperation at the interruption Susannah tipped tesserae on to a sheet of white card. After what had seemed to her the most tiresome waste of a day, she hadn't felt in the least bit creative when she'd finally got into the studio – the trivial duties of the day had sucked her dry of inspiration – and she had only just begun to get absorbed in her latest design when Paul barged in.

An artistic mood, she was discovering, did not automatically befall you the minute you had time to devote to your craft. Paul's suggestion of watching a video came as a strong temptation not to bother at all, if he did but realise it. She was tired, and drained . . . but this would never do.

'I can't, Paul. Really I can't. I've got to get this table top started.'

'But . . . you can do that any time, surely?'

'Actually, I can't.' She drew a long breath. 'I've got someone coming to see my work. Tomorrow, in fact.' Though as she spoke she wondered whether she had dreamed Harvey's phone call after all. 'And if I don't get a move on with this there'll be nothing for them to see.'

She looked up in time to read astonishment on her husband's face, and the small glow of triumph that flared inside her was soon extinguished by guilt; it seemed wrong to feel so good inside when Paul was so clearly dismayed.

His mouth had been working loosely. 'Who?' he finally came out with. 'Who have you got coming to see you?'

'Just someone from the village. They're new-comers like us, I think.'

'They?'

'Well, he. I mean they both are, he and his wife – newcomers, I mean. But he's the one that's interested.'

'Oh, he is, is he?'

'Interested in mosaics,' she stressed.

'Sounds a right poofty type to me.' He frowned. 'Do you think I'd better be here? I could take the afternoon off if you –'

'Oh, don't be so damned ridiculous!' she snorted. Then, remembering how she had once thought Harvey Webb might not be thoroughly honourable, she added, 'The children are here, anyway. I'm sure I'll be perfectly safe.'

'Well, all right, if that's the way you want it. So –' Paul moved round the table to study her design with the air of one who knew about such things – 'he's commissioned this wonderful table, has he?'

'Well, no, not exactly. He just wanted to have a look at the sort of thing I do. Maybe, if he likes what he sees, then he might decide to commission something. That would be really wonderful, wouldn't it? Now do you think I could have a bit of peace, Paul? I'm finding it hard to concentrate.'

'OK.' Paul backed away with hands held up in surrender. 'But if you ask me, you've enough on your plate with the family right now, and . . . good lord, what on earth's that dreadful noise?'

As they were talking they had been partly aware of an arc of light piercing the flimsy blind and sweeping all round the room. Now they realised that a car had come up their drive, its engine revving hard.

'There's a damned great van outside,' Paul growled, having twitched back one edge of the roller blind.

'A caravan,' Susannah corrected, peeping through a gap on the other side.

United against imminent invasion, they stared out into the gloom. Then they exchanged puzzled glances.

'More visitors you haven't told me about?' was Paul's caustic suggestion.

CHAPTER 12

'Well, I didn't know they were coming,' Susannah wailed. 'And I certainly don't want them here.' She watched in dismay as her father's caravan sank into a rut behind the wood-pile, never to be moved again.

Seconds later, Jan – a spry, spidery figure in black stirrup pants, despite her years, and a close-fitting black woollen sweater – climbed out of the passenger seat of the Volvo that had towed her most treasured possessions almost non-stop from the south of France, and turned to look at the cottage. She seemed to know instinctively that Paul and Susannah were watching her and she waved both arms in the air.

Susannah couldn't hear from where she stood but she knew that Jan's arms would have jangled with bracelets as she hailed them, and if she had not been wearing gloves a collection of large rings would have flashed in the light of the moon. Jan never went anywhere without her jewellery.

'I don't believe this!' Susannah breathed. 'What does Dad think he's playing at? He gets me to run his errands for him, then turns up to do them himself.'

'Obviously thinks you aren't capable – if that's really why he's come.'

Winter blew into the kitchen ahead of the new arrivals and Susannah hugged herself against the chill as she stood waiting on the doorstep. She unwound only briefly to embrace her father and step-mother, and there was no enthusiasm in her greeting.

No one seemed to notice, though; there was too much going on, what with Justin waking at the commotion and Jan and Frank's delight on finding that both their grandchildren were at home.

'And you've got another cat!' Jan exclaimed, unable to choose between taking Justin from Simon's arms or Gazza from his bean-bag bed. She doted on children and animals, and although she had had a number of pets over the years she had never had children of her own. She had put her career before anything else, and had not even intended to marry. Frank had been something of an after-thought, though all in all not a bad one, she often congratulated herself.

'The cat belongs to Simon and Natalie,' Susannah explained.

'Ah, yes! Natalie. Where is the dear little girl?' Jan looked round the kitchen and Susannah cringed: Jan couldn't help but notice the sorry state the place had got into over the weekend, and although Susannah professed not to care two hoots for Jan's opinion on anything, she didn't like to be thought of as a slut.

'Oh – er – Natalie?' Susannah repeated. 'Yes, why hasn't she come over, Si? I thought you said she was going to join us?'

'I only said she might.'

'And how's my favourite granddaughter?' Jan went on, having darted Simon a closer look than she'd so far spared him. 'I thought you were up in London, Katy. The big bad city and all that. What are you doing here?'

Jan was rapidly brought up to date on the latest news. She commiserated where necessary – telling Katy about a friend who had worked in a post office and got a similar condition through banging a rubber stamp – and made all the right noises, while Frank was slowly helped over the journey with a generous glass of malt whisky.

They had crammed together in the sitting room by then but the conversation soon faltered and died; there were one or two obvious questions to be answered before they could all move on.

'Well –' Jan glanced round at the family in the heavy silence that followed, her gaze resting pointedly on her husband. But he merely indicated with a turn of his head that since this was all her idea she could expect no help from him. He had been persuaded to fall in with her plan on condition that they dump themselves on no one but Susannah; she was at least family, which was better than having to lose face in front of their friends.

But to expect him to have to explain everything . . . no, that was best left to Jan.

'I – er –' Jan twisted a silver bracelet. 'We suppose you're all wondering what we're doing here. Well, the fact is we were wondering whether you'd mind very much if we were to camp for a while in your garden. Just for a week or two . . .'

'What – camp – outdoors . . . in this weather?' Paul laughed at the notion outright. 'But this is the middle of winter.'

'We can see that, Paul,' Jan told him in the tone with which she used to put down her over-confident pupils, 'but the weather is immaterial. We have power – although it would be useful if we could plug into your garage supply or something – and we therefore have plenty of heat. We can cook, and wash, and – well – everything, really. We're thoroughly self-sufficient. As you know, we lived in the van for several months while the farmhouse was being gutted; we can very easily manage.'

'Yes, but –' Paul balanced an extra-large log on top of the fire – 'that was in summer in the Dordogne . . .'

Ever ready with a practical view, he was doing a good job of discouraging his in-laws, Susannah decided, even if that wasn't his intention. But she couldn't resist a contribution of her own, for good measure. 'And what would you do for water?' she said. 'We've found that the outside tap freezes up if we leave it on.'

'Water . . . well, yes.' Jan bit her lip. 'That could

139

be a bit of a problem. Look, we know you don't have much room, which is why we've decided not to impose . . . just as well, really, isn't it, what with Simon and Katy back home . . . but maybe we could come into the cottage now and then? To do a bit of washing in your automatic, Susannah? Or to take a shower or a bath? And – well – you know. But we wouldn't get in your way, of course. We could come in when you're out at work.'

'Wouldn't you be better off on a proper site?' was all Susannah could think of to add.

'At this time of year? Don't be daft.' Paul poured more Glenfiddich into Frank's glass and lavishly helped himself. 'They'll all be closed in winter, won't they? I can't think why you don't book into a hotel, though, rather than camp outdoors. But I can see you've made up your mind, Jan, what you want to do, and far be it from me to argue. Would you like me to help you fix things up outside, Frank? Before it gets any colder?'

Jan sat back with relief. 'Thank you, Paul, that would be lovely,' she said on her husband's behalf. She had thought she could count on Paul. She hadn't expected an ecstatic welcome from Susannah, of course, and she certainly hadn't got it, but Paul was always a perfect gentleman.

'You still haven't said why you've come,' Katy felt compelled to point out. 'I mean –' she glanced doubtfully at her mother and father before confronting Jan once more – 'you don't often come to see us, do you?'

'Katy . . .' Paul felt uncomfortable enough at his daughter's bald statement to rumble a parental warning. It was an accepted fact that Frank and Jan didn't visit much, or expect to be visited in return – between them they barely marked the usual rites of passage – and everyone knew it was because Susannah wished it that way. But these things were not usually mentioned.

'It's OK,' Jan was quick to assure him. 'Katy has every right to ask. And we should have explained it all sooner.' She looked to Frank again but he had just found something interesting at the bottom of his glass. 'The fact is . . . we've had to give up on the farmhouse. We've tried – nobody knows how hard we tried – but . . .' she shook her head with a kind of shudder . . . 'we really had no choice. Yesterday – or was it the day before? I've lost track – we decided to call it a day and put it in the hands of an agent. Though if it ever gets sold, the way things are, I'll eat my woolly hat.'

'But why?' Susannah was sufficiently intrigued to question her step-mother directly. 'Why do you want to sell it? And why might it not be sold?'

Frank shrank lower into his chair; how he hated being reminded of his unbelievable failure, of his abysmal handling of the whole damned affair!

Jan looked into the fire. 'It's rather a long sad story. When we found the farmhouse it was just what we'd been looking for, although it needed a lot done to it, as you know. Well, we didn't want to lose it but we hadn't sold our house here in

England, so the only way we could be sure of getting the property was by putting our life savings into it and purchasing it like that. We could then use the money from selling the house here, which we had no doubt we would do in no time, to replenish some of our savings and pay for the renovations.'

Simon was one jump ahead. 'But the housing market crashed and you couldn't sell the house for ages. And when you finally did you didn't get as much as you were expecting?'

'Exactly. Not nearly enough by half.' She reached up to pat Simon on the cheek. 'Having been in the business you would know all about that, dear, wouldn't you?

'But that's only part of our troubles. We've been taken to the cleaners by shoddy workmen since then, *and* got involved in a legal wrangle about the land. We've had to pay a fortune to a solicitor who could be conning us hand over fist, for all we know, because we can't understand a word he says. And the place turned out to be more derelict than we realised, too. Oh, I could go on and on about it all night, but I won't. Our money's just trickled away.'

'So,' Paul enquired of Frank, 'that's why you were so hopeful of inheriting from your brother?'

'We could have finished the building work,' Frank growled from the depths of his chair, 'and taken in holidaymakers to try to recoup some of our losses.'

'Not that we fancied that idea very much,' Jan

pointed out, 'since we aren't as young as we were. And to be honest it was all a big mistake anyway.'

'A mistake?'

'We were never truly happy there! We missed England, you see; missed it terribly. We're both so glad to be back.'

'The proceeds from selling Bert's house could still solve a lot of problems, though,' Frank said. 'We've only got our pensions now; nothing to fall back on at all. No luck on that score, I suppose, Susie? You would have said by now, if there was.'

'With – with the solicitor, you mean?' Susannah had been dreading the question, and she hesitated while thinking what to say, but Paul took it upon himself to answer.

'I don't think you stand much chance of contesting the will,' he told Frank soberly. 'You would need to prove that your brother was incapable of rational judgement through mental illness, for example. Or you would need to have been a dependent of his, and of course you're clearly not that. Or there would have to have been obvious errors or ambiguities in the wording of the instructions . . .'

He spread his hands as if to say there was little point in his going on, while Susannah sat motionless and stared at him. If he knew so much on the subject, she was wondering, then why the hell couldn't he have told her about it, before she trudged up to London for nothing?

'Is that what the solicitor told you?' Frank

was asking her now point blank.

'Er – no, not exactly.' She saw her father exchange a knowing look with Jan, and wondered at it. Did they discuss her weaknesses and foibles in private behind her back? 'I – er – didn't actually get to see the solicitor after all.'

Now it was Paul's turn to stare – at his wife: a stare that said she must be losing her marbles. 'But you went up to town just to see him!' he protested. He couldn't believe what she'd said.

'Yes, I know, but I changed my mind.' Trying to ignore Paul she turned to her father with a pained expression. 'Well, I couldn't bring myself to do it, you see. Not after calling on Dora Saxby.'

'You – you went to see that woman?'

'Yes, on the spur of the moment. I really didn't intend to. I don't know why I did. Maybe I was just plain nosey. I wanted to see what she was like.

'And I recognised her, Dad, as soon as she opened the door. She *was* that old lady we saw at the funeral; the one I thought had got left behind by another funeral party.'

'I didn't even notice her.'

No, Susannah reflected, Dora wasn't the sort to invite attention. Faded and weary in her threadbare clothes, she was hardly the scarlet woman one might have expected. During their short chat over tea and biscuits, Susannah had warmed to her immensely. A more gentle, caring and selfless person would be difficult to find. Small wonder that Bert had loved her. Perhaps she could discuss this with her father in private some time; right now she would stick to the facts.

'Dora was very nice and invited me in. She looks after a sick old husband, and has done so for many years, which is why she never left him for Uncle Bert. She couldn't. She's poor, and a decent sort, and terribly unworldly in many ways; didn't want to even think about her inheritance.

'I think the thought of owning her own house scared her half to death. She didn't know what to do about it. Well, to cut a long story short I persuaded her to consider letting it out or selling it, because she doesn't want to move. She'll need the money one day, for nursing costs and so on. I think she saw sense in the end. So after that . . .'

'You couldn't dream of going to see the solicitor,' Jan said in full sympathy with Susannah, 'and possibly making things more difficult for the poor old dear. I don't think I could have done that either.'

'*If* we can believe her story,' was Paul's aggrieved comment. Women could be so damned soft! 'The "poor" woman's story I mean, not Susannah's. I wouldn't put it past my hopelessly gullible wife to have –'

'I think it's time to sort out the caravan now, my dear,' Jan butted in. She swiftly rose to her feet and put her hand on Frank's shoulder, after darting glances at Susannah and Paul. Little escaped Jan's antennae, and they had been doing overtime that evening.

There were definitely several undercurrents

around, she decided, shoo-ing the men from the cosy cottage and out into the chilly night; but she didn't know quite what to make of them.

CHAPTER 13

Jan was woken by a bird on the caravan roof – just one, hopping about and scratching with sharp little claws, but it was enough. She stared at the painted ceiling, wondering how a bird could make so much noise; she had forgotten what camping was like.

'Not the most comfortable of mattresses,' Frank grumbled, squinting in the half-light beside her. 'Feels a bit damp to me, too.'

'But at least we're back in England.' Jan struggled out of the sheets, grabbed her thick padded anorak, and began to make some tea, her heart swelling with pleasure at being home again at last. Let birds hop about on the roof if they wanted to. They were British birds, weren't they? They were home!

But what had they actually come home to? A family in dire straits?

'I don't suppose you noticed, Frank,' she said over her shoulder, 'that things seemed not quite right?'

Frank watched her fill the kettle and plug it into the wall. Used as he was to picking up Jan's scattered thoughts and gluing them into a coherent whole, this time he was struggling. 'Come again?' he said, rubbing sleep from his eyes and trying hard to concentrate.

'The family. Got problems,' she said slowly, as though he were deaf.

'Families always have.' He shrugged. 'What business is it of ours?'

'Well, of course it's our business! It's one of our reasons for coming back.'

'Is it?' Frank looked bemused.

'Yes! Oh, come on, Frank; we missed not being involved, didn't we? And that means going along with the good and the bad. Not that Susannah let us be all that involved, but still . . .'

'Hmm. I suppose you're right. So what's wrong with our wonderful family then? They seemed all right to me.'

Jan tutted to herself; men were as blind as bats. 'For a start, there's poor little Katy. What's to become of her I've no idea. And then there's Simon and Natalie: something's going on there. Simon couldn't look me in the eye when he spoke about the girl. And why has she gone to live with a girl friend? For a young mother to go off and leave her baby with its father . . . But the most worrying thing of all is Susannah and Paul.'

'You can't be serious.'

'I could sense trouble between them, like a big black cloud. Trouble with a capital T. He was rather rude to her, I thought, which surprised me very

148

much. I know he can't be an angel all the time – how many men are? – but I've never known him to be discourteous to anyone, least of all to Susannah. And they obviously haven't been communicating with each other . . . Oh dear, I didn't expect this. It's come as rather a shock.'

'Are you sure you aren't imagining things?'

'Yes, Frank, I'm sure!'

As soon as she walked into the office Susannah became aware of an unusual atmosphere, but couldn't immediately identify it. Could it simply be that she was late and therefore unused to everyone else being at their desks with nothing better to do than cast virtuous glances in her direction? No, there was more to it than that. These weren't mere glances she was getting; there was something afoot, something to do with her, and she was the only one not in on the secret.

'Go on,' she whispered to Molly, trying to shrug off her uneasiness with a smile, 'tell me my underwear's showing, or whatever it is. I can't stand the suspense any longer.'

But Molly wouldn't even look her in the eye. 'Rather late in the day,' she commented, raising her head from her work and ducking it again. 'I was beginning to think you weren't coming in.'

'We *are* on flexi-time,' Susannah reminded her. Something in Molly's voice told her it might have been preferable if she hadn't come in at all. What was going on?

She began to shed layers of clothes, throwing off her coat and her non-slip driving gloves, unzipping her fleece-lined boots, and unwinding three long loops of blue rib-knit scarf. But she couldn't discard the feeling.

'So what was it this time – an influx of visitors?' Molly wanted to know, her nose in a batch of claims.

'What?'

'Well, your weekend hasn't exactly rejuvenated you, has it?'

'Thanks, Molly. I can always rely on you for the feel-good factor.' Susannah sat down and located her pen; began clicking the end up and down. 'It *was* visitors actually. Sort of.'

Molly's head came up again. 'Go on, spill the beans,' she said, one hand poised for effect with a pen above a claim form, the other dipping in and out of a bag of crisps at regular intervals.

Susannah launched into her saga.

'What?' Molly exclaimed when she'd finished, 'your father and Jan too? As well as Simon and the baby and Katy? Flipping 'eck! And doesn't it seem a bit odd,' she went on, 'about Natalie not turning up, and going off on her own to her friend's?'

'Yes.' Susannah sighed; that worry had been niggling her too. She had hoped that Paul might have learned something of Simon's problems on their trip to the pub. Vain hope. From what she could gather they had discussed nothing more enlightening than where to go for the cheapest petrol, who would be the next Prime Minister, and Formula One racing.

Susannah had intended to have a quiet word with Simon herself, but there had been so little time over the weekend, and he'd been asleep when she'd left for work that morning.

Justin hadn't been asleep though. He had woken her up at ten minutes to five. Not by hollering, but by snuffling and whimpering and thumping about in his cot. Even through the solid old floorboards of the cottage the sound had managed to penetrate. At least, it had beaten a path to *her* room; it apparently drew the line at Katy's door. And why it hadn't gone the other way and bored through the wall to his father in the next room remained a mystery.

At first Susannah had lain silent and motionless next to an equally oblivious Paul, fully expecting to hear stirring sounds from Simon so that, happy in the knowledge that all was under control, she could squeeze in a few more minutes of sleep. But it was soon clear that she might more realistically expect hell to freeze over: Simon was temporarily but thoroughly deaf – a comatose heap under two zipped-together sleeping bags.

In the end she had given in, creeping downstairs, tip-toeing past Simon in search of a jar of baby food, and noting with rising despair a collection of dirty crocks in the sink and that the cat had made an evil mess in its tray – or beside the tray to be precise; he'd not got the hang of it yet.

There was nothing 'breakfasty' in the baby bag but Justin didn't care; he accepted each micro-waved spoonful of creamed rice with a beam of gratitude and a clapping together of hands.

Thank goodness he was as eager to get it inside him as she was, she thought, wiping his hands and face afterwards with kitchen roll and trying to make it seem fun. Then she scouted in the fridge, poured milk into a saucer for Gazza who had kept up a dogged leg-weaving exercise for the past ten minutes, and gave Justin some in a bottle to hold for himself, though not without suffering pangs of guilt because all the baby books she'd ever read said it was wrong not to nurse a baby in your arms.

'Bollocks to that,' she muttered, chipping a block of lean mince out of the freezer, 'I had more time to myself then. And I thought those days were the worst!'

Would she be expected to feed her father and Jan, she wondered, sizing up the meat. She tracked down another pack and left them both next to the sink to defrost.

There wasn't much time for anything else after that. After a change of nappy Justin had been content to go back to his cot with a yellow plastic hammer, leaving Susannah free at last to take a shower. She had stepped into it seconds after Paul stepped out, and when she had rushed back down-stairs, her hair still damp, her clothes slung on anyhow, and her nerves stretched almost to breaking point, Paul was leaning over Justin's cot looking spruce in his office suit.

'No trouble at all,' he was saying, 'are you, little chap?'

And he'd not looked so happy in weeks.

'Susannah –' Molly broke in on her thoughts – 'I didn't want to have to tell you this but – well – Duffy came in this morning, just a few minutes before you arrived. Said he wanted you to see him as soon as you got in.'

The radiator in Mr Duffy's room did not bring out the best in him. The atmosphere was laden with body odour; stale alcohol fumes tainted the air.

'Ah,' he said when he discovered who had come to see him. There was no politeness injected into the word as he glared at Susannah across the desk, and certainly no pleasure.

'I won't keep you long.' He made no attempt to offer her a seat. 'Perhaps you can throw some light on these.'

Swivelling a heap of papers so that the writing was Susannah's way up, he peered up at her from under his grizzled brows. 'I take it you know what they are?'

'Of course,' she replied as coolly as she could. 'They're forms ACS 6B. They're – er – for manual payments.'

'Quite so. I thought you'd be familiar with them. Been using quite a few of them recently, haven't you?'

Susannah swallowed hard before launching into her explanation, but he swiftly cut her short.

'It's not your reason that interests me for the moment. It's the signature at the bottom. I presume you recognise it?'

'I ought to –' she tilted her chin – 'because it's mine.'

'Precisely. And do you know on which date these forms were signed?'

'Not exactly . . .'

'Oh, come!'

'Well, it might have been – um – Friday. I think. Possibly.'

'You are correct. It was Friday. Last week. And where was I on Friday of last week? Was I here, or was I on leave?'

'You were –' she looked about her vaguely – 'here somewhere, I suppose.' She hadn't searched too hard for him, having been ninety-nine per cent certain that at that time of day, and on any day of the week come to that, he would be enjoying a long and entirely liquid lunch at the Huntsman's Arms.

Duffy held her with disdainful eyes. 'Mrs Harding, you are allowed to sign ACS 6Bs when – and only when – you have been authorised to sub- stitute for me. Friday was not such a day. Please remember, in future, that you must work within the rules.' He waggled his narrow head in a kind of exasperated shudder. 'And by the way . . .' He stopped her as she headed for the door, sighing deeply as though troubled by a wayward child.

'You keyed out in core time that same afternoon. I do hope it won't happen again.'

Susannah didn't attempt an answer. She contented herself with letting off an explosive 'Paugh!', once out in the corridor.

'I must be mad to put up with this,' she muttered on her way back to her desk. All those years of incessant toil, and what thanks did she get for it?

It had only been the thought of Paul and his TESSAs, his PEPs, his shares and his building society accounts, that had stopped her telling Duffy exactly where to get off. Paul would not be at all happy if she lost her job and could no longer contribute to his precious retirement fund.

Then she remembered that Harvey Webb was coming to see her mosaic work that afternoon and a thrill ran through her. He might give her her first commission! And after that there were sure to be others. It might not be long before she was back in Duffy's room, handing in her notice and telling him a few home truths . . .

She floated back to her office, smiling at her harmless dream.

If there was one thing that annoyed Harvey it was the advertising junk that fell out of magazines. Today a ton of it slithered across the carpet when he attempted to clear a space for himself on the sitting-room sofa.

Not bothering to scoop it up, he settled down with a cup of coffee and began to consider how he might fill in time until his appointment with Susannah Harding.

Susannah . . . Harding.

A smile curved his lips as he called her image to mind. It was her tip-tilted nose that did it. It was only slightly turned up at the end, but he'd always had a weakness for noses like that. His first girlfriend had had one.

But what did he think he was playing at? Playing away from home – or thinking about it, at least? He was pretty certain she wasn't the type. Neither was he, really. Julia had always been enough for him. And anyway, with his current difficulties, a bit of hanky-panky was out of the question. He was just after a bit of harmless amusement, wasn't he? And he was genuinely interested in what she was doing. His foot skidded about on something on the carpet.

That junk mail again . . . or was it? He picked up the booklet. Exam notes! The kind of thing keen parents bought their offspring in the hope that they'd get good results. How such a thing should have found its way inside one of Julia's weeklies, he couldn't imagine. Thumbing through the magazine produced no answers: there was no feature on exams and they weren't giving exam notes away as free gifts! So the booklet had to have been put there by Julia.

But Julia? With exam notes? He couldn't be more shocked if he'd found her in bed with another man.

His coffee forgotten, Harvey rubbed his chin. At times Julia seemed nine-tenths a mystery to him; at others he felt that 'what you saw was what you got' and he knew all there was to know. Suddenly he felt he didn't know her at all. What was she up to behind his back?

'I'm going now,' Julia told him briefly from the door. She had part of her hairdressing kit in her hand and was about to disappear again, but decided after a moment's hesitation to go over and kiss him goodbye.

Harvey nudged the exam notes under the sofa with his foot. 'How long do you think you'll be?'

'I won't be back until dinner-time, I suppose.' She turned and began to mince out of the room, her brief skirt a tight band round her upper thighs. 'Oh, and that bathroom, Harvey . . . it's beginning to get on my nerves.'

'Yes. Yes, I know.' Harvey couldn't help but agree with her. It tended to bug him too. Being at the top of the stairs it was forever in full view. Even with the door closed it was hard to ignore what lay behind it. The men had been remarkably quick in installing the new furniture but the walls had been scraped bare of the old tiles and left as ugly plaster.

'I don't know why you had to send my nice tiles back,' Julia grumbled. 'And as you've nothing better to do today you'd better go and choose some more. Or – what was it you said about a mural?'

Harvey's thoughts raced: perhaps fate, through Julia, was giving him the go-ahead. He was meant to see Susannah Harding again.

'But it's not as if we use that bathroom much,' he

157

countered by way of testing his theory. 'We can take as long as we like over it. Even if it is a bit irritating.'

'No we can't,' was her parting shot. 'Christmas'll be here before you know it, and so will my mum and dad.'

'So they will,' Harvey muttered when she'd gone. That seemed to settle it.

CHAPTER 14

Accustomed to finding the cottage as tidy as when she left it, Susannah's shock at discovering an unqualified mess was compounded by the fact that Harvey Webb had already arrived. He couldn't have been there long, she conjectured; he was standing in the middle of the kitchen with Katy gawping up at him. But he couldn't help but notice . . .

The floor was littered with toys, an accumulation of dirty dishes and baby bottles huddled round the sink, and a block of cheese that should have been wrapped up and returned to the fridge hours ago was going stale on the draining board next to the defrosting meat. A day's living had taken place on the pine table, and the arrangement of dried flowers that normally occupied the centre was lost amid the clutter.

Justin – barely noticeable among his surroundings – was heedless of both the stranger's arrival and the effect he was having on his young aunt. He was sitting under the clothes airer, absorbed in pulling off row upon row of socks, with Gazza crouched close by, watching him.

When he saw Susannah, he let out a squeal and tried to hide his face with his hands. But he couldn't conceal the stains down the front of the vest he was wearing.

Susannah gazed about her in dumb disbelief – until Harvey coughed politely.

Lifting a quizzical eyebrow at her across the room he looked larger, more real, and more disturbingly attractive than she remembered. Heat surged to her cheeks.

'Oh,' she began to blurt out, a hand fluttering to her throat, 'I thought you wouldn't be here.'

'Is that what you were hoping?' He smiled ruefully down at her. 'That I wouldn't bother waiting and would be gone before you got back?' He helped her slip off her coat.

'No, no, of course not.' She took another furtive glance round the room as she took her coat from him and draped it across a chair; was the place really as bad as she'd thought on first opening the door? But it was, it really was.

'I'm so sorry I wasn't here first,' she rushed on, making a helpless gesture to indicate her sorrow for the muddle, but Harvey merely smiled and put a hand on her shoulder. Presumably he had meant to soothe her but it had quite the opposite effect.

'It's my fault for being too early,' he said. 'One thing I have plenty of these days is time. Of course, if it's inconvenient . . .'

'No, no of course not . . . it's not inconvenient at all.' Lord, what an outrageous lie!

Her vision of this meeting had been so different. To begin with she would have smartened up a little beforehand and would have let him in through the front door, which was hardly ever used. Harvey Webb wasn't the kind of person to be let in through the side entrance and entertained in the kitchen. Whatever had Katy been thinking of?

Well, then they would have sat over tea and shortbread fingers for a while – all served on the best bone china from the sideboard, of course. And they would have made intelligent conversation – about art, maybe, or music. She was sure they would have similar tastes in music. After that they would have drifted into her studio to study her work and he would have expressed delight at the quality of –

'Tea!' she said suddenly aloud. 'Good heavens, Katy – you've met my daughter Katy, I presume? – couldn't you have offered our guest a cup of tea? Or – or coffee, perhaps, if he prefers?'

Katy closed her mouth for the first time since setting eyes on the visitor and dragged her attention to her mother.

'There isn't any milk left,' she muttered through the side of her mouth. 'You didn't order enough.'

'I –?' Susannah was gaping now. 'But you must have heard the milkman come. Or Simon must have done if you didn't. Surely one of you could –' She stopped; her voice was beginning to rise, and Harvey Webb hadn't come to listen to family squabbles. He must already be wishing he hadn't come at all. 'Where is Simon, by the way?' she asked. 'And your grandad and – and Ganjan?'

Ganjan was the name Jan had been given since Katy and Simon's babyhood – it was a compromise of Susannah's, since Jan wasn't their grandmother by blood. It had seemed a good idea at the time; right now it sounded plain silly.

'Simon's out.' Katy shrugged. 'I don't know where. Ganjan and Grandad have gone out too. They've been out all day. They said they had things to do.'

'I'm sorry.' Susannah turned to Harvey again. 'There appears to be no milk . . .'

'Black coffee would be fine. Instant,' he added before further complications could arise, 'and I don't take any sugar.'

'Oh. Good. Well, Katy, would you mind putting the kettle on while I see Mr Webb through to the sitting room? Oh, but you can't, can you? I forgot . . .'

'Sorry,' Katy mumbled. She lifted her useless hands. 'And Mum, I've made myself an appointment – you know – for these, like we said.'

'Oh, yes?' Susannah brightened a little; at least *something* had been accomplished that day. But her face soon fell when she realised what Katy was trying to tell her: she had promised she would go with her to the doctor's and the appointment was right now.

'Yes, I was lucky,' Katy said. 'It's the last appointment of the day, five fifty-five this evening.

And you did say you'd come, you know.'

Susannah's eyes flew to the clock on the wall. She hadn't dreamed the appointment would be so soon; usually you had to have a premonition of when you would be ill and book up well in advance.

Harvey glanced at the watch on his wrist, and Katy looked at her mother. It was ten past five already.

'I –' Susannah began, but Harvey put up both hands to her, his smile as yet undiminished.

'No problem,' he said, 'don't worry. I can always come another time.'

But Susannah was determined that something would go her way for once. 'No, I won't hear of it. We have just about enough time; the surgery isn't far away. Please, Mr Webb, won't you come through to the sitting room?'

She started to push open the sitting-room door but stopped and banged it shut again. 'I'm so sorry,' she said, closing her eyes. 'I'm afraid I can't take you in there after all.'

One brief glance had informed her that whatever calamity had befallen the kitchen had not been confined to that room; it had spread like leaking water – probably throughout the whole cottage. Simon's bedclothes were precisely where he'd crawled out of them. The chairs and sofa hadn't been reassembled, and the curtains looked as though they hadn't been opened all day.

As if that weren't enough, Paul hadn't been able

to get into the room, with Simon sleeping there, in order to perform his usual task of cleaning away ashes and re-laying logs, and it hadn't occurred to anyone else to do it. In short, the room was a dark, unwelcoming tip, giving out a stale and musty smell.

'We – we'll have our coffee in the studio,' Susannah decided. 'That's –' her eyes flickered doubtfully to her ever-patient guest – 'if you don't mind having it there?'

'Not at all,' he said, still smiling, and he stood back so she could show him the way.

'I've managed to put something together for you,' she said, clicking on the strip light and indicating the table on which her work was laid. And he would never know how difficult it had been, she thought, watching his face for his initial reaction. She had had precisely thirty-seven and a half minutes to herself the previous day – she had measured it by the kitchen timer. In that time she had drawn a rough cartoon of a design and laid out some samples of tesserae. She had been thrilled with the result, even with those early beginnings, but Harvey was looking puzzled. What was wrong?

Drawing her eyes away from their contemplation of his handsome profile, Susannah followed his gaze. And there, where once her work had been, lay quite another kettle of fish. Some of the tesserae had been rearranged into a matchstick man lying down, while the rest formed a ragged word: B-O-R-I-N-G.

Susannah's knees turned to water.

'Oh, no!' she managed to gasp. 'I don't know what to say. I'm so very, very –'

'Sorry?'

Something relaxed inside her; she managed a rueful grin. Thank goodness he was being understanding about it.

'That's better,' he said. 'Now promise me you'll stop apologising.'

'But what on earth can you be thinking? The place looks like the aftermath of a jumble sale and I can't even offer you milk. And I hope you don't think that I –'

'Did that?' His eyes twinkled at the matchstick man. 'Of course not. And I can see you've got your hands full at the moment. You must be rushed off your feet.'

'Yes, you could say that.' She began to regroup the tesserae. 'My family has run into difficulties. They've all come to stay for a while. Look –' she pulled the stools from under the table – 'these aren't very comfortable to sit on, but please, feel free. I'll soon have this sample looking something like it was intended to be.' She glanced up at him, suddenly apprehensive. 'Do you know anything about the techniques for this work? I mean, if you're an expert in this kind of thing . . .'

'Good lord, no. I haven't an ounce of artistic knowledge in my entire body. I've spent all my life in the world of finance.' He fixed her with his clear grey eyes and pulled a self-deprecating face.

'Boring, as your daughter might say. I – er – presume she was responsible for this sabotage?'

'Well, it does have her stamp on it, I must admit. I don't think it could be my son's work; that sort of thing would be a little beneath him now he's a father. The baby's his, by the way.' Which gave away the fact that she was a grandmother, but never mind.

'Mmm.' Harvey made thoughtful sounds with his lips. 'And how old is Katy now?'

'Twenty-one . . . and a half.'

'And she expects you to take her to the doctor's?' He was clearly incredulous.

'Yes. Well. I am her mother, you know.'

'I know.' He considered the matter for a moment. 'All the same, I should have thought there was a limit. I mean, when do you stop taking children to the doctor's? When they're thirty? Forty? Till you're no longer around to do it?'

Susannah refrained from answering. It was all too easy for people to criticise when they had no children themselves.

'You see,' he went on, 'what I mean is, if you don't let them stand on their own two feet, won't they always rely on you?'

'Katy's got problems at the moment,' she said tersely, 'problems with her hands. You don't have any children, do you?'

'No,' he said, not looking away quickly enough. Pain had shown in his eyes and she wished she hadn't asked. 'We wanted to have some, and the doctors said there was no reason why we shouldn't. Somehow it just never happened.'

Mortified, Susannah arranged a section of the smallest tiles. They blended from the deepest of blues to the palest aquamarine. All that animal magnetism, she thought as she worked, and he couldn't produce a child. Or maybe the problem was with his wife.

'This is going to be the top of a coffee table,' she said, changing the subject. 'When the tesserae are all laid out here I shall apply a special glued tracing paper to the design, dealing with it section by section. If it's divided up like that it will be easier to handle.'

'I see.' Harvey was watching intently.

'It's simply a means of lifting the design,' she explained, sensing his mystification. Why men would never admit that something was beyond them she would never understand. 'I'll then carry each section across to my ready-glued table top – when I've finished making it – and lay them down in order. That's why I use tracing paper, you see; I can keep an eye on the design.'

'Ah-ha.'

Then a board is used to level them. And when it's all hardened nicely, the paper can be peeled away. After that it's grouted and finished off.'

'Simple,' he declared, 'if rather finicky. And I can see you're very good at it. Now what I want to know is whether you could apply this to a wall.'

'A wall?' Susannah mentally consulted her *How*

to Make Mosaics book. 'Well, of course it could, yes, although the technique would be a little different. Depending on the materials used, mosaics can be put anywhere: patios, paths, outside walls; floors, ceilings, windows. There really is no limit.'

'Good. Then how about my bathroom? I'm having it done up at the moment and something like this would look terrific over the bath.'

Her stomach lurched at his words; he surely wasn't going to suggest she take on anything that ambitious? But he was. He really was! She was about to get her first order, and she couldn't wait to see Paul's face when she told him the news.

'I wonder whether you could quote me for it?' he went on, as though it were as simple as ordering carpet. 'Something – oh, I don't know – perhaps about four feet or so by three?'

She swallowed hard on her euphoria, trying to keep a level head. What should she charge for labour? And it would take many hours of work – at least . . . but her dream began to disintegrate while it was still taking shape. She clenched her hands with frustration.

'Mr Webb,' she said, shaking her head, 'I'm not sure I have the time for this sort of undertaking . . .'

In the next room she could hear Justin winding up towards his most irritable period of the day. If Simon didn't come home soon the baby would have to accompany them to the doctor's.

'I work full-time,' she went on, 'at C & G

Electronics. I'm in the salaries section.' Her mind dwelt for a second on the wretched BMDs – the bane of her life – and of the 'punters' who were always so swift to condemn on the odd occasion when their pay was wrong. Her thoughts must have shown in her face.

'Pity,' he said, casting a calculating eye round the well-stocked studio. 'I should have thought this was more your scene. Haven't you ever thought of giving up the job and concentrating on this? I'm sure you could make a success of it.'

'Oh, I wish . . .' she sighed, getting to her feet. 'Now I'm afraid I'm going to have to hurry you . . .'

'Sure.' He made a move to the door. 'Is that a definite no, then? Could you really not find some time?'

'I –'

'Think about it, at least. Come and look at the room. You may not find it as daunting as you think. I'll leave you one of my cards.' His smile as she opened the front door for him was enough to make her swoon. 'I do hope you decide you can do it,' he said, before striding off down the path.

'Wow–ee!' Katy yelped when she wandered back into the kitchen. 'So where did you find him?'

'He's much too old for you,' Susannah admonished, 'and you should never trust charming men.' She bent to pluck the baby from the pile of socks, which were now almost as grubby as he was. 'Ye gods and little fishes . . . couldn't you at least have put a clean top on him?'

169

'What for?' Katy paused on her way out of the kitchen. She was making a bee-line for her bedroom so that she could smarten herself up for her appointment.

'What for?' Susannah retorted. 'Because he can't go to the doctor's like this, can he? Just look at the filthy state of him!'

'You mean, he's coming with us?' Katy watched with a vacant look on her face as her mother snatched a striped garment from the airer and felt it all over for dryness.

'Well of course he's coming with us. You don't expect him to stay here, do you? What's he supposed to do – clean up this mess and start the dinner while we're out?' She tugged at the jumper and Justin's head popped through. 'And where on earth's that brother of yours got to?'

'How would I know?' Katy shrugged. 'I've got to go upstairs.'

In the time it took Katy to get ready, Susannah dressed the baby for outdoors and did a whirlwind clean round the kitchen. She was ready herself, in her coat and boots but chopping onions to make use of every available second, when Katy reappeared.

'I hope no one thinks he's mine,' she grumbled, glaring hard at the baby. 'And I hope no one thinks he's yours either.'

'That,' Susannah growled back at her, 'is the least of my concerns.'

The driveway at the side of the cottage was

beginning to look like a West Country traffic jam on a bank holiday weekend.

Paul pulled on his hand brake and carried out a survey by the beam of the security light: there was Frank's Volvo and the caravan; Susannah's little car as well as Simon's – which he had hinted was out of petrol but so far no one had stumped up for; and now there was his own. If anyone were to park in the garage they would never get out again.

He reached for his briefcase beside him but something caught his eye: Jan was weaving her way through the vehicles with all the appearance of an over-eager squeegee merchant intent on cleaning his windscreen.

She rapped hard on his side window and mouthed for him to open his passenger door. Seconds later she was sitting beside him, bundled in a thick old cardigan.

'I hope you don't mind, Paul, but I was hoping to have a quick word. I've been watching out for you.'

'Nothing's the matter, is it?'

'No, well, not in the way you mean. Everyone's all right as far as I know. Frank and I have been out on business most of the day, trying to sort out our own little problems, and now we're thoroughly exhausted. We're going to have a light supper and an early night. We shan't be troubling you.'

Paul nodded understandingly. She and Frank could hardly be over the long journey home with the caravan, without the day's outing on top. He sat clutching his briefcase, waiting for her to get to the point; already the car's heat was evaporating.

'You're no trouble at all, Jan,' he said, trying to move the conversation along. Jan seemed to be finding it difficult to say what she felt she must say.

'Are you sure?' She bit her lip, looking dubious. 'I – er – I've been wondering whether we were. I mean, I must be the last person Susannah wants around on top of Simon and Katy. You know how she's always been.'

Paul sighed deeply. 'I wish Susannah would put an end to this ridiculous feud. It's gone on far too long, and it really isn't like her.'

'I know. But . . . if you'd rather we went away, we'll do our best to oblige. Frank will have to swallow *his* pride and beg shelter from some of our old friends.'

'No, no, of course not. I won't hear of you moving on. As far as I'm concerned, you're family, and this is where you ought to be. Don't let Susannah put you off; she's just going to have to lump it.'

Paul propped his elbow against the window ledge and gnawed at one of his knuckles.

'Paul –' Jan couldn't help noticing his sudden irritation with his wife, and put out a comforting hand. 'I hope you don't mind my asking this, but what's been going on? Oh, don't look at me as though I've discovered the world's best-kept secret; it doesn't take much to see that things aren't right between you and Susannah. I noticed it straight away.'

Paul smiled grimly out through the windscreen. So that was why Jan had waylaid him! He really ought to have guessed.

'I suppose we've just hit one of those rough patches people talk about,' he finally admitted. 'I expect we'll get over it soon.'

'You've never hit one before,' Jan pointed out. 'At least, I don't think you have. You always both seemed happy enough.'

'We were. Yes, you're right. We always have been content. This is something new.'

'But you don't want to tell me about it, do you?'

'There's not that much to tell. It seems such a little thing, really.'

'So there isn't . . . someone else?'

Paul shot her a glance. 'Certainly not on my part. And not on Susannah's either. At least, I don't think there is; I haven't really thought of that, to be honest. No, this isn't a some*one* else; it's more a some*thing*.'

He thought about it for a moment. 'You've heard of golf widows, and football widows, and that sort of thing? Well, this is similar, I suppose; a compulsive hobby taken up by one partner that excludes the other completely. All Susannah's spare time's taken up with mucking about in her so-called studio these days, making things with mosaic tiles. She just won't leave it alone.'

'That's a new one on me.' Jan looked mildly surprised. 'Mosaic-making, eh?'

'I didn't mind at first. Thought it was a good

173

idea. I helped her fit out the studio, as a matter of fact. It was something for her to do. Only now . . .' he shrugged expressively. 'She's going at it as though her life depended on it. She's got no time for Katy or Simon, and seems to have forgotten about Natalie altogether. Of course, I don't get a look-in either. It's beginning to get me down.'

'She's always made things, hasn't she?' Jan nodded slowly and speculatively. 'Yes, she always had the creative urge. Been very good at it, too. I think I'm beginning to see . . .'

'Creative urge, my foot. Creating a family's enough, surely? I don't know; women these days – they want everything, it seems to me.'

Jan sucked in air as though she'd touched a nettle. 'You think they should be there when their families want them, don't you?'

'Right.'

'And see *their* happiness as their main concern.'

'Yes.'

'And achieving that should be fulfilment enough for them.'

'Yes. Yes! I only wish Susannah could see it that way.' He turned to appeal to Jan. 'I suppose you couldn't possibly have a word with her?'

'Now when could I ever speak to Susannah, Paul? You might as well ask me to cuddle up to a hedgehog. Look, if I get the opportunity, then I'll do so. But to be honest with you, it would be pointless. Anyway,' she wrapped her cardigan about her and began to get out of the car, 'it's hardly *advice* that she needs.'

When Jan's parting shot had penetrated, it left Paul a little confused. Her tone had been snappy, rather than sympathetic. Why? He'd thought he'd been gaining an ally; now he wasn't so sure.

CHAPTER 15

'Dad!' Katy threw her arms round her father the minute he stepped into the kitchen.

'Hi, honey-bun,' he said, 'hi, Gazza,' and she was relieved to see, on releasing him, that the glum face he'd had on arrival had relaxed into a little smile. But she also noticed that, although he had peered round the steamy kitchen and couldn't have failed to see her mother at the sink, he'd said nothing at all to her.

Katy watched as he put his briefcase by the back door. He seemed rather preoccupied; would he remember that she'd been to see the doctor this evening? She had phoned him at work to tell him she had an appointment, and he didn't usually forget things.

'Well,' he said at last, 'how did it go this evening?'

'At the doctor's?' She beamed her delight at him; of course he had remembered! 'Well, the one I saw was absolutely ancient – must have been eighty at least. But he was quite nice really, I suppose. Actually, he seemed a bit depressed. He was called out three times last night and he's on call again

176

tonight. And his wife gives him nothing but stick for it. Isn't she mean? It's hardly his fault, is it? She must have known what she was up against when she married him. And –'

'Hey, wait a minute, Katy!' Her father was chuckling now. 'The doctor was supposed to listen to *your* complaints, not the other way round.'

'Yes. Yes, I know.' She clammed up a little at this. So maybe she hadn't handled the situation as well as she might; he didn't have to say so, did he?

'Well, he did listen to me – sort of.'

'I should jolly well hope so, too. And what does he think you've got wrong with you?'

'I don't think he really knows.'

'Well –' her father shook his head in that exasperated way of his – 'is it RSI or isn't it?'

'He said that doesn't exist.'

'Oh . . . for heaven's sake.'

'He said it might be carpal tunnel – er – syndrome. Or it might be arthritis, or something. But it can't be RSI. Well, it can't be, can it, if it doesn't actually exist?'

'But people are suing for RSI these days,' he spluttered, *'and* getting compensation. I'm still looking into that, by the way. How can he say it doesn't exist?'

He looked across at her mother, but all the response he got was a shrug. Were these two not speaking, she wondered? Ever since she'd come home there had been a bad atmosphere. And even when they did talk to each other they didn't sound too friendly. What was going on?

'Well, I don't know about other people,' Katy went on, seeing that her mother had no intention of contributing to the discussion, 'but *he* said there's no such known medical condition.'

'Oh, that's just terrific. But he can't dispute that you've got *something*, so what does he intend to do about it?'

'He's sending me to a hand clinic.'

'Oh, really! Now I've heard just about everything. Can there be such a thing?'

'He would hardly be sending me to one if there wasn't.'

'No, I suppose not.' Her father rubbed the back of his neck and glared down at his black office shoes. He looked as if he was mentally drumming up an army of top solicitors to fight his daughter's cause.

He sighed. 'I suppose all this is going to take months. What are you expected to do in the meantime, I wonder? Go about with a begging bowl?'

'I don't know, I'm sure.' Katy flapped her hands at him. 'I suppose I just wait around.'

'But didn't you ask him what was best for you? I mean, should you exercise your hands or rest them? Keep them warm or put them on ice?'

'I don't *know*. I didn't *ask*.' She felt her face going sulky, but couldn't help it. Treat me like an incompetent child and I'll behave like one, she thought.

She'd already been grilled like this by her mother

and had been looking forward to her father coming home with his endless stock of sympathy, not a list of nit-pickings.

It was all her mother's fault. She was surely to blame for the bad atmosphere in the house; the 'vibes' were definitely coming from her. Could it be – Jee-sus! – that she was having an affair with that man? And did her father know about it? She looked carefully from one parent to the other and found that her father had put on his resigned look.

'The world's full of absolute idiots,' he was saying. 'And what does that doctor think he's up to? Anyone could do that job with a medical encyclopaedia in one hand and the other tied behind his back.' He rounded on his wife. 'I thought you were going to go with her.'

'Oh, I thought it'd somehow be *my* fault,' her mother snapped right back at him. 'Well, I did, as it happens. But Katy didn't want me to go right into the doctor with her; she's much too old for that. So I stayed outside with Justin. And he taught himself to walk, holding on to the furniture.'

'Did he? So soon?' He smiled in spite of himself. 'At least someone in this benighted family's a credit to me. I suppose Simon will have put him to bed by now? Where is Simon, by the way?'

Katy jumped as a lid banged down on a saucepan.

'We don't know where Simon's got to.' Her mother spoke through her teeth. 'But Justin's finally dropped off under the sideboard and I don't dare move him in case he wakes up. Katy's supposed to be keeping an eye on him.'

'Dinner going to be long?' Katy saw her father look pointedly at the table; normally a gin and tonic was waiting for him there, but tonight her mother hadn't made him one. And she wasn't taking the hint.

If her mother was having an affair *secretly*, she thought, then she wasn't very good at covering it up; she ought to be being extra nice to him.

'I suppose I'd better get changed,' her father muttered after a while, and he went unhappily upstairs.

Susannah threw salt into the pan. Paul hadn't even said hello to her, let alone give her his usual kiss. As for asking how *she'd* got on . . . well, he seemed to have completely forgotten about Harvey coming to see her.

And Simon was taking advantage . . . how could he keep leaving her to cope with the baby like this? If he'd gone to see Natalie why hadn't he taken Justin with him? And what did Natalie think she was up to?

It was all getting too much for her. They'd had to wait ages at the doctor's, and Justin had got so tired. The minute they got home she'd had to rush around bathing him, trying to feed him, and getting him ready for bed . . . but that must be Simon now.

'Ah, the wanderer's returned!' Susannah turned from the cooker, hands on hips, and waited for an explanation. But none was forthcoming. Simon merely grunted in the general direction of his mother and sister and sat down on a chair at the table.

'I didn't mean to be so long,' he said eventually. 'Has Justin gone to bed?'

'Yes, he has as a matter of fact. He said he was feeling rather exhausted after a hard day and apologised for not being able to wait up for you.'

Simon looked at her and blinked.

'Actually,' Susannah amended, 'he's dropped off under the sideboard and was too tired to eat anything I offered him. He's been learning how to walk.'

'No, really?' Simon brightened for a second, then lapsed back into the cloud of despondency that had hung round him, since he'd shambled in, like an over-large coat. 'Ssh . . . I missed it! His very first steps!' He slumped down in his chair and began to play with a fork.

Susannah had laid the table ages ago; it fooled people into thinking the meal would be ready any minute. She hoped.

'I've been to see an old friend,' he said, making tramlines on the cloth with the fork prongs. 'I wanted to find out about signing on. Toby – the friend I saw – works in one of the Job Centres. He knows all the ins and outs.'

He turned to Katy who had taken up a TV magazine crossword puzzle. 'You'd better sign on too, Katy. And you'd better do it soon.'

Alarm sprang to the girl's eyes. 'Do I really have to?'

'Well, of course you do. Noodle.'

'What for? And don't call me Noodle.'

'To get money, of course, sister dear. How else are you going to eat?'

'Well –' Katy's gaze gravitated naturally to the cooker and came back to her brother's face. Clearly she thought the question superfluous.

'I take it you'd like some dosh, though? You know –' he lowered his voice, wishing he hadn't veered so close to the unmentionable topic of sponging off one's parents without appearing to do so – 'for clothes and . . . well . . . things.'

Katy showed interest for a moment then shook her head. 'Not if I have to beg for it. Mum –' She appealed to her mother, her lip curling in disgust at the idea. 'I don't have to go and beg, do I?'

'It's not called begging, Katy, and it isn't. You've a perfect right to claim in times of trouble.' Susannah lifted the saucepan lid and threw a generous amount of chilli into her concoction. 'Heaven knows, your father and I must have put enough into the national cake over the years to support this whole village. It's about time we got a few crumbs of it back.'

'A few crumbs of what?' asked Paul, coming back into the kitchen.

'I don't have to go to the DSS, do I, Dad?' Katy sprang over to her father. 'I don't have to go and beg?'

'No, no, of course not.'

'Wha-a-t . . . ?' Susannah began.

182

'But why not, Dad?' Simon jumped in. 'I'm signing on.'

'Yes, I thought you might,' Paul said, 'and I've been meaning to have a word with you about it. There's no need for either of you to claim dole money; I'd really rather you didn't.'

'But, Paul –'

'I don't want children of mine having to ask for handouts. I'll give you whatever you need.'

Katy threw her arms round her father again, but Simon was looking embarrassed.

'Dad,' he mumbled, digging ever more deeply with the fork, 'I don't want to depend on you . . .'

'It's better than joining the queue, Simon. We've never depended on the State for anything and we're not going to start now. Your mother and I can look after you. Can't we, Susannah?'

But Susannah could only flounder. 'Katy,' she said, suddenly rousing herself, 'and you, Simon – hadn't you better go and see what the baby's getting up to? I think I heard him wake up.'

Simon and Katy exchanged glances, as if to ask each other how anyone could 'hear' a baby wake up, unless it actually yelled. Did its eyelids go clunk, or something? But they realised they were being got rid of and wisely took the hint.

'I can't believe you just said that!' Susannah exploded when she and Paul were alone.

'Said what?' he asked, dipping a teaspoon into the chilli to taste it. His face was a mask of innocence.

'You've stopped Simon and Katy claiming benefit,' she accused him, 'when they're perfectly entitled to do so.'

'They may be entitled, but they don't need it. They've got us to help them out.'

'Yes, but . . . they won't *always* have us, Paul, will they? And anyway, you've paid a fortune in taxes for this sort of thing; why dip further into your own pocket?'

'No one will ever be able to say that *I've* failed to support my children when they needed it.' He made it sound as though she *was* failing them.

Susannah glared at him impatiently while the chilli glued itself to the pan.

'Paul,' she said eventually, 'I know you mean well, but I don't believe you're doing either of them the least bit of good, cushioning them like this. They have to learn to stand on their own feet, and the sooner they do it the better.

'They won't thank you later on in life for depriving them of the lesson; they'll just look back and see you as some sort of soft great idiot with more money than sense. What you're doing,' she added, unable to resist a jibe, 'looks to me suspiciously like trying to buy love.'

'Well, no one's ever going to accuse you of that!' he flung back at her. He inclined his head towards the pan of chilli. 'And any mother worth her salt would have remembered that her son is a vegetarian!'

*

Paul and Susannah hardly exchanged a word throughout the evening, but when they went to bed she realised she wouldn't be able to sleep until she had told him about Harvey's proposed commission. It might help mend the rift between them, she decided, some good news like that.

'Harvey Webb came this afternoon,' she told him while he was tinkering about at the vanity unit with a yard of dental floss.

'Who?' he asked, turning from the mirror at last and kicking away his slippers. He threw back his side of the duvet to reveal Gazza curled up in a ball.

'*You* know – I told you about him; he's interested in my mosaics. Which is more than I can say about some people,' she added tartly, unable to stop herself. So much for mending rifts.

'Oh, him,' Paul said, moving the cat to her side of the mattress.

'Yes, him. And you'll never guess what: he wants me to make him a mural.'

'He does?' Paul sank thoughtfully down, swivelled his head on the pillow, and eyed her for a long minute.

At that moment she was imagining a sun for the design. A sun rising up over a hill.

'Yes, a mural for his bathroom. He's doing it up. He wants most of it done in plain tiles, but a panel over the bath in mosaics. That's where I come in,' she added unnecessarily. The look in Paul's eyes was fish-cold.

'You haven't got the time,' he said, turning back to look at the ceiling. End of daft subject, as far as he was concerned.

'Well, I've been thinking about that, actually.' She tickled Gazza behind one ear. 'I could take some of my annual leave.'

'You haven't got any left.'

'I know. I used a lot when we were decorating. And that long weekend finished it off. So I was thinking I might anticipate some.' It would mean going cap-in-hand to Duffy, and she didn't relish the thought, but it seemed to be the only solution.

Paul was quick to point out all the pitfalls. 'Look, you already get less leave than I do. You'll have nothing left for our holidays. And how long do you think you would need?'

'A week, I'd say. Yes, a week.'

'That long? And how much would you be paid?'

'I was wondering how long it would be before you got around to that. But I haven't worked it out yet. It's going to need a lot of thought.'

'Well, whatever figure you come up with, it's bound to be prohibitive. Either that or you'll end up doing it for next to nothing. Really, darling, you can hardly expect to make a living out of this kind of thing. And we *are* still coming out of a recession.'

His tone implied that she'd be better off selling ski-suits in the Sahara.

'Thank you so much for your kind encouragement,' she snapped. 'Harvey happens to think I'd soon get plenty more commissions, once people have seen what I can do. He thinks I'm on to a good thing and that I should give up my job to concentrate on it.'

'Oh, he does, does he? He's going to chip in with all our bills, is he, while you play at being creative?'

'But you don't need help with the bills, *do* you? You've got plenty of money to squander on your children. So why can't you use it to support me? Or don't I count as much?'

But Paul refrained from answering that one. He rolled over and feigned deep sleep.

CHAPTER 16

As soon as Julia had gone to work Harvey pulled on his thick cable sweater and snatched up a bunch of keys. This was the second day of following her, and he hoped it would be better than the first.

He had always fancied himself in the role of private eye but already had reason to be glad he'd never taken it up as a career. Yesterday he had nearly frozen, sitting in one side-turning after another waiting for Julia to emerge from her various hair appointments. And the boredom had been excruciating.

Worse still was the niggle at the back of his mind telling him that snooping on one's own wife – or on anyone else's, come to that – was hardly cricket. There was something horribly pathetic about it too: he ought to be able to ask Julia outright what she was doing, not be going about things like this. That they couldn't discuss matters openly did not bode well for their marriage.

No, it all left a nasty taste in the mouth. But he couldn't stop. The thought that today might be the day he discovered how exam notes fitted into

Julia's life spurred him to go through the whole sad business again.

Of course, even if he were to accomplish his mission, he would still be left with the whys and wherefores to work out. But he would worry about that later; one thing at a time.

Stepping into his shoes he put a hand out to the door-latch – just as it was lifted from the other side. Oh no! He let it go as though it had burned him. Julia had come straight back! Today, of all days, she must have forgotten something.

'My – er – records,' she told him, rushing into the kitchen. 'If I don't make notes of who pays what, I'm lost. Oh –!' She reappeared with a large ring binder tucked under her arm, and stood looking him up and down. 'I thought you said you were staying in today – to sort out the utility room?'

'I – er – was only going to pop out for a minute or two. I need to fetch that special paper. You know – the one with all the jobs in?'

'Oh. Yes. But I could have got it for you. Save you going out. Why didn't you ask me to bring it home with me?'

He shrugged. 'Well . . . I'd lose a whole day then, wouldn't I? When I've finished the sorting out I can be getting on with some more applications. Anyway, I could do with a breath of fresh air . . .'

He bent to look through the peephole in the door with the exaggerated eagerness of a condemned man in his cell; only a fool or someone really desperate would want to go out in such a downpour if they didn't absolutely have to.

'Right,' Julia said, still eyeing him a little doubtfully.

'Right,' he said too, opening the door for her. He stood watching her with an awkward smile on his face while she walked out ahead of him. And didn't let it relax until he was certain she was gone.

'Phew!' he breathed, locking up behind him and hurrying round to his car. Deception, he reminded himself, was far from an easy option. Little lies led to big lies; you could be out of your depth before you knew it.

He had left the car at the ready in front of the garage, facing out towards the road. And that, too, had elicited comment: Julia had wanted to know why it wasn't under cover, when he was always so particular about it being so. And why was it back to front?

He had stammered a bit, and waffled, and finally got out an answer, but his explanation had been far too long-winded to sound convincing, although Julia hadn't seemed to notice. Julia, apparently, wouldn't smell a rat if it got up on its hind legs and shook hands with her. Which was all to the good, under the circumstances.

So here he was, trailing her again, because he had to know what she was up to behind his back, and why she was keeping it from him.

Now then, he murmured to himself, pay proper attention. There she is, just ahead of a delivery van.

Driving straight through the village as per yesterday, and forking left at the church by the green. Now out through the fields to the junction, and indicating . . . left or right? Ah, right towards Bath – that's different – and picking up a bit of speed.

Thank heavens for a lot more traffic. Julia didn't look in her rear-view mirror overmuch – except perhaps to check her make-up – but there was always the chance that she might. She would know his car immediately if she did so; there couldn't be that many green Mercedes Sports around.

There weren't many purple Fords either, which made Julia's easier to spot. 'Ever wondered what kind of people go in for bright purple cars?' he had often joked with his colleagues. 'You should come home and meet my wife!'

Right now he was glad of the colour; he could let a couple of cars come between Julia and himself and still keep her in his sights. He needed all his concentration to keep up with her though; she handled that car pretty well. She drove fast. And maybe a little recklessly. And – damn! – she'd swung off the road.

Harvey stamped on his brake. His body strained hard against the seat belt and his tyres protested with a screech. He had almost run into a cyclist, and the near miss left his heart knocking against his ribs. Of course, he was thankful for avoiding actual damage but inwardly he let out a groan; the game must surely be up now. Julia *must* have looked round. But no. The whole world was looking in his direction, but thankfully Julia was not.

Shielding his face with one hand – a pointless exercise if he'd thought about it – he began to ease forward again, peering as he did so through the passenger's side window. Julia had parked in one of the ten spaces in front of a parade of shops and was scurrying through the rain towards a serve-yourself greengrocer with a purse in her hand.

That made sense, Harvey thought, rubbing his freshly shaved chin: last night they'd run out of potatoes and had had to make do with some clapped-out pitta bread from the freezer. Grilled plaice, peas and pitta bread; not to be recommended.

He turned into what he believed would be a quiet side street further along the route and parked so that he could see Julia when she passed. Looking around to relieve the monotony of his wait he spotted a traffic warden in the distance.

The man, poor chap, was leaning into the wind, hunched inside his coat with the edges of it flapping open. Fine mood he would be in, Harvey decided, over even the most minor of offences. Then he looked at the road markings and found he was illegally parked.

'Blast,' he muttered, about to pull away again, but a lorry-driver decided to unload his goods right in front of him. He couldn't see a thing and neither could he move; a milk float had pulled up behind.

The lorry then managed to get stuck. Its trailer was half on the pavement, half off it, and the driver couldn't swing round properly without demolishing a phone booth. All Harvey could do was sit there, fuming at the stupidity of the hooting traffic behind him, and darting his eyes between the lorry and the traffic warden. Julia could be anywhere by now, and if he didn't get away soon he'd never find her again.

By the time he finally shot out of the hell-hole the traffic warden was striding down the street at a rate of knots to see what all the fuss was about, and had almost reached the Mercedes. Harvey's final view of the man was him jotting something in his notebook with grim determination.

'Brilliant,' he muttered, scanning the traffic on the roundabout ahead. 'That's just about made my day.'

But, setting the wipers as fast as they would go, his luck suddenly changed. There was Julia in front of him. Just three cars ahead! And this time he was going to stick to her no matter what; she wasn't going to get away.

'What we need to do is build ourselves a nice big fire,' Jan said. 'That'll cheer us all up.' She put down Justin and let him toddle about the sitting room; he was getting very wearing and she needed to catch her breath.

'It'll take a lot more than a fire to cheer me up,' Simon grunted. 'I'll never be happy again.'

'Me neither,' Katy said. 'Even my best friends have deserted me.'

'Your London friends?' Jan asked, kneeling down at the grate and busying herself with a shovel.

'Yes, the ones I knew in this area have all gone different ways. But the London ones said they'd bring my stuff down for me, and they haven't even phoned. When I ring them in the evenings they always seem to be out. All busy enjoying themselves, I suppose. Without me.'

'They can't have been very good friends, then,' Jan said briskly, 'if they can't be bothered keeping in touch. It's at times like these that you discover who your real friends are.'

'That means I haven't got any, then.' Katy twiddled her lock of hair. 'Mum and Dad are no help, you know.'

'No?' Jan's ears went on special alert.

'They keep having horrible rows. Don't they, Si?'

'Yes.' Simon lay back on one elbow, plucking tufts of wool out of the hearth rug. 'They were having another one last night. Well, not exactly a row, I suppose, but a pretty hostile argument. I don't know . . . nothing's the same any more. It never used to be like this. I can't think what's got into them.'

'Oh dear.' Jan stopped shovelling and sat back on her heels. 'Oh dear,' she said again as Justin sat in some ash.

'You don't think it's because of us, do you?' Simon wondered aloud.

'It's nothing to do with *us*,' Katy said scornfully.

'It's because Mum's got the hots for another man.'

Jan stared at the girl in horror. 'Katy, I'm sure that can't be true! Whatever do you think you're saying?' She shook her head so vehemently that her chin wobbled – and all the skin underneath it that she usually took pains to hide. 'No, I think it's something entirely different, my dear. Nothing to do with a *man*.'

'Well, he's ever so good-looking, you know...'

'Who? Who is? Who do you mean?' Jan's eyes flew open wide. 'You mean, you've actually *seen* this person?'

'Well I wouldn't have made him up, would I?' Katy told her about Harvey's visit while Simon frowned and went dark in the face.

'You really are a pillock,' he told his sister as soon as she'd finished.

'Simon!' Jan reproved him. 'That's not a very gentlemanly way to speak to your sister. I'm sure you've never heard your father speak to your mother like that.'

'Oh no?' Simon's face showed all his recent disillusion. But underneath lurked a certain amount of shame: why did he revert to his silly childhood ways the minute he walked into the parental home? Katy did it too, he'd noticed. And they fought each other like cat and dog when their parents were around, although really they were quite good friends.

'Well, anyway,' he said, 'if Mum was carrying on with a bloke, she wouldn't do it under our noses.

She'd be having mysterious meetings and phone calls, not entertaining him at home.'

'But I could tell by the way she looked at him . . .'

'Katy, I think Simon does have a point . . .'

Katy conceded sulkily, and yet felt greatly relieved. She didn't want her mother to hurt her father like that; she couldn't bear the idea. And if Jan thought there was nothing in it, then there couldn't be.

'Oh dear,' Jan said again after a long and thoughtful silence. 'And you, Simon,' she went on, moving aside so that he could lay twigs and paper in the grate. 'Things aren't well with you either, are they? What a sad little family we are.'

Simon jerked his head by way of an answer.

'Sore point.' Katy spoke up for him. 'He doesn't like to talk about it.'

'Chance would be a fine thing!' Simon burst out. 'Mum doesn't even want to know. I keep trying to talk to her but I can never pin her down lately. She always seems too busy.'

'Well, she *is* busy, isn't she? She's out at work all day. You know, you two could –' But Jan bit back the homily that had come to mind; if she was to get close enough to Simon and Katy to help them she would do well not to antagonise them right now.

'I wonder, Simon, whether *I* could help at all with your particular problem? Of course I can see that it might look like gross interference on my –'

'Oh, would you, Ganjan? Could we talk?' Simon emerged a little from his gloom. He wrested a bunch of twigs from Justin's grubby fist and threw them to the back of the fire. 'You know, I don't like to admit defeat over this, but really I feel out of my depth. I just don't know what I can do.'

'Come over to the caravan this afternoon when your grandfather's out,' Jan shouted above Justin's protests. 'We'll talk it all over then. And I think we can drop the Gan, now, don't you, dear? From now on call me Jan.'

'What about me?' Katy muttered. 'No one can do anything for me.'

Jan patted Katy's delicate hands with her speckled, time-worn ones. 'If the pain's getting a little less each day, as you say it is, then surely that's a good sign? All it probably needs is time. Perhaps you've been *given* time to completely rethink your life. Who knows?'

But Katy was not to be encouraged and Jan had to rack her brains.

'You know, you could do with getting out of the house more,' she finally came up with. 'If I give you two some petrol money, perhaps you could take Justin for a drive? It would keep him out of mischief for a while, and give you both a break.'

'Whoopeedo,' was Katy's ungracious comment. 'I can hardly contain my excitement.'

It was six o'clock when Harvey got home. In slow motion he dropped his keys on to a table and stepped out of his shoes one by one. He'd been driving around for ages. Just driving. And thinking a lot. And he was numb all over, again, but not from cold. This time it was from shock. And no matter where he had driven, and no matter how appalling the weather, all he'd been able to see was Julia tripping up to the door at the City of Bath College, lugging a big bag of books.

Nothing wrong with that, of course, incongruous though it may be; it was what happened next that had stunned him.

He had been standing against a wall, trying to look inconspicuous among the swarm of students hurrying to their lectures, and intending to make a dash for the entrance as soon as Julia had passed through it. He had planned to follow her movements inside the building if he could. But before he had been able to carry out his intention, a young man of about Julia's age, who had been striding across the forecourt, suddenly caught up with her. And put a hand on her shoulder. And didn't take it away again.

The two were laughing into each other's faces as they entered the building together, obviously enjoying each other's company and looking as happy as Larry. But Harvey had not been amused.

Slumping into his armchair he played the scene again. And again. It hurt him every time he did it, but he couldn't help himself. Julia. With another man. Would you credit it?

Well, he decided, finally calling a halt, what was sauce for the goose . . .

His face unusually grave, he reached for the phone and dialled.

It was a man's voice that answered; well-spoken but with traces of London in it, and definitely pin-striped.

Harvey looked down at his socks and dredged up his bank-manager's accent. 'I'd like to speak to Susannah Harding,' he told her husband. 'My name is Harvey Webb.'

'You're very late tonight,' Paul called out when Susannah arrived home that same evening.

'Well, I did phone to warn you,' she shouted back at him from the lobby, where she was shedding her outdoor clothes. She put her head round the sitting-room door. 'I told Katy I had to do some overtime. Katy, didn't you tell Dad I phoned?'

'Oh,' Katy said, her eyes on the TV screen. 'Sorry, Mum, I forgot.'

Susannah sighed heavily, but let the matter drop. To remonstrate further would be a waste of effort. She needed to go to the bathroom, run a comb through her damp hair and get her feet inside fluffy slippers. Then she might feel a bit more human. Oh, and she must give Harvey a ring; let him know her decision. If she didn't give him an answer soon he might start making alternative arrangements for his bathroom wall.

She began to edge her way round the crowded room, stepping over Simon's feet, avoiding the cat on the rug, and being careful not to knock into

Katy's legs where they dangled over the arm of a chair. But as she was squeezing past the telephone table she noticed a message scribbled on the pad. The name Harvey was spread across one corner with the pen thrown down upon it. In the opposite corner a phone number stood on its head. She snatched up the pad and turned to face the family.

'Did I have a call?' she asked, her pulse beginning to flutter.

Katy's eyes slid sideways. 'Dad took it earlier on,' she mumbled, raising the volume on the TV with the controller.

Susannah looked wildly at Paul. 'When did he call? What did he want? Did he tell you what it was about?'

'Yes.' Paul paused to dip into a bowl of peanuts at his elbow and she now saw that they all had a snack of some sort: Katy a bag of Frazzles, Simon popcorn, and Paul the nuts. Even Gazza had a saucer of Kitbits on the hearth.

Paul began feeding himself the nuts one by one, tipping his head back like a hungry fledgling and crunching at aggravating length until each was completely gone. 'Yes,' he went on. 'He phoned about two hours ago, I suppose. He was hassling you about this wretched mural; wanted you to get stuck into it as soon as you possibly could – like yesterday, from what I can gather – *if* you'd made up your mind you were going to do it, that is.'

'Oh?'

'Yes. So I told him.'

'You – told him – what?' she said with ominous care.

Paul cleared his mouth again. 'That you'd decided you couldn't manage it, that you simply don't have the time.'

'But – but – how on earth could you say that? That's not what I'd decided at all!'

Her tone must have cut through the languorous atmosphere of the sitting room, because the TV suddenly went dead. Then Katy and Simon slid simultaneously from their armchairs and melted into the walls. Susannah was left standing over her husband, quivering from head to toe.

Paul glanced up at her somewhat belatedly with a nut half-way to his mouth. 'What are you so uptight about? It's what we agreed last night.'

'What *we* agreed? *We*?' She stabbed a finger at her chest.

'Yes! We discussed it all in bed . . . if you remember.'

'Oh, I remember it very well. Discussing it, that is – if your pouring cold water on everything can be considered having a discussion. We aired the matter, certainly, but never for one moment did I consider turning down the job. That much was perfectly clear.'

'But –'

'Well, obviously it wasn't clear to *you*. But of course you only see what you want to see; you always have. The proverbial ostrich in the sand, *you* are. And how you had the bare-faced cheek to go over my head like that and discuss *my* business with *my* client . . . well, it really beggars belief!'

She stormed off into the studio and banged the door. Snatching up the wall-phone she jabbed out a number.

Calm down, she told herself, smoothing her hair and gulping down breaths of air. I must sound normal by the time Harvey gets to the phone.

But her efforts at normality were wasted: an endless ringing tone was all she could get.

'Mum!' Simon whispered loudly from the door. 'You're going to wake Justin if – oh, you already have. Now he'll be up all night.'

'Mind if I come in, folks?' It was Jan calling now, from the kitchen.

Susannah sank on to a stool.

'Ah, there you are.' Jan came into the studio – but not without some difficulty; she was dragging a large cardboard carton behind her, and making heavy weather of it. 'I felt I simply had to go out and get you this. So Frank and I ran over to that big Argos they've just opened up – you know the one?' She looked up guiltily. 'I'm afraid we'll have to juggle the cars round again for the morning . . . but you ought to have one of these, you know. Before there's a nasty accident.'

'A fire guard.' Susannah's voice was faint. 'How lovely. You really shouldn't have troubled . . .'

'Thanks, Ganjan – I mean Jan,' Simon said. 'It's absolutely perfect. Look, Justin, what a lovely fire guard! Your Great Ganjan went and got it for you.'

Paul appeared on the scene. 'You must let me reimburse you,' he said, a hand plunging into his pocket. But the pocket held nothing but a handkerchief so he just stood there looking uncomfortable.

'There's no need for that right now,' Jan assured him. She looked round at the ring of faces; how stiff and stilted they seemed! Susannah looked about to commit murder; Paul equally so. Simon seemed embarrassed for them both, while Katy could be seen hanging back doubtfully in the sitting-room doorway. Things seemed to have gone from bad to worse in just one day. She smiled at them all awkwardly in turn and rapidly excused herself.

'Fancy a game of Happy Families?' Frank teased her when she reported her findings to him. He pretended to reach for a pack of cards from the shelf where they stowed a few games.

Jan couldn't raise the smallest smile. 'You can keep your feeble jokes to yourself, Frank May. I'm beginning to wish we hadn't come home, honestly I am. And that's no laughing matter.'

Katy slumped down on the bed and looked at her stack of possessions – three boxes and two carrier bags containing all her worldly goods. Andrea had finally turned up with them late that afternoon – and with Spike in tow.

They hadn't stayed long, and it was pretty obvious why: Katy had fancied Spike herself and had been working on him in London but now, would you believe, it seemed that he and Andrea

203

were wrapped up in each other. To be fair they'd tried not to flaunt it but it had shown all the same. So that put the lid on keeping a link with the London lot. There was no place for Katy there now.

And to add insult to injury Andrea had seen fit to pass comment on Katy's hair, just as they were getting into Spike's car.

'Nobody's wearing it like that any more,' she'd hissed, presumably thinking she was doing Katy a kindness by keeping her up to date – now that she lived in the sticks and couldn't possibly know about such things.

'So what?' Katy had found herself snapping back. She was aware that the style had gone out of fashion some time ago, but it had taken her a while to cultivate the extra odd length and she was reluctant to part with it. 'The whole idea is to be different, isn't it?'

'Yes, but –' Andrea had shrugged; she'd had no answer to that.

Katy nudged one of the carriers with her toe. Two bags and three boxes wasn't much to show for a lifetime.

She got up, snatched the dressed doll off the window-sill and tossed it on to the top of the wardrobe. In its place she arranged her collection of CDs, tapes, cosmetics, and baby spider plants. That was a bit better. But even when she'd unpacked everything and found new homes for it all, black despair still enveloped her.

She threw herself back on the bed. For two pins

she could take the entire contents of the Disprin bottle that had just rolled out of a shoe. Wait a minute though – forget the two pins. She wouldn't need them where she was going, would she?

CHAPTER 17

The sleeping-bags rustled as Susannah crept past.

'Oh, so you're awake?' she said.

'Nnngh.'

'Well, I don't know why I'm tip-toeing about anyway; you ought to be getting up.'

Simon unglued his tongue from the roof of his mouth sufficiently to mutter, 'Why?'

As if he had no child to feed, no reason to stir himself! But Susannah's patience had worn thin by now – with her whole family. Last night had been the giddy limit; not just because of Paul's incredible nerve and Jan's well-intended interference either.

To be fair, Paul had attempted an apology. At least, that was what she had supposed it to be. With hindsight it might have been another opportunity to point up her failings. Whatever, Paul had found her in their bedroom soon after Jan had left, where she had gone to be alone, and asked her if she wanted some pancakes.

'Pancakes?' she'd repeated, puzzled.

'Yes, we're making some in the kitchen. You – er – there didn't seem to be any dinner.'

Just as she had suspected: they had been sitting around waiting for her to come home and make them all a meal. Peanuts had just been the hors d'oeuvres.

'I don't want any, thank you,' she said primly, though her stomach, with unbelievably bad timing, let out a groan. It must have been the thought of lemon juice and sugar, plus the smell drifting up from below.

'But you haven't eaten anything.'

'I'm simply not at all hungry,' she'd insisted, and he'd shrugged and gone downstairs. She'd got into bed soon after that, resolutely not thinking of pancakes and, quite surprisingly, had slept the whole night through.

'Well –' Susannah began bustling round the sitting room in an attempt to straighten the usual mess – 'are you going to get up and feed that baby of yours or are you going to lie there and let him starve?'

'Mum, he isn't even awake yet.'

'He . . . isn't he?' She stopped tidying to listen. And could hardly believe her ears. There wasn't a single sound. Trust Justin to sleep in when she had decided not to be on duty.

She hurried into the kitchen, which looked as though it had been used as an all-night café, and began to clear debris from the sink.

'Mu-um . . .' Simon said, coming up behind her.

She turned to find him hugging himself against the cold that tended to steal into the room when the boiler went down overnight. 'Mum, I've been wanting to talk to you, you know.' Well, why not, he thought, rubbing sleep from his eyes? Jan had been very helpful and would keep her promise, he knew that, but she might not get around to seeing Natalie for a while. Perhaps his mother would.

'Have you, dear? About what?' Susannah reached distractedly for a tin of cat food and flipped off the plastic lid.

'About us of course – me and Natalie.' He looked down at his big bare feet and stroked Gazza with one of his toes. 'I thought you'd know what to do about her, and all that.'

Susannah looked from the cat food, to her son, to the spoon in her hand. Talk about bad timing! 'Well, of course we must have a chat. But couldn't it wait till this evening?'

'Well, actually, I've already had a talk with Jan . . . and she's promised to go and see Natalie. But I thought it might be better if *you* went. You see . . .'

Simon quickly filled his mother in on all the things he had discussed with the oh-so-sensible Jan, unwittingly overwhelming her by the sudden avalanche of his problems. She hadn't guessed the half of it; she had thought it no more than a little tiff that would soon blow over.

'I'll . . . do whatever I can,' she said, swallowing hard when he'd finished. And she would, she told herself. She'd sort Natalie out before Jan could put in an oar, even if it killed her.

'Oh, thanks, Mum, you're a wonder.' Simon gave her a hug. 'I thought you'd say you couldn't possibly; you wouldn't be able to find time. You've never got time for any of us these days, have you? Katy was only saying so yesterday.'

Susannah opened her mouth to protest, but Simon went on.

'We didn't tell you we went for a drive yesterday, did we? Jan gave us some petrol money. And Katy wanted to go and look at Windy Ridge, so that's where we went.'

'For heaven's sake, why?' And what had that to do with anything right now?

Simon jerked a shoulder. 'She just did. Anyway, we sat outside the house, just looking at it, and wishing we were still there. We were happy in that house, Katy and I. So were you and Dad. You didn't argue like you do these days, and –'

'Simon . . .' Susannah shook her head, bewildered as to why he had seen fit to bring up such a topic at quarter past six on a dark November morning. And she despaired that her offspring seemed so ill-prepared for life that all they could do was look back. Where was their grit, their drive, their ability to cope? Was life so much more difficult these days? She had always thought that a happy family background was enough to set children up for dealing with practically anything, whereas all it had seemed to succeed in doing was over-protect them. Oh, parenthood was impossible.

'We'll talk about all this later,' she promised him

guiltily. 'I'm sorry, Simon, but . . . we will. Here, give this to Gazza, would you? I really have to fly.'

Susannah glanced round the office before lifting the receiver. Private calls were frowned on unless they were absolutely essential, in which case you were supposed to get permission, though nobody did. Well, she could just imagine Duffy's reaction if she were to ask if she could phone a man about a mural: he'd blow a gasket.

As she listened to the ringing tone, she pulled a print-out of that week's dummy pay-slips towards her and flipped straight to her group of shift-workers. Their statements looked a bit odd with the same amount of money being shown twice. But hopefully the men would realise that the two amounts cancelled each other out and only appeared like this for record purposes. Hunching over them she pretended to work. Fortunately no one was close enough to hear what she would be saying on the phone. Even Molly was out of the office at the moment, giving blood.

A woman came on the line. Thrown, though she should have been prepared for Harvey's wife to answer, Susannah gabbled that she needed to talk to Harvey. Urgently. But he was out at the moment, apparently; Julia didn't say where. 'Would you tell Harvey I'll call him later?' Susannah said.

'But *not* on the office phone,' a voice came from behind her as she replaced the receiver. 'And *not* during office hours.'

Susannah looked up to find Mr Duffy peering down at her with grim disdain.

'Mrs Harding,' he said, 'do you think we could have a quiet word?'

As soon as they were in his office Susannah offered to pay for the call. But he batted her words to one side.

'It's not just a matter of the phone call, is it?' Gravely he wagged his head at her.

'Then what –?'

'*What?*' he repeated incredulously.

'Yes, what?' She was supposed to be a mind-reader?

Duffy stood in front of her with his mouth open, two old gravy stains below the knot in his tie. 'Well now, you had your statements in front of you; you tell me. Or were you so engrossed in your conversation that the penny failed to drop?' He went to sit in his chair, tipped himself back in it and fixed her with cold eyes. 'Perhaps "pennies" might be more appropriate in the circumstances. And rather a large number of them too.'

Realisation came to Susannah like an icy hand on her spine. The statements had looked odd for a very good reason: they were wrong.

And it simply wasn't fair. She had tried so hard with the wretched forms, filling them in with the utmost care to get the figures right, and what had she forgotten, for all that? To mark the debit box.

'A plus and a minus cancel each other out,' Duffy lost no time in reminding her, 'whereas a plus and a plus means we have forty-three overpayment cases on our hands. Or, to put it another way, forty-three men who'll be getting money in their banks to which they are not entitled, and from whom we'll have the devil's own job recovering it – especially with Christmas nearly upon us. They'll hang on to it for dear life, even though they know they can't keep it for ever. So you see, Mrs Harding, it isn't only a question of cheating the company out of money for a phone call. Heaven knows what Management are going to say when they're presented with all this.'

It was at that point in the interview that Susannah discovered she couldn't give a tinker's cuss what Management might have to say. She couldn't care less about the error. In fact, she couldn't care less about the job, and hadn't for a long, long time.

It was strange, but not caring was so much easier than caring, and far from hammering her into the ground, Duffy's words were having the effect of lifting weights from her shoulders. A bubble of recklessness enveloped her and would have floated her to the ceiling if it hadn't been for that one degrading word 'cheating'. *That* kept her feet on the carpet.

OK, so it had been dishonest of her to make the phone call; but talk about the pot calling the kettle black!

'Cheating,' she said, with jerky nods of the head. 'Do you plan on telling Management about that too? Well, perhaps you'd better show them the Flexi print-out while you're at it. They might be interested in an entry on the print-out that appears under the letter D.'

Duffy's gaze met hers. His mouth fell open and stayed there, confirming Susannah's wild shot in the dark – wild, because only he normally saw such print-outs. But a sudden vision of Duffy lurking around the Flexi machine had sprung into her mind, and with it had come the notion of what he had probably been up to. Not watching over his staff and keeping them up to scratch as they had all naturally concluded, but fiddling the system himself!

'Everyone in the office knows you spend an hour and a half in the pub each lunch-time,' she went on. 'What Management hasn't cottoned on to – yet – is that you key yourself out and in again for exactly the obligatory half-hour *before* you swan off to the pub. You've been cheating the company of an hour of your services each day, for years and years. And *that* makes my overpayments pale into insignificance.'

Duffy chewed over these facts for a long time. Susannah could almost see cogs grinding inside his ugly head.

Finally he said, 'Well, I've got proof of your inadequacy, haven't I? But where's your proof against me? A print-out can't prove anything; everything looks fine on that. You'd need witnesses prepared to support your story – for "story" is all it is.'

Susannah saw too late the impossibility of her case. Everyone in the office moaned like hell about injustices until given an opportunity to do something to put them right; then they stuck their heads in the sand. And of course they couldn't afford to put their jobs on the line the way she had done.

Duffy was smiling grimly. He had always resented her working here for pin money, she felt, when the less well-off could have had her job. And now he could do something about it. 'I think you've just about made it impossible for us to work together in future, don't you? Looks like one of us had better walk away from all this. And it sure as eggs won't be me.'

The Old Dairy looked as quiet and deserted as the rest of the village normally did, mid-morning on a week-day.

Would Harvey be at home, Susannah wondered, sitting at the kerb in her car. She chewed the thumb of her glove. He simply *had* to be there. And he must be persuaded to let her do the mural. No doubt he was fed up with being messed around, first by her own prevarication, and then by Paul's negative response to him on the phone, but she was now desperate to retrieve the situation. Throwing away her job at C & G as she had just done would not go down at all well at home. But if she could tell Paul that at least she had work of a kind . . .

Wrapped in the same cloud of unreality that had transported her from Duffy's office to her desk, from her desk to her car and all the way home to Upper Heyford, she climbed out on to the pavement and let herself in at the Webbs' white picket gate.

Her first timid knock went unanswered; her second, more resolute one, brought Harvey to the door with a newspaper in his hand and a pencil tucked behind one ear. The accommodation now partly revealed behind him was open-plan, and it was instantly apparent that she had disturbed his coffee break.

'Oh,' she said, her eyes drawn to the steaming mug he'd left balanced on the arm of a chair, 'I do hope I'm not intruding.'

His face had relaxed into a smile on seeing her. 'Actually you're a welcome relief,' he assured her, stepping to one side as she transferred herself to his doormat. She stood shivering inside her coat while he shoved the door shut with his shoulder. 'Care for a cup of coffee? There's plenty left in the pot.'

'Please!' She nodded nineteen to the dozen. Coffee was something she badly needed right now. Her nerves were so strung up following the morning's drama that she could barely control her limbs.

But watching Harvey's easy, confident movements as he made his way over to the breakfast bar she wished she hadn't agreed to the cup of coffee – appetising though it promised to be since the smell of fresh-ground beans hung in the air. Being here alone in this attractive man's company – and for all she knew alone in the whole village – an uneasiness was stealing upon her. Cautious by nature, and having spent most of her life with one man, she was not at all sure of this one's trustworthiness. She resolved to gulp down the coffee, get her business over with as soon as possible, and quickly make her escape.

But the coffee was scalding hot.

'I'll put it down on this table,' Harvey said, after a glance at her trembling hands. Clearly she was in no fit state to handle dangerous liquids. 'You'd better come over to the fire.'

Under his guidance Susannah gravitated towards a wood-burning stove set under an unusual old chimney-piece. 'I'm not cold,' she said, afraid that his arm was about to go round her. She sat down on the sofa abruptly.

'Not cold?' he said, smiling again. He looked her over in a leisurely manner, his eyes twinkling with secretive humour. Then he suddenly broke away, loping across the carpet to the other side of the fire.

'I was browsing through the "Situations Vacant" before you arrived,' he told her conversationally. He snorted as he picked up the paper only to throw it aside again. 'Situation's hopeless, if you ask me.'

'Oh dear.' Susannah sought out a hang-nail she'd recently discovered and began to pick at it. If Harvey had been counting on getting another job soon and was beginning to discover the unlikelihood of this happening, wouldn't he think twice before lashing out money on a useless mural?

She crossed one leg over the other and tugged her skirt as low as she could. 'Harvey –' speaking his name brought a smidgen of pink to her cheeks – 'I want to come straight to the point . . .'

But it seemed that Harvey didn't. Far from giving her the silent encouragement she expected he carried on down his own track.

'Do you know,' he said, 'I've written forty-five letters already? Cost me a fortune in postage, too; because you don't stand a chance of a reply unless you enclose a return SAE. And I've had practically zilch come back to me. Not a single solitary crumb of an offer. It seems to me – don't forget your coffee – that –'

'Harvey, I don't want to take up your time –'

'No, no, of course not. I'm sorry, I'm rambling on.' He got up from the tapestry-upholstered chair in which he'd been stretched. 'You don't want to listen to my woes, do you? You've obviously got plenty of your own.' He plumped himself down beside her. 'I could see *that* the minute I saw you on the doorstep. But I wasn't going to pry – unless you want to tell me what's wrong? And what are you doing away from work in the middle of the week, anyway? Don't tell me you've been given the grand order of the boot as well?'

She winced. 'Er – not exactly. But what I really wanted to ask you –'

'Shame, because they'd have been doing you a favour if they had. I told you the other day that you're wasted there. With your talents . . . well, you should be using them. Life's too short for not doing the things you were born to do.'

'I know!' Her soul flew out to him. Why didn't Paul say things like this? 'Look –' she covered the painful hang-nail – 'what my husband told you last night when you phoned . . . well, it wasn't right at all. He shouldn't have said what he did. I'd actually made up my mind to take some leave to do your mural, only –'

'Your husband had other ideas.' Harvey raised his eyebrows at her. 'Bit high-handed of him, wasn't it?'

'High-handed isn't the word. Downright arrogant, presumptuous, outrageous . . . ugh!' Anger flared inside her. 'Well, anyway, I can do your mural if you still want me to. I can start any time you like.'

'I consider myself very flattered.' He flashed her a disarming grin.

'Fl—? But why?'

'That you should contemplate giving up your leave for me.'

'Oh. Well . . .' She took a peep at the hang-nail. 'Actually, it's not going to be quite like that.'

'Sorry?'

'I mean –' she needed to take an extra breath – 'I've just walked out of my job.'

Harvey's face had begun to take on a wooden appearance, but she barely registered the change; she was too busy rehearsing the tidings that she must later break to Paul. 'I had a bit of a run-in with my boss this morning – we didn't see eye to eye over something – and the interview ended with him giving me the equivalent of "this town ain't big enough for the both of us". So –' she laughed a little too gaily – 'I'm the one who backed down.'

But her smile soon froze on her lips. Why should Harvey be looking so utterly appalled at her news?

'Oh!' Her hand went up to her mouth. 'Oh, I'm sorry, I didn't think! There you are, desperate to find a job, and here am I jacking mine in. How insensitive can you get?'

'No, no. It's not that.' He waved the suggestion away. 'It's just that I feel so terribly responsible.' He got up and began to pace the room, smoothing the hair at the back of his head as he walked blindly from wall to wall. 'I've been shooting my mouth off, telling you you're in the wrong sort of job – and you seem to have taken me at my word. God, I feel awful.'

Susannah glanced sideways at him. Had he influenced her? Or would she be in this position in any case? And – horrid thought – had he not really meant what he'd said about doing what she liked best? Had he only been humouring her?

'I've done the wrong thing, haven't I?' she said bleakly. 'I should have kept my nose to the grindstone, stuck to the wretched job. My place is with my family. They still need my support. I've been foolish and reckless and stupid. And I should –'

'For heaven's sake, Susannah! That's not what I'm saying at all.'

She jumped to her feet to challenge him. 'You don't really want your bathroom wall done, do you? I don't think you ever did.'

'But I do!' He clutched his head. 'Women! Give me strength! Sit down and listen to me. What kind of man do you take me for?' he went on in a more normal tone. 'Of course I want you to do my bathroom. It was my idea, wasn't it?'

She looked at him for a long time.

'You're not just saying you'll have it done – to boost my flagging morale?'

'Now why would I do such a thing?'

Why indeed, she wondered, looking into his eyes and trying to ignore the sensation of treading the deepest of waters. Never trust a good-looker, a voice said inside her head.

Harvey suddenly went over to his cup and drained the last of his coffee. 'I'd better take you upstairs.'

'W-what?'

'To take a look at the job,' he added, grinning at her stricken face.

'Ah. Yes. Right.' She followed him up the polished treads, part-fitted with sisal matting.

'Oh good, I'm glad it's a white suite,' she murmured, taking a notebook, businesslike, from her bag. 'Victorian style, too. I think I can see –' she screwed up her eyes – 'something like stained glass for your panel. Perhaps even vaguely religious. What do you think of the idea?'

'So long as it's not too pi.'

'Mmm. Or how about something like those old cave-paintings? Charging bulls – that kind of thing?'

'I'm imagining a mermaid . . .'

'Or a lion with a mane . . .' She would have liked more time to consider, but Harvey was standing so close . . .

'I have to go,' she said, heading back down the stairs. 'I have to go over to Bristol.'

'That's a good idea,' he said. 'New chapter in your life; new wardrobe. Go and have a lovely splurge.'

'I didn't mean to the shops! Heavens, I've got far better things to do.'

'Such as . . . getting some tiles for my mural?'

'No, I've plenty of those to be going on with. No, I must go and see our young Natalie. She's my son's girlfriend, you know. The mother of baby Justin. They've got problems, and I promised I'd try to help.'

'Can't they sort out their problems on their own?'

She shook her head. 'If a mother stays away from her own baby for days on end then there's something seriously wrong. And I'm that baby's grandmother. I can't simply stay out of it, can I?'

He made mock tutting sounds. 'An artist has to be single-minded, you know; devoted to his craft and nothing else. He can't afford to get side-tracked by other people's problems.'

'You've hit the nail on the head there,' she said grimly. 'Note: *his* craft.'

She flashed him a cynical smile. 'Ever wondered why there've been so few great female artists in the world? Well, I'll leave that one for you to work out.'

She left him shaking his head and ran outside to her car.

But although she waited half an hour in the car park of the school where Natalie taught, she didn't spot the girl. Perhaps Natalie stayed at school for lunch; perhaps she'd already gone home. Susannah had no idea, and trying to find someone inside the building who knew where she might be proved impossible. All she could think of was to come back at going-home time and hope to catch up with her then.

So she ended up passing time in the shopping centre after all, and spent an excessive amount of money on two dresses she didn't need.

Do I have to do everything Harvey Webb tells me? she demanded angrily of herself as she waited for the clothes to be wrapped. But she couldn't really lay the blame for these mad impulse purchases at his door. If anyone was to blame it was Paul. Resentment against him had been building up for days, and this was one way of getting back at him.

And so what if she'd lost her job, and hadn't the money to spend? Might as well be hung for a sheep as for a lamb.

CHAPTER 18

One blue Volvo ought to look like any other, Natalie considered, but this one didn't. Something about it was distinctive; familiar even. Why?

Maybe, she decided, as she watched it nosing round the school car park in search of a space, it was the arrangement of stickers in the back window that had caught her attention. She had seen them somewhere before. And she was certain, even from her distant position at the staff-room window, that none of them were of a frivolous nature. No. They were the sort that promoted worthy causes: the preservation of historic buildings; the rights of the unborn child; wild life, etc, etc . . .

Of course! A brief vision had sprung to her mind, a picture of that very car receding into the distance and a group of people waving it away. That was it. She had last seen the car taking Simon's grandparents off to their new life abroad almost two years ago.

So what was it doing here?

Remembering that she was supposed to be meeting Lara in a few minutes, Natalie drew away from the window and began to pack her straw shoulder-bag. She could only assume that Jan and Frank had sold the car to someone else. But no, that couldn't be possible, because they were still out of the country. Unless they had met English people out there and . . . She ran through a series of possibilities and gave up with a little shrug; the car, and its current owner, were the least of her concerns. She had plenty of other problems queuing up to take their place.

But, casting one last glance out of the window while thrusting the final batch of test papers into her bag, she saw that the vehicle had been backed crookedly between a hedge and a Honda, half in and half out of a space. And Jan – Simon's gran – was emerging from the driver's side.

Natalie's heart beat fast as she slipped down the stairs and jogged across the car park to meet the visitor – not so much from the small exertion involved as from nervous speculation. What could Jan possibly be doing here? What had brought her back to England? Had Frank – heaven forbid it – suddenly died? Or had something worse still happened to someone in the family . . . to Simon, perhaps, or – or to Justin . . . and they were all too distraught to come and break the news to her themselves? Oh God, don't let it be that!

'Natalie, how lovely!' Jan stopped the girl's momentum with outstretched arms. 'I was wondering how I'd track you down.' Her eyes swept the sprawling sixties building of drab concrete and tinted glass. 'What an enormous school this is. It'd be like looking for a needle in a haystack, though I'm sure the secretary would have helped me.'

'I'm not often in this building,' Natalie said. 'You were really lucky to catch me.' Relief had begun to flow through her; Jan didn't appear to be a bringer of bad tidings. In fact she looked very well – full of her usual confidence. Her woollen hat, which would have resembled a knitted tea cosy on most women her age, looked stylish on her, and her scarf was draped in a chic arrangement about her shoulders. Smiling and exuding L'Aimant, she held Natalie in her grasp while she studied her.

Jan had always had time for Natalie – they shared the same profession, after all – and had taken an interest in her ever since Simon, in his first decent car, had proudly driven her down to his grandparents' home in Potter's Bar to show her off. That was three years ago. The two had hit it off immediately, Jan revelling in reliving school life which she badly missed in her retirement, and Natalie lapping up the older woman's affection like a half-starved stray.

Natalie's parents had never been close to her. Her father had been a naval officer and they had travelled the world, leaving Natalie at boarding school in England much of the year. By the time they had completed their last tour of duty and settled down, Natalie had started at training college; and the day after she received her teaching diploma they announced that they were to divorce.

It was as though they had waited until such time as Natalie had the means with which to support herself before making their announcement; though why they thought she would have been adversely affected by the split was beyond her. Feeling that she hardly even knew them, what they did or did not do made no difference to her at all.

'Dare I hope that you've finished for the day?' Jan was saying as she finally let Natalie go. She nodded at the straw bag. 'Or are you dashing off again to extra-mural activities?'

An electric bell sounded somewhere in the building, followed by a rumble of imminent evacuation as chairs were scraped back and desks cleared of work.

Natalie chewed at her lip. She drew her coat more tightly round her. 'I'm supposed to be meeting a friend . . .'

'I badly wanted to talk to you,' Jan urged. 'It's really rather important.'

Something in her tone brought Natalie's fears back. 'It's not Simon, is it? Or Justin? They are all right, aren't they?'

'They aren't hurt or in any danger, if that's what's bothering you.' But Jan's carefully chosen words hung between them; clearly she knew that all was not well in Natalie and Simon's relationship, and Natalie quickly changed tack.

'What are you doing here in England?' she asked. She cast a grim look up at the sky. 'I thought the whole idea was to escape the British weather,

226

not to come back for a winter break.'

'Oh . . .' Jan gave a shudder and shook her head. 'France hasn't turned out well. I'll give you a quick run-down on the situation on the way to a rather nice-looking tea shop I noticed out of town.'

Natalie hesitated again, but only for a second. Jan's coming like this, out of the blue, was not at all convenient, but she could hardly be refused. A reluctant driver – especially of the Volvo because she claimed it was too big for her and was afraid of incurring Frank's displeasure by scraping its paint-work – Jan had obviously put herself out to make the trip over to Bristol.

So Natalie followed the older woman to her car and silently got in. Lara was bound to be livid, she thought as Jan revved, stalled and flooded the engine. Well, Lara would just have to put up with it.

'So it was Simon who sent you to see me,' Natalie said bluntly, sitting back from the corner table at the Little Pantry and folding her arms with an air of disgust.

Jan had just finished explaining how she and Frank came to be living at Upper Heyford in the Hardings' back garden, so it was pretty obvious that Simon had been bleating to all and sundry about their affairs.

'Well, yes,' Jan admitted, flipping up the lid of the stainless steel hot water jug and peering in. She let the lid clatter back in place and topped up the teapot. 'I'm sure he'd rather not have had to do it, but he seemed to be at the end of his tether.' She glanced across at Natalie. 'So do you, if you don't mind my saying so.'

Natalie was used to Jan calling a spade a spade. Nevertheless she minded very much, but couldn't find her tongue to say so.

'I – er –' Jan went on – 'wonder whether you'd like to talk things over with someone? Like me, for instance. I'm a very good listener.' She smiled. 'And I also happen to be very fond of you. But I think you know that, don't you?'

Natalie blinked back sudden tears. This she could do without! The least little thing could start her blubbing these days: sentimental films, beautiful tunes; kind words – as much as harsh ones. She was developing into a proper little cry-baby, and she hated it.

But if Jan noticed her fumbling for a tissue and blowing her nose ostentatiously, as if it was only the cold wind that had got to it, she made no comment; she just took over the conversation for a minute or two while Natalie gulped tea and tried to compose herself.

Jan's next words, however, were enough to start her off again.

'You've produced a sturdy enough little boy, though. He's been fairly wearing me out, has Justin.' She let out a puff of breath to demonstrate her exhaustion. 'Bringing up a baby must be one of the most difficult things in the world, I think, but of course I never had to do it. I don't know how you young women cope these days, what with your careers to consider as well as the child.'

Natalie thought her skin must have been unzipped, so raw and exposed did she suddenly feel. Further concealment of her emotions was useless: she let them all bubble up from the pit of her stomach and spill over in great wracking sobs. Even a tiny wail escaped her, so that an elderly gentleman at the next table turned round and stared in alarm.

'Oh dear,' Jan muttered, surprised at what she'd unleashed. She had thought she was on safe ground, beginning the conversation by talking about babies and things. 'Perhaps it would have been better if we'd gone somewhere more private for our little talk?'

'No – no – it's all right.' With an effort Natalie pulled herself together. 'I feel a bit better now. Honestly.'

She looked quite ill, however, with a blotched red nose, pink eyes, and her pale face swollen with tears. There were rings of shadow under her eyes too, and her normally thick, glossy fringe showed signs of neglect.

'When did you last see a doctor?' Jan asked baldly.

'A doctor?' Natalie attempted a laugh that came out wrong. 'What would I want a doctor for?'

'Well I don't know . . . they have some uses. Did you have your post-natal check-up, for example?'

'Of course I did. And everything was as it should

be. Nothing wrong at all.' Natalie regarded the older woman from under her fringe. 'For someone who's not had babies of her own you seem to know a lot about it.'

'Well, I have had quite a few women friends in my time. And I told you I'm a good listener; what I haven't heard about the baby-making business would fit on a postage stamp.'

She was silent for a moment, stirring her tea to the accompaniment of several other teaspoons around the tea room and the strains of some slow Vivaldi. A bored waitress strolled past brandishing long silver tongs and pushing a cake trolley with a squeaky wheel. She looked at Jan and Natalie but they both shook their heads, though Jan followed the display with her eyes as it rolled on its way.

'So it's something else getting you down, is it?' she asked when the cakes were out of temptation.

'I never said anything was getting me down, did I?'

'No, you never *said* . . .' Jan was tired of beating about the bush. 'Natalie, do you mind if I ask you something? Something very personal? It concerns this friend of yours – Lara, I think her name is.'

'Yes, what about her?' Natalie watched Jan's face for clues. What had Simon been saying about her friend? Nothing to the good, that was for sure.

'I don't know how to put this.' Jan bit her lip. 'My generation isn't used to talking about this sort of thing. When I was your age I swear I didn't even know it existed . . .'

Now Natalie was bewildered; she seemed to have lost the thread. 'Sorry?' she said, with a frown.

'Well, *you* know.' Jan shifted in her seat. ' "Sexual orientation" is one of the phrases they trot out. Or perhaps sexual preference.' She took a breath and came out with it. 'Is Lara a lesbian, is what I'm trying to get at. And – and –' but she couldn't say any more.

And Natalie was too taken aback to speak. She sat clutching her teacup in both hands, the hot china a mild comfort to her as she let Jan's words sink in. Then she let out a snort that spluttered into a laugh – her first laugh in many weeks, and it threatened to become hysterical.

'Oh, Jan, you've got it all wrong,' she told her, drying more tears from her eyes, and she forced herself to be serious again. 'That's not what Simon's been thinking, is it? Because he couldn't be further from the truth. Lara does have a problem with men, it's true, but only because they ignore her. Secretly I think she's desperate for a boyfriend, but she – well, she's not terribly attractive, you see, and on top of that her attitude puts men off; she has strong feminist views. So she pretends she hates all men, and – well, she's really rather mixed up.'

Jan pressed a hand to her forehead and loosened her scarf a little more. Her hat was making her scalp prickle but if she were to take it off her hair would look a mess. She pressed on with the conversation.

'I see. At least, I think I do. Lara's a lonely, awkward soul and you feel sorry for her. Is that it?

But that didn't mean you had to move in with her and keep her company, did it? Not when you had Simon and the baby to consider?'

Natalie felt her face darken. How could she explain? 'It all seemed to be for the best. I wasn't up to scratch at work . . . I was tired but I couldn't really sleep . . . I wasn't even much good with Justin . . . And when Simon lost his job Lara said . . .' She leaned her elbows on the table, squeezed her eyes tight against more tears and put her hands over both her ears. How had she let Lara convince her that she'd be better off without Simon, and that the baby would be better off with him? Was she out of her mind?

'It was Lara's suggestion that I get away from it all,' she finished lamely, 'to give myself some space.'

'Oh yes, of course – space.' Jan's mouth twisted on the modern buzz-word. And she didn't need to hear much more; she could fill in the rest for herself. A fine 'friend' Lara was, if she had judged the situation correctly.

It sounded as though, jealous of what Natalie had, Lara had been doing her utmost to rob her of it, and Natalie, rendered vulnerable by probable post-natal depression, was putty in her hands. Gentle probing of Natalie confirmed all this – or most of it.

'I feel so terribly guilty,' Natalie cried when everything had been dragged out of her. 'I'm a terrible dreadful mother; I don't think I even love

Justin. And I've behaved abominably to Simon at a time when he really needs my support. But how can I support *him* when I feel I can't cope myself? Oh, what am I going to do, Jan?'

'I'll tell you what you're going to do.' Jan's tone was decisive. 'First of all you must give me your doctor's phone number. And then ... well, we'll take it from there.'

CHAPTER 19

The caravan was in darkness and the Volvo missing when Susannah got home from Bristol. Lights were shining in the cottage, but she could derive no comfort from the fact. She wasn't looking forward to seeing any member of her family – not one of them.

The entire afternoon had been a total waste of time – as well as money – because she never got to speak to Natalie after all. So on top of Paul's displeasure over her losing her job – and 'displeasure' was probably putting it mildly – she would have Simon's disappointment to contend with. Not to mention Katy in one of her moods.

At length, gathering up her shopping, she went into the cottage via the kitchen door and found the family grouped round the pine table.

And to think, she thought grimly, surveying their accusing faces, that I dared hope for a change of heart.

On the journey home in crawling traffic, jammed between a horse-box and a menacing van, she had pondered the possibility that they might be pleased for her when she told them about doing the mural. They might decide it would be good to have a more interesting wife/mother, now that they'd got used to the idea: an artist in their midst, rather than a pay-clerk . . .

Pure fantasy, of course. *She* might have changed, but they certainly hadn't.

'You've been ages,' Paul lost no time in informing her. 'We had to go out and get ourselves a Chinese.'

'Poor you,' she grunted unsympathetically, 'I hope you made sure he was well-cooked.'

Katy pushed a foil dish of congealed remains towards her. 'Yours is Szechuan Beef.'

'Yes,' Simon sniggered from behind his hand, 'we didn't like that one much.'

She glared at her tormentors; she was in no mood for badinage, no matter how harmlessly intended.

'Where have you been all this time?' Paul wanted to know. 'Earning another nice lot of overtime?'

'N-no . . . I went over to Bristol to see Natalie.' She dared not look at Simon. 'But I'm afraid I couldn't track her down.'

'Oh, Mu-um!'

'Well, it isn't my fault, Simon! I did my best for you.'

Simon's expression told her it just wasn't good enough.

'I went to the school to see if I could meet her

coming out – twice, I'll have you know. Then I went to her friend's flat and parked outside for ages but neither of them ever turned up. I didn't know where else to try after that.'

'There are two separate parts to the school,' Simon told her in a world-weary tone that implied she surely ought to have known. 'Natalie normally works in the west block –'

'That's where I went.'

'– but not every day of the week. And today's her day for meditation. She does *that* straight from work, with her friend.'

Meditation! a voice shrieked inside Susannah's head. The girl had time to swan around *meditating* while others were left holding the baby? She felt too stunned to explode.

It was then that Katy noticed the shopping bag, still dangling from her mother's wrist.

'Ooh! You've bought something nice,' she said, pointing at the bag. 'Is there anything in there for me?'

Susannah closed her eyes. 'No. No, there isn't, Katy. I'm sorry, I –' But why on earth should she apologise? She straightened her shoulders and lifted her chin. She knew it was all going to come out far from the way she'd planned it, but – well, what the hell.

'Actually,' she told them, 'I've been thoroughly and unashamedly selfish. And I really don't give a damn. Today I bought myself two expensive dresses that I don't need; I informed Mr Webb that

I'd be doing his mural, no matter what; and I told Mr Duffy where to get off. Oh, and I had a whole cream eclair in the coffee shop. Entirely to myself. Now, does anyone have any objections?'

But if they had she didn't wait around to hear them. She ran upstairs to get changed.

'What exactly was it you told Duffy?' Paul asked before she'd even discarded her coat. He'd abandoned his bag of prawn crackers and shot upstairs after her to their room.

'To stuff the —— job,' she replied calmly, inserting a suitably unpleasant adjective that was guaranteed to make his ears go red. Paul hated to hear her using bad language.

'You told him to . . . ? You didn't!'

'I did.'

'And what did he say to that?'

She undid her skirt and stepped out of it. 'Not much he could say, was there? Anyway, I hardly gave him the chance to say anything. I walked right out and left him to it.'

'You mean . . . you've actually lost your job?'

'I mean precisely that.'

Paul took a step towards her. 'You've thrown away a perfectly good job? When your children would give their eye teeth . . . ? And on top of that you come home flaunting two brand new frivolous dresses?'

'It was *my* money I was spending! Mine! My uncle left it to me. He left me five hundred pounds, if you must know.'

Paul's eyebrows disappeared. 'Well, you've kept damned quiet about that. But it's *your* money now, is it? Since when did we cease to share? And if it's each to his own from now on, how far do you think *you're* going to get on five hundred measly quid? Especially if you're going to squander it on clothes left right and centre. Oh, but I forgot: you'll be getting paid for the mural, won't you? That should help a whole lot.'

'It's a start, Paul, a start. Everyone has to start somewhere. Even –' she raked up an idol of his that came in useful from time to time – 'even Margaret Thatcher! And I bet Denis wasn't an old meanie during *her* early career. I bet he gave her his full support.'

Paul spluttered a simulated laugh. 'That's hardly in the same league . . .'

'The principle's the same. Denis had faith in his wife and – and vision. He wasn't to know she'd end up one of the most famous women in history. Not at the beginning. He didn't quibble when she contributed less to the family income than he did. And anyway, I *have* contributed as much to this marriage as you have. I've been a wife, a cook, a cleaner . . . a-a nanny, and a laundry-maid and a shopper. *And* I worked full-time. All on top of being a mother, of course, and that's no meagre achievement. So I reckon you owe me, Paul. I reckon you owe me a lot.'

Paul jabbed a finger at the floor. 'Haven't I got enough people to support right now without worrying about you as well? And don't forget you're *still* a mother, not *were* one once upon a time. How about actually behaving like one, or is that too much to expect?'

'I can't be expected to mother them for the rest of their lives!'

'But you can't simply stop being their mother, can you? You can't turn it off like a switch. They're yours for ever.' He turned to flounce out of the room. 'And it was you who wanted them in the first place.'

Susannah threw the two dresses to the back of the wardrobe – she would hate them for ever more – put her coat back on and slipped out of the cottage by the front door. She couldn't face either Paul or the children right now: Paul had managed, as usual, to make her feel so bad about herself, and as she stepped into a soft mizzle she could barely hold back tears.

Never before had such a chasm opened up between them; never had love turned to bitter dislike. Because she didn't like Paul the way he was now; in fact she almost hated him. Why wasn't he on her side? Why weren't the children? It wasn't as if she was asking much. And she'd never asked for anything before.

Perhaps that was the trouble. She had been too easy-going. And now that she *was* asking, now that she was sticking her head above the parapet, she was getting it blown off.

She headed down the lane, making for the centre of the village where the street lighting was more generous. She needed brisk activity that would burn away some of her anger, but walking after dusk in thickly hedged shadow – even in respectable, burglar-proofed Upper Heyford – was not a good idea.

The Golden Fleece, already decked out with its extra lights for Christmas, beckoned through the mist as she hurried past the terrace of old weavers' cottages. It was then that a shape loomed up from nowhere.

Startled, she let out a gasp, then saw who it was, though she barely recognised her father slouching towards her with bent shoulders, his feet shuffling along. Since having to admit that he was unlikely to influence the outcome of his brother's will he had aged considerably.

'Susannah!' Frank accompanied her name with a fit of painful-sounding coughing.

'Heavens, Dad, it's you! You gave me quite a scare. But what are you doing here?'

'Just been down to the pub.'

'Bit early to be coming back, isn't it?'

'Well . . . didn't much fancy their grub.' Frank pulled down the peak of the cap he always wore for playing golf, but nothing was a match against the dampness. The fine drizzle that enveloped them could only be seen when caught in the beam of a lamp, but it managed to seep through clothing in no time at all. 'Paul offered to get me a takeaway, but I don't like that muck either.'

Susannah recalled the deserted caravan. 'Why aren't you eating with Jan? Where is Jan, by the way?'

'Didn't she tell you where she was going?'

'Er – no. No, she didn't.' Susannah nudged a heap of sodden leaves with her toe, the dank smell of mould drifting upwards.

'Not had another bust-up, have you?' Frank came straight to the point.

She glanced up sharply. Her father was fingering his ear. 'Now why would you think a thing like that?'

Frank tried to come out with 'Huh!' but ended up coughing again. 'Perhaps,' he said as soon as he was able, 'it's something to do with the fact that Jan goes on about you and Paul, and Simon and Natalie and Katy, ad nauseam. You surely didn't imagine you were keeping it to yourselves, did you?'

'No, I suppose not. Not with Jan around.'

'Now Susannah . . .' he reproached her from under his peak. There was real hurt and concern in his eyes.

'Sorry,' she said shortly, taking her father's arm. 'I think I'd better see you home to bed. That cough doesn't sound too healthy. And where did you say Jan had gone?'

'I didn't. She went over to Bristol some time ago. She warned me she might be late back; she didn't know how long things would take. It all depended on Natalie.'

'Natalie!' Susannah's free hand clenched round a fifty pence piece in her pocket, its edges digging into her palm; so Jan had been running around after the girl too. But would she have been any more successful? Sod's law told Susannah she probably would.

She saw her father to the door of the caravan, waited for him to find the light-switch, and put her head inside. 'Are you sure it's warm enough in there? You could come and sit with us, you know.'

Frank turned to look at the cottage, its windows cosily a-glow. 'Snug as a bug in a rug,' he assured her, not very convincingly, 'so long as you get a move on and put 't wood in 't 'ole. Don't you worry about me, now.'

But she did. She had seen the temptation on his face. Prone to mild asthma and the occasional 'chesty cold' her father had denied himself a log fire and Paul's best malt, rather than face the chilly atmosphere of the Hardings' living room.

And she felt awful all over again.

CHAPTER 20

Susannah glanced round the studio with satisfaction. A pale sun lit her work table and gently warmed her hands. The cottage was still and quiet. A whole day lay ahead of her; a whole day to herself. And there would be many more. Casting aside all thoughts as to the cost of this achievement – the disapproval of the family, the rift between herself and her husband, the loss of her job – she set to work on a design. But with only her hands fully occupied, her mind kept returning to matters she would rather ignore.

This morning – her first day of freedom, as she saw it – she had hidden under the bedclothes until Paul had gone to work. Positively childish of her, of course, and the sight of her still curled up under the duvet while he had to go to his office must have infuriated him no end, but she decided that getting up and joining him for breakfast might have appeared hypocritical under the circumstances. And what was the point? They were communicating in snatches of cold politeness – and then only when they had to.

Simon had been up and dressed when she finally went downstairs. He hadn't realised, until she eventually told him the previous evening, that Jan had gone over to Bristol as well.

'But don't raise your hopes,' she'd advised him. 'If I couldn't find Natalie, then perhaps Jan won't have been able to either.'

But of course Jan had. Hardly had Susannah finished speaking than the Volvo lumbered up on to the drive and Jan got out. Her face, as she peered into the kitchen, revealed how successful she had been.

She had got to the heart of the mystery, she said. She had spoken to Natalie, found out what was troubling her, and got her an emergency appointment with her GP. Natalie was starting immediate treatment for depression. She had been signed off work and would be seeing the practice counsellor, but – best news of all – she wanted Simon to fetch her from the flat in the morning and get her away from Lara.

Simon had hugged Jan so hard her feet had left the floor, and she let out a little scream. Even Susannah had had to laugh at the sudden easing of tension, at Simon's sheer euphoria, and could bear her step-mother no grudge for succeeding where she had failed.

Simon had gone off, whistling, that morning as soon as was practicable, taking Justin with him, followed only minutes later by a thoughtful-looking Katy.

Coming across Katy in the lobby, fully dressed in light blue jeans and a denim jacket that would have been suitable for an early summer's day but which was madness in November, Susannah found her winding a long blue knitted scarf round her neck.

'Yes, you can borrow it if you like, Little Girl Blue,' Susannah told her, but her hint was wasted on Katy. 'And where are you off to so bright and early?'

'The doctor's.'

'You too? Again? I didn't know he wanted to see you again.'

Katy merely shrugged.

'You – er – don't want me to come with you?' Susannah saw her time being eroded again, but with for ever and a day ahead of her, it hardly mattered now. She could easily afford a few hours.

'No thanks. I'll go on my own.'

She studied her daughter more closely; Katy was avoiding her eyes. 'Well, if you're sure.' She shrugged. 'I don't know... what with you, Natalie and Grandad... thank heavens for the NHS.'

Thinking of doctors, Susannah glanced up from her blank sheet of paper and took herself over to the window where she knew she would be able to see one end of the caravan – as if that would tell her how her father was today! He had certainly sounded rough last night. Being out in the mist and rain wouldn't have helped his condition at all.

But, leaning with her nose almost touching the

glass, what caught Susannah's eye was Jan. She was standing on a ladder with a shiny black sack in one hand, her body bundled up against the cold, and as Susannah watched she struggled to maintain her balance on the highest step while attempting to smooth the plastic out flat on one corner of the caravan's roof. Susannah threw down her pencil and hurried outside.

'What on earth do you think you're doing?' she called out in the way an exasperated mother might remonstrate with a wayward child. 'You'll break your neck if you're not careful.'

'Oh, hello, dear.' Jan smiled down at Susannah as though there wasn't a soul in the world that she would rather see. 'Got a day off? That's nice.'

Susannah passed no comment. Jan didn't know about her throwing in her job yet, and Susannah did not feel like enlightening her.

'I hope you don't mind,' Jan ran on, busying herself with the plastic again, 'but I saw the ladder through the garage window and didn't want to interrupt you in your work.'

'Of course I don't mind your borrowing the ladder. But what are you trying to do? You shouldn't be clambering about like that.'

'Not at my age, you mean. Well, I don't like heights much, I must admit, but I really don't have any choice. I can't ask either of your men-folk to do this, can I? Simon's tied up at the moment and Paul's out at work all the hours of daylight. And Frank isn't feeling too good.'

Susannah let out a sigh. 'I guessed as much. Chest playing up again, I suppose?'

'Yes, and the van's got a leak which isn't helping. Our mattress has been soaking up rain since we got here and we've only just realised.'

'Jan –' Susannah ran a hand through her hair. 'You're wasting your time with that.' She picked up the roll of parcel tape, with which Jan had no doubt intended to fix the waterproof in place. 'It would be like mending a burst pipe with an Elastoplast – no earthly use whatsoever.'

Jan came down the ladder and sighed too. 'You're right, of course. This is silly. I'm going to have to get someone in to do it properly.' She looked at her boots, then at Susannah. 'Could I – er – pop in for a moment, do you think? I'll be needing to use your phone.'

Paul picked up the receiver and put it to his ear. 'Harding,' he said, and took a sharp breath; it was Wesley Morris's secretary, telling him his boss wanted a word.

While he waited for Wesley to come through, Paul wondered whether this was just another routine call, or whether it was to do with the matter they'd discussed in London. He hoped it would be the latter. The wait for news had been unnerving. And he had had to endure it alone.

Of course it need not have been like that, and it was Susannah's fault that it had. She was making things so damned difficult. If only he could talk to her! But every time he opened his mouth the words came out all wrong.

He wanted to show her how reasonable and fair he could be – pander to her odd little whims once in a while; tell her he understood; show her that he loved her in spite of everything – but she managed to rile him at every turn these days. No sooner had he resolved to try to make things up with her, than she went and upset him again.

'Paul!' Wesley's voice burst in on him. 'Won't keep you in suspense. Just this minute got word. Hold on to your hat and listen up; *you* are about to be made an offer you simply *cannot* refuse.'

'You won't expect miracles, will you?' Natalie sat down on the Hardings' settee, her hands squashed between her knees. 'It could take a little while . . .'

'No.' Simon slid to the floor in front of her and took one of her hands in his. 'I won't be looking for a sudden transformation. Oh, but I'm just so glad to have you back! These past few weeks have been hell; I never want to go through anything like that again.'

'We aren't out of the woods yet, you know. We've still got problems to solve.'

'I know.' He looked round the room. 'This is hardly ideal, is it? But I won't be out of work for ever. Something's bound to turn up.'

'Simon . . . it's not going to be that simple.'

'Well, let's not think about it now. First of all we must get you fit.' He looked deeply into her eyes. 'Is it really just post-natal depression?'

'Just?' She forced out a laugh. 'If you knew about the black hole I'm beginning to climb out of, you wouldn't speak of it so lightly. You're not the only one who's been to hell and back, you know.'

'Poor thing.' Simon put her hand to his lips.

'I know it must be difficult for you to understand how I've been feeling. Mothers are supposed to be ecstatic over their babies, aren't they? But I was shocked when Justin was born.' She screwed up her face with the effort of trying to describe her feelings. 'It was nothing like I expected – so messy and unromantic. And then, after all the effort of having him, I didn't know what to do with him. I would stare at him in his cot and hate him. Simply hate him for being there; for yelling and yelling and yelling at me and making his constant demands.'

'Yes, he was a miserable little bugger.' Simon recalled all the crying. But he hadn't known what to do either. Looking back he realised he'd been glad to get off to work each day and leave her to manage on her own. He'd always thought her so capable, and she'd never let on how she felt.

'I couldn't feel anything for him; only how he'd come and ruined my life. I didn't know you could get real depression from having a baby – only the baby blues. The doctor I saw yesterday said it was mostly down to hormones. Lots of women get it, you know, some of them worse than me.'

Simon reached for Justin with his free hand and

hugged him so that their three heads were bent together in close communion. Everything was going to be all right now. But the child immediately struggled to be set free.

'It doesn't look as if he's suffered, much.' Simon grinned and let him go. 'Not exactly screaming for love and attention, is he?'

'I hope not, I really do.' She set her face firmly. 'I'm going to make it up to him, you know, if it takes me the rest of my life. I don't want him to grow up like I did – with his mother not caring a toss.'

'Of course he won't.' Simon soothed. 'Poor you – you didn't have much of a role-model, did you? You don't really know how to be a mum.'

'No.' With an effort, she held back more tears; she had shed enough of those lately to float the QE2. 'And *your* mum makes me feel so inadequate.'

'Mine?' Simon couldn't make that out at all. 'Well, I suppose she was all right when we were young. She doesn't seem to care much about us now.'

'But she's always been terrific with Justin. And you've turned out well enough, haven't you? You don't know how lucky you've been. And you're a man now. Gosh, if I thought Justin was still going to need me running around after him once he's eighteen, well –' by a trick of the lips she blew her fringe off her forehead – 'I'll be on anti-depressants for ever!'

Simon kissed her, feeling uncomfortable.

'Anyway –' Natalie nodded her head in the

direction of the door – 'what is it your mother's up to in there?'

'In the studio?' Simon looked glum. 'She's going through an arty-farty phase. Driving my dad up the wall. The two of them are hardly speaking – mainly because she's chucked in her job. This, I have to warn you, is not the happiest of homes. I only hope you don't find you're sorry to have been rescued from Lara's clutches.'

'No chance of that.' She gave him a playful nudge. 'I still can't believe what you've been thinking about Lara. Poor girl.' She sighed for her friend. 'She only wants to be loved, you know.'

'So do I,' Simon said with a rush of feeling, and wondered how soon, and where, they could get down to it.

The receptionist looked up suspiciously. 'Was it with Dr Llewellyn?'

'No.' Katy flicked back her hair. 'My appointment's with Dr Platt this time.'

'Ah, yes. Dr Platt.' The receptionist ran her pen down a column of spidery scribble, and crossed out Katy's name. 'I'm afraid he's running rather late as usual; you may have to wait a while. Unless you'd like to see one of the other doctors, of course . . .'

'I'd rather see Dr Platt.'

Katy scanned the benches of waiting women and found a seat by the radiator. She hoped her red nose would have gone by the time she was called in to see the doctor. Dr Platt was absolutely gorgeous – much more to her taste than that old fogey Llewellyn – and she wouldn't want him to see her like this. That would never do.

'She's absolutely insufferable!' Susannah banged clenched fists.

'Hey, hang on!' Harvey leaned across the bath tub. 'That bit's not quite straight.'

'Sorry. There. That better? My mind's not on the job.' She sat back to survey her work, reflecting on the past three days. 'And that's my problem in a nut-shell. How on earth does the woman expect me to concentrate when she's always beavering about?' She leaned out of the bath to pick up the next sheet of mosaics.

'But –' Harvey tried to puzzle out the way women's minds worked – 'this so-called wicked step-mother of yours sounds more like a fairy god-mother to me. I mean, isn't she just what you need right now? Someone to do all your chores for you?'

Susannah looked at him pityingly from the pile of blankets he'd thoughtfully provided for her to kneel on; he didn't understand. In a way he was perfectly right, of course: she did need someone to relieve her of domestic chores. The cottage was even more chaotic now that Natalie was with them. Also, Jan and Frank had had to squeeze in too until their bedding – which was also their day-time seating – had dried out. Oh, yes, she certainly needed help. But the last person from whom she wanted help was Jan.

On the second morning of her 'freedom' Susannah had shut herself in her studio; she had been side-tracked enough the previous day and she wasn't going to let it happen again. She would get on with Harvey's mural, come hell or high water or even both, and everything else could go hang.

But, pondering over a possible colour scheme for what she and Harvey had finally agreed would be two fish swimming towards each other through rocks and reeds, she had become aware of the Hoover groaning into reluctant life.

Now Katy claimed she was incapable of pushing the Hoover, because of the pain in her hands; and Natalie had been ordered to rest. Simon had declared that Justin was phobic and would go bananas if his father so much as got the machine out of the cupboard; and even if Frank had been fit enough he didn't know one end of a Hoover from the other, nor had he heard of 'New Man'. So there was only one person who could be responsible for the noise.

'What on earth do you think you're doing?' Susannah demanded, much as she had the morning before. She had found Jan poking about under the kitchen table with the nozzle and a circular brush.

'Just having a little clean around, dear.' Jan's good nature never once wavered. 'That cat's fur gets everywhere, doesn't it? As for that horrible litter . . .'

'But there's absolutely no need for you to − I

mean, well obviously it's got a bit messy. But you really don't have to do it.'

'I know I don't have to do it. But I like to feel useful, you know. And you've got better things to do with your time, now, haven't you?'

Susannah flushed and ground her back teeth. Simon, returning with Natalie from Bristol the previous day, had spilled the beans about his mother losing her job, making her look not only a fool for not having owned up to Jan immediately, but a liar for letting her think she had only taken a day off.

Now, looking down at Jan as she bent to unhook more flex, she could detect no malice, criticism or sarcasm in her step-mother's words, but she was sure it must be there all the same.

'Where's Katy?' Susannah wondered aloud, thinking that even she would find it difficult to sleep through all this activity. Looking round for the familiar pink dressing-gown, her gaze took in the old orderliness that Jan had quickly reinstated. There was a smell of Mr Sheen and disinfectant, and the table was clear of junk. Even the cat was neatly curled up on a chair, the tidiest of black furry balls.

'Katy's out,' Jan said, 'getting me some things from the village shop. She's taken young Justin with her.'

Susannah blinked in disbelief. Katy – up early again? Unbelievable.

But that was only the beginning. By the time Paul got home from work a mountain of ironing had disappeared from the bottom of the broom cupboard, the lounge looked like a lounge, and a meal was almost ready for the table.

Paul had looked over to the cooker expecting to see his wife there, but Jan was busy in her place. He had then glanced into the workroom, found Susannah still bent over her heap of tesserae, and deduced that she had not been re-converted in his absence.

'Still fiddling,' he'd muttered caustically, 'while Rome burns, I see.' And he'd gone off to look for the rest of the family.

'I don't want to like Jan,' Susannah fumed to Harvey. 'I want to hate her. She's taking over my role. And she does everything better than me!'

She tapped at the bathroom wall, evening up the mosaics and making more noise than she needed to. 'The cat flap was taking things just a tad too far.'

'What's all this about a cat flap?' Harvey obligingly enquired. He was sitting on the bathroom stool with his feet propped up on the bidet, looking relaxed and handsome in a black stretch jogging suit. He had watched over all the proceedings in much the same distracting manner, which was why Susannah had done as much of the work as she could at home. Of the two major distractions in her life at the moment, Jan was actually the least disturbing.

Susannah applied adhesive to the next section to be worked. 'The cat flap. Well. To cut a long story short, she got her handyman to mend her caravan roof, then got him to fit a cat flap in our door – having consulted Paul, of course, who had been dead against it in the beginning even though I said it was a good idea.'

'Ho-hum,' Harvey said, trying not to take sides. He wasn't at all sure whom Susannah was most at odds with: sometimes it seemed to be her step-mother, sometimes he wondered whether it was her husband.

'It's the story of my life,' she went on. 'Nobody takes any notice of me. But I know I have only myself to blame. If you behave like a doormat you get treated like one, don't you?'

'Whatsoever a man soweth, that shall he reap . . .' Harvey frowned because the words didn't sound quite apt but he could think of nothing better. Or maybe it was the sentiment that disturbed him: ten seconds earlier he had been thinking about marital infidelity. Julia was never far from his thoughts. He seethed with anger against her; could hardly bear to share the same home. And he couldn't find words with which to confront her.

He stared hard at his fingernails. 'Actually,' he said, 'it's not a good idea to have cat's mess around – not with children about. I saw something about it on *This Morning*. Or was it on *Animal Hospital*?' He caught Susannah's expression and grimaced. 'OK. I know. So I need to get a life. Just you tell me how.'

'You're asking me? I'm only just beginning to learn.'

'And you've got glue coming out of those edges,' he said, rising to show her where.

She turned her head at his close proximity and held herself very still.

'Nice perfume,' he murmured, taking her finger and guiding it up to the glue.

'I –' she swallowed as he wiped her finger on a rag – 'I think I can hear your phone.'

When Julia came home from yoga she asked Harvey how it was going.

'What?' he said. He looked up at her but straight through her; he seemed to be miles away.

Julia hesitated before speaking again. There seemed to be no way of getting through to him lately. He was remote, and even cold whenever he so much as looked at her. And his words came out all sarcastic-like. Or perhaps she should say ironical. That might be a better word, she thought, because until recently she hadn't been sure what it meant, but now she did so she ought to practise using it.

'I said, how's the work on the bathroom going?'

'No you didn't,' he told her, his face held aloof, 'you were your usual vague little self. You never say what you mean.'

'There's no need to get hoity-toity!' She put her hands on her hips. But all he replied was, 'Isn't there?' and she didn't know what to make of him. Shrugging her shoulders, but with a frown, she ran upstairs to see the mural.

Golly, she thought, studying it reverently. It was looking really fantastic. She reached out and touched the stones, fascinated by the feel of them under her finger-tips and the way they swirled and fanned to make pictures. Then she clattered back down the stairs and hovered round Harvey again.

Perhaps he really needed some help – from a professional counsellor, or something. All his natural optimism had vanished; he was sinking into a pit of despair. She'd never seen him in need of help before and she felt so horribly helpless.

'Is she nice, this Mrs Harding of yours?' She perched on the arm of his chair and began to run fingers through his hair. Normally he wouldn't have refused a head massage, but now he ducked to one side.

Julia got up again, more alarmed than ever. 'She's doing a wonderful job, isn't she?' She tried to keep her tone light. 'I know! Why don't you ask her and her husband to dinner one evening? You're always saying we should invite more people round – get ourselves known in this place.'

Harvey gazed at her in silence, his eyes flickering over her face. It was as if he was trying to read something, but could find nothing there to be read.

'Yes, that's it,' Julia struggled on. 'We should invite more people round; give you someone different to talk to. You're getting quite good at cooking now, aren't you? We could have – ooh – how about, say, cannelloni and custard?' But he didn't even react to her little joke. 'Well, anyway,' she wound up, at a loss to know what more to say, 'it would give you something to do.'

'I'm really not in the mood,' he said. He pulled himself out of the chair and went and sat in the study.

CHAPTER 21

Jan popped her head round the studio door. 'Can I come in?' she wanted to know.

Susannah had been staring at the wall.

'I won't intrude if you're working,' Jan went on.

'It's pointless cleaning this place.'

'I wasn't going to.' She spread her hands wide. 'Look, no duster; I've finished for the day. I thought we might have a little chat.'

Susannah summoned her most discouraging expression; it wasn't very difficult.

'I know you don't want to talk to me,' Jan said, 'but you haven't anyone else, have you? The children don't seem to understand what you're trying to do, and Paul . . . well, he seems so terribly preoccupied about something, doesn't he? Is he worried about his work, d'you think?'

Guilt rose up in Susannah. Was Paul worried about his job?

'And I couldn't help noticing . . .' Jan went on, 'I mean, it doesn't take a genius to see that things aren't right between you.' She sat down on the other stool and twiddled one of her bracelets, but having launched herself into the conversation she seemed unsure how to continue it.

'What are you doing at the moment?' she asked, glancing about the room. 'You don't seem to be working on anything. Is Mr Harvey's mural finished?'

'Webb. Harvey Webb.' Susannah forced the name through tight teeth. The man was becoming quite a problem. 'I just have to finish it off in situ – grout it and clean it up.'

She had actually been plucking up courage to go over to his cottage and complete the job that morning, but the thought of what her visit might lead to was causing her to think twice. Damn the man! Damn him for making her feel like a teenager with a crush every time she thought about him. He was a good listener as well as a good talker, and she was getting to like him a lot. Too much, really, and she realised that her rift with Paul made her dangerously vulnerable right now. If she was in a position to do so, she'd refuse to finish the mural; but at this stage of her venture she couldn't afford grand gestures.

'Has it turned out as well as you'd hoped?' Jan prompted.

'Oh, yes. Far better than I'd expected. I wasn't really sure I could cope, to be honest. And now,' she picked up a pencil and began to doodle with it, 'I've even been given another commission. A neighbour of Mr Webb's – a Mrs Titchmarsh – saw what I'd done and decided she must have something made in mosaics, even though her bathroom's not suitable. She's settled for a plant stand for her conservatory, and she knows absolutely everyone for miles around so I hope more work will follow.'

'But that's wonderful news! I'm thrilled for you, Susannah. I am. Thrilled and very proud.'

Susannah looked up in surprise.

'I can see you don't believe me.' Jan gave a helpless shrug. 'You've got cynicism all over your face. You think I'm simply buttering you up because you're letting us park in your garden. And that isn't so.'

'No?'

'No! Oh, Susannah —' She put out a friendly hand. 'I'm completely on your side. Can't you see that? Haven't I always been one for equal opportunities? Haven't I always been in favour of women developing their talents to the full?' She smiled. 'I know I'm not a very religious person, but I've never been able to forget the parable of the talents . . .'

'Spare me,' Susannah groaned. She covered her face with her hands. It was bad enough having Harvey quoting the Bible at her, without Jan joining in.

Jan shook her head. 'Oh, I know those talents aren't the sort of talents I'm talking about — or are they, I was never quite sure? — but I've always believed they should be put to good use, not buried out of sight and left to rot.' She sighed. 'Your father and I were so disappointed when you refused further education. We wanted more for you. Oh, I know that was partly our fault. Your father and I decided to marry at precisely the wrong moment, didn't we? And all too soon *you* were married, and tied up with two little children. But why am I telling you this?'

'It's hardly news to me, is it? I've heard it all before.'

'Yes. Yes, I know. But now you're free of your children –'

'Wwha-a-t?' Susannah spluttered.

'Sorry. Sore point. But you must see this as only a glitch, surely? Simon and Katy will be off again before you know it. They won't be here for ever.'

'Oh no? Want to bet on it? Haven't you heard? There aren't any jobs out there. Can you see the housing market recovering? And what can Katy do? We don't even know if she can be cured. One thing's for sure: she'll never be able to pound a keyboard again. And look how many jobs need keyboard skills.'

Jan looked worried. Things weren't like this in her day. 'Well, anyway,' she said with sudden brisk-ness, 'I just wanted you to know that you have my full support. And I'm sure Paul will come round soon. He's feeling a bit put out, I think, because you haven't time for him at the moment.'

'He's never going to understand.'

'Well –' Jan looked doubtful – 'it's really not up to me to try to tell him. And I can't interfere between husband and wife.'

'Why not?' Susannah muttered ungraciously. 'You've interfered with everything else.'

'Susannah!' Jan got up from her stool, her voice trembling.

'Oh, I'm sorry, really I am. I didn't mean . . .' Susannah buried her head in her hands, disgusted with herself. But when she looked up again, Jan had left the room.

Harvey was looking scrubbed and ultra-clean as he let Susannah into the cottage. He was wearing a green denim shirt tucked into corduroy jeans and had one arm down the sleeve of a suede jacket.

'I thought you weren't going to come today.' His eyes were fixed and staring. She might have dropped in from another planet.

'I . . . got held up,' she told him. He need not know how close she had been to not coming at all. 'But I said I would finish the job today, so here I am.'

Discouraged by his look she added, 'It won't take long; I won't bother you.' And she hurried past him to the stairs, acutely aware of his presence. She expected him to follow her as he normally did, but when she got to the top of the stairs and looked down through the stair-well he was still standing where she'd left him. He had put his other arm in the jacket now and was shrugging his shoulders to settle it.

'I – er – have a dental appointment,' he said

without turning his head, 'so I'll have to leave you to it.' He sent a glance her way. 'Sorry.'

She nodded slowly in acknowledgement of this obvious untruth.

'Look,' he rushed on, 'I'll leave you this key by the phone here. Would you lock up when you leave and put it through the letterbox?'

'I take it Julia's not here then?' She thought she must be somewhere; her being in the cottage was the only explanation she could think of to account for his shifty behaviour.

'No. No, she's out doing some manicures, or something. Um . . . how long do you think you'll be?'

'About two hours, I think. That should do the trick.'

'Two hours. Right. Cheerio.'

Susannah heard the front door clang on its latch and the Mercedes start up outside. What on earth was the matter with him? She had thought they were getting on so well. Had she said something to offend him? But, casting her mind back to the last time she'd seen him she could think of nothing at all.

Puzzled, and more than a little bothered, she searched in her hold-all for grout.

Once clear of the village Harvey thumped the steering-wheel. By mistake he caught the horn and made himself jump in alarm. The car swerved and righted itself, leaving him shaky.

'This is bloody ridiculous!' he said aloud. He was being an utter fool. If you fancy the woman, he told himself, then *do* something about it.

And he did fancy her – badly – even though she wasn't really his type. Susannah wasn't overtly sexy in the way that Julia was. She was more sophisticated. Understated. And older, it had to be said. But that didn't seem to matter; she was wearing pretty well. And he had caught enough glimpses of ninety-nine per cent of her neat round breasts as she bent to pick up mosaics, to instil desire in him. He had had ample opportunity to admire the curve of her bottom as she'd worked on the wall as well. And one slanting glance from those soft grey eyes of hers could turn him to quivering jelly.

Added to that the fact that her marriage was undoubtedly dodgy – he had picked up that much from her conversation – and so, it seemed, was his own, and there really was nothing much to stand in his way.

So why was he running like this? Why wasn't he making a move? But the answer to that was obvious; renewed interest in the trouser department was no guarantee of success. Just supposing that Susannah was willing: what if he got it up all right but couldn't keep it there? Then what a fool he'd feel. What a dope.

But that wasn't all. Susannah, he was pretty certain, had always been faithful to her husband. She'd probably only ever known one man. She didn't seem the sort to have played around, before her marriage or since. Quite frankly he didn't know how to go about seducing so fragile an object without scaring her half to death.

For the next two hours he drove around, fantasising about being with her, and when he finally got back home to find her car had disappeared from the kerbside, he didn't know whether to be glad or sorry.

'I can only do three things,' Katy protested. 'Three things, then my arms'll drop off.' She plonked the iron down on its stand and hammered the plug into the wall with her foot.

'Three things will do very nicely,' Jan told her, her mouth firmly set. 'Every little helps. But you can do them later, if you please, dear. We're having a family conference in the lounge in a minute. And that includes you.'

'Bloody Nora,' Katy muttered, throwing down Justin's sailor-top. 'What's this all about then?'

But Jan would say no more until they were all gathered together.

Susannah was last to join the meeting. She sat on the arm of the chair that her father occupied, because there was nowhere else to sit, and Paul failed to perform his usual gentlemanly act of offering her his seat.

She rolled down her sleeves, smoothed her hair, and glanced round at her family. It was like seeing them for the first time, and they were all looking slightly self-conscious, like an Al-Anon group meeting.

Were they all contemplating their problems, she wondered, and about to confess their weaknesses? Should she kick off the proceedings by divulging her heartfelt thoughts?

Hi. My name's Susannah and I've made a mess of my life. My family doesn't understand me and now my client's taken me for a ride . . .

Well, how else could she explain his odd behaviour that afternoon? With the work about to be completed she could reasonably have expected to be paid. Was that why he'd beaten a hasty retreat? Oh, how Paul would smirk at her if she never got paid for the job!

Her eyes drifted to Paul. He didn't quite fit into the Al-Anon scene because he had a whisky in his hand. He and Frank seemed to spend a lot of time lately sampling Paul's collection of malts. Whisky was their only common ground.

Paul was looking – she searched for the right word – yes, he was as Jan had remarked: pre-occupied. Whereas her father had the air of one who has been deeply injured by life.

Natalie and Simon had commandeered the sofa and were sitting arm in arm, looking as though they were wondering how soon they'd be able to have sex again, irrespective of the fact that the whole family had to listen in whenever they got together. Katy was examining a swollen finger, and Justin was squirming on Jan's lap because his teeth hurt.

Gazza was perched on the window-sill with his back to everyone, planning his nocturnal excursion.

Jan put the baby down and cleared her throat. Everyone looked expectant.

'I just wanted to say . . . that is, Frank and I wanted to say . . . that things can't go on like this. It's obvious: the cottage can't cope with us all. The system doesn't heat enough water for a start; the bathroom situation's impossible; there's nowhere for us all to sit while our caravan's drying out, and –' her gaze rested on Simon and Natalie – 'there are other things to consider. Meals are a bit of a problem too, what with all the washing-up. And as for the washing and ironing – well, it sometimes seems like we've got the whole village's wardrobes to contend with. So what we were both wondering is . . . well, what are we going to do about it?'

It took the family some time to realise they were not about to be told something, but were being asked a question. They had not been expecting to have to think. They all looked at Jan until she felt compelled to go on.

'We've racked our brains,' she said, 'but we can't come up with an answer.' She threw Frank a worried look. 'If we had anywhere to go, we'd move out. I'm sure Simon and Natalie would too, but at the moment that isn't an option; Natalie can't cope with that yet.'

Simon and Natalie looked relieved. And smug and rather special.

'I expect Katy would prefer to be with her

friends,' Jan went on, 'but of course she can't if she can't pay her way. So –' she tried an encouraging smile – 'do we have any other suggestions?'

'I suppose we could move into the studio with Justin,' Simon offered, but then noticed his mother's expression. 'Sorry, Mum.'

'No, that isn't an answer,' Jan confirmed.

'Perhaps we could build an extension?'

'Or do up the garden shed.' Katy let out a snigger after her contribution. 'It's got a lovely en suite water butt.'

'We could go into Bath for a bath,' Simon added, beginning to get in the mood. He grinned. 'I meant, to use the facilities at the sports centre.'

'And we could fill the boot of Dad's car with washing, and take it to a launderette.'

'We could each have a machine to watch over.' Natalie spoke for the first time.

'And hire Molly Maid to iron it all!'

The younger members of the family were now rolling helplessly all over the furniture, even though nothing funny had been said.

'Really, I don't find this amusing,' Jan scolded, but her acid tones had no effect.

'I think you've lost your touch, love.' Frank spoke drily from the depths of his chair. 'Your class is out of control.'

'I wish you would all be serious!' Jan rasped. 'We do have a real problem to solve.'

Susannah looked across at her. 'I don't think there is a solution, Jan.'

Then Paul spoke quietly from his corner. 'Oh, but there is, Susannah. There is.'

CHAPTER 22

Paul drained his whisky glass and looked round at the family. Assured of their full attention he began to explain his claim.

'Susannah and I won't be here much longer, so the rest of you will be able to spread out.'

Katy's jaw dropped open at the news. 'Dad, you aren't that old,' she protested, 'you've both got years to go!' Then she realised by the look of scorn on her brother's face that she had jumped to the wrong conclusion. She poked her tongue at Simon before turning back to her father. 'I thought for a minute you meant . . . but you can't be going on holiday again already.'

'I wasn't talking about taking a holiday, Katy, any more than I was thinking of leaving this world. What I was trying to tell you was that –' he turned his head away from his wife – 'I'm being transferred to Glasgow.'

'Glasgow!' The word was chorused by everyone except Susannah, who found herself struck dumb.

'But you never mentioned a word of this,' Jan said, shifting round on her chair to confront her step-daughter. 'Oh –' She bit her lip. 'I see this is the first you've heard of it.' She turned back to Paul. 'That was rather naughty of you, Paul, springing it like this. Shouldn't Susannah have been the first to be told? And – I would have thought – in private?'

'Chance would be a fine thing,' Paul growled, his face darkening under the rebuke. When did Susannah ever want to listen to him? She was in a world of her own.

'Yes. Quite.' Jan had misunderstood him. She was already on her feet. 'You haven't had much privacy recently, have you? But you shall certainly have some now. Come on Frank – and you children – we're all going down to the pub.'

'Frank looked at his glass of whisky; it seemed a bit pointless going out in the cold and paying for something he could get indoors for free. And surely Paul and Susannah could go upstairs to talk? He was about to suggest as much when something in Jan's face made him think better of it. He allowed his wife to usher him from the room, shaking his head as he went.

Paul and Susannah remained sitting like statues while coats were found, feet were thrust into shoes, and Justin bundled off to bed. They didn't even move when the back door finally banged.

A minute or two ticked by before Susannah could trust herself to speak, and then she could only do so in a low, strangled tone.

'What the hell are they sending you to Glasgow for? You told me you were staying put. You said it was unlikely they'd ever want to transfer you again – and you wouldn't go if they did. You said you were winding down to retirement. You said, Paul!'

Paul looked down at the carpet; he'd half-forgotten all that. Of course, he hadn't been sure how she would take his news, but he had hoped she might be pleased. After all, it would solve most of their problems. And a fresh start away from the family could bring the two of them together again.

'Nothing in this world's ever certain, Sue . . .'

'And what the hell's up in Glasgow, for God's sake? Why are they sending you there?'

'We have quite a large dep—'

'It's bloody miles away!'

'Not all that far really, and the roads are pretty g—'

'Couldn't they send someone else? Someone young, and willing, and keen?'

'They need someone experienced.' And he still saw himself as young, and willing, and keen.

'Well, it doesn't have to be you.'

'I'm sure you'll soon get to like it there.'

'Whether I'll like it or not is immaterial. Because I flatly refuse to go!'

'You're talking nonsense now, and you know it. You can't refuse to go.'

'I beg your pardon? Can't I? How will you make me go?'

'Susannah, please be reasonable. Of course you'll have to go. Look –' he tried to sound calm and reasonable – 'this is the answer to our problems –

274

can't you see? And it's only for two or three years.'

'Two or three *years*? And no, I don't see at all. This would solve nothing for anyone; it only makes matters worse.'

'Not if we rent somewhere in Scotland, it doesn't, and let all the family stay here. They could pool together to pay us rent. And we'd still have this place to come back to.'

Susannah had just discovered how the phrase 'hopping mad' came about; she was literally hovering from one foot to the other in her agitation.

'You really think you've got it all worked out, don't you?' she said. 'But you're forgetting one rather important thing. I happen to have a life of my own now, Paul. I've work of my own to do. I know it means nothing to you, but it means a lot to me. I'm beginning to pick up commissions – just beginning to get off the ground. I can't just walk away from it all.' She turned her back on him. 'And I damn well won't.'

'And I have no intention of walking away from a promotion,' Paul calmly put in.

Susannah's head swung round. '*Promotion*? This is a *promotion*? But – but – you said you wouldn't want it – the extra responsibility! You said no amount of money was worth it. And you weren't going to take it – even if it ever came up.'

Had he really said all that? He couldn't remember. Must have been one of those 'off' days. 'Well, now it has come up. And I have to take the opportunity. I really don't have any choice. I might have thought better of it if you still had a proper job. But with the kids on our hands again we need the money. We need it more than we ever did.'

'But I do have a proper job! There's more to a job than just . . . Oh, what's the use. You'll never understand, will you? I don't think you even try. Well, I'm not going to Glasgow and that's final. If you go, it'll be on your own.'

As was the way with most work colleagues, Susannah and Molly had spent more of each twenty-four hours in each other's company than did many husbands and wives. They thought they knew each other through and through, yet in reality there were vast areas of their lives about which the other was hardly aware. Walking up the path to the door of Molly's little house, Susannah realised with a flicker of surprise that she had never been there before.

'Hello, stranger,' she said when Molly came to the door. 'Long time no see, as they say.'

'Heavens! I wasn't expecting you.' Molly's hand flew to her hair.

'Is it all right?' Susannah had sudden qualms. Perhaps she should have phoned first.

But Molly wouldn't hear of her going away again. She drew her over the threshold.

The first thing Susannah noticed was the row of neatly polished shoes lined up inside the door, the three, almost fully grown children, seated quietly at a table in the front room, heads bent over their homework.

Molly despatched the eldest to fetch tea for the visitor, as Susannah glanced around in confusion. She had never imagined Molly's taste to be for frills and fussy flowers, nor had she expected such orderliness.

'It seems a shame to disturb them.' She nodded at the children. She could hardly take her eyes off them, so unnaturally studious they appeared.

'We can go in the other room,' Molly told her when everyone had been introduced. 'Let these monsters keep their noses to the grind.'

'Monsters?' Susannah spluttered the word. These young people were veritable saints.

Bemused, she followed Molly to the back room and sat down on a chair patterned with tiny dots. Molly's son brought in a loaded tray.

'I'll bring you the pot when it's brewed, Mum,' he said, practically bowing from the room again. 'Is there anything else I can get you?'

'Would you mind if I borrow him for a few weeks?' Susannah laughed and then grew serious. 'I honestly meant to give you a ring, you know – give you the gory details . . .'

'About your abrupt departure, you mean?' Molly poured milk into delicate cups. 'I must say I've been dying to hear your version of things. But I thought you might want to be left to lick your wounds for a while so I didn't try to get in touch.'

'Lick my wounds...' Susannah considered Molly's odd choice of words.

'Yes, but I wouldn't do it for too long, if I were you. I was only going to give you until the week-end.'

The teapot arrived and Molly busied herself with it.

Susannah took the proffered cup but declined the plate of French Fancies. 'I don't think I get your drift, Molly.'

'Well, the longer you leave it the more difficult it'll be to come back.'

'But I'm not coming back!' Susannah paused with her cup half-way to her lips.

'Oh, but everyone's expecting you to.' Molly scooped sugar into her tea and tinkled a spoon round and round. 'We all know roughly what went on between you and Duffy – a couple of the girls were ear-wigging through the partition. And Duffy knows he's been rumbled. So we reckon that all you have to do is turn up soon and things will carry on as normal – or even better, considering you've got Duffy over a barrel.'

'What a charming notion!' Susannah smiled grimly. 'But I'm afraid this is all too late for me.'

She filled Molly in on what she had been doing: how she had taken up mosaics, and how she thought she could make it a going concern. She didn't mention anything about Harvey, though. 'You see, things have moved on since I saw you.'

'Good lord!' Molly sat back in her chair, her big

knees a little too far apart. 'I'd no idea you were interested in that kind of thing. You old dark horse! But I must say it's more you – sort of arty-crafty. And I suppose Paul's thrilled to bits.'

'As thrilled as a dog without a bone.'

'Oh.'

'For some reason he's always resented my having this interest. And then when the children came home he resented it even more.' She leaned one elbow on the arm of her chair and dug her fingers into her hair. She struggled with her emotions, dreading that she was about to howl in front of Molly.

'Is . . . everything all right?' Molly asked. 'Sorry – seems a stupid question. I can see something's troubling you.'

Susannah blew her nose. 'I just don't seem to matter to anyone. Paul wants us to go to Scotland, would you believe, and I want to stay here and build up a business. I want a chance to do my own thing. But he can't see it my way.'

She went on to tell Molly everything, then there was a silence while they drank second cups of tea.

Eventually Molly said, 'If you came back to work then Paul would have less of an excuse for going to Scotland, wouldn't he? He couldn't claim that money was an issue then. So you could stay here. And do the mosaic stuff, if you really must. But it would have to be in your spare time.'

'I can't.' Susannah thumped the arms of her chair. She was not in a mood for compromise. She knew that, before long, for the sake of a quiet life she would gradually drop the mosaic work and be back to square one. 'It would be fine for everyone else, but what about me?'

'Ah, yes, "me".' Molly nodded her head in sympathy.

'Yes, I know. I've got the dreaded "me" disease.'

'So, what are you going to do about it?' Molly was looking very serious now. 'You aren't going to do something really stupid, are you? Not – let Paul go to Scotland on his own?'

'That's what I've already threatened him with.'

'Oh, Susannah, you haven't! You can't! It would break up your marriage in no time – and probably your family too. Oh, please think what you'd be giving up.'

'That's rich coming from you, I must say. Wasn't it you who walked out on Les?'

'Well, he *was* carrying on with another woman. But Paul's been a damned good husband to you. And a good dad to your kids. Les was neither of those things; and when he asked me to take him back I said no. But I'll tell you something I've never told anyone: I regret to this day that I did.'

'In heaven's name, Molly, why?'

Molly drew herself up with dignity. 'Because I've been lonely as hell, that's why. You see, it wasn't just him I lost. I used to be friendly with his sisters. And with his dear old mum. I fell out with my mum over it too; she thought marriages should be worked at, no matter what. So you see, my support mechanism, as it's fashionable to call it these days, was totally smashed to pieces.'

'Support mechanism,' Susannah scoffed. 'Is that what it's supposed to be? I think I could manage without mine.'

And Molly couldn't persuade her otherwise. But as Susannah walked away from the house to her car, she wondered whether she could really cope on her own half as well as Molly apparently did. Molly seemed to have her life – which must have been tough at the best of times – neatly sewn up now. And it was amazing how well she controlled her children. She ought to be running the country, Susannah mused, unlocking her car and ducking into it; she was certainly wasted as a clerk.

CHAPTER 23

Katy found her father packing a small nylon hold-all.

'You're not going so soon?' she gasped, watching him roll up a red sweater and fit it down the side of the bag.

'Just a preliminary visit,' he said. 'I'll be back again in two days.'

'I wish I was coming with you.' She sighed. Jan could be such a pain, making her do this, that and the other. She was far too bossy by half. If she could escape from her clutches she would. And now that it turned out that Dr Platt was a happily married man there was nothing at all to keep her here.

'It's a long way to go just for two days,' her father was saying.

'I know. I didn't mean now; I meant when you go permanently.'

'But Katy . . .' Paul frowned. 'There's nothing much up there for you.'

'That's what Mum says too.' She folded a shirt for him in two, and then into four. 'But there's nothing down here either. You're going to be awfully lonely, aren't you, if Mum's not going to go with you?'

'But of course she'll be going with me!' Paul shook out the shirt, lay it on the bed and folded the sleeves to the back.

'But Mum keeps saying she's not.' Katy was thoroughly confused.

'What your mother says and what she actually does are two separate things. She'll come round in the end, you'll see.'

'If you say so, Dad.' She stared hard at her father; she wanted, with all her heart, to believe he knew what he was talking about. The thought of her parents parting like this made her feel sick, but she couldn't push it away. Somehow, deep down, she had the feeling that for once he'd got it all wrong.

'Mum,' Katy said, her mother having just come up to the bedroom with a heap of clean towels, 'are you going to Glasgow with Dad or not?'

Susannah looked at them each in turn, and looked away again.

'I've made my intentions quite clear,' she said.

'Well, I don't think Dad –' Katy took one look at her father's face and decided she was needed downstairs.

'You *have* to come with me, Susannah,' Paul rasped, when Katy was safely out of earshot. 'Everything's been arranged.'

'How can everything be arranged?' Susannah demanded. 'I've told you, I'm staying right here.'

'You're being thoroughly selfish, you know. I suppose you realise that?'

'Oh, and you're not? This has nothing to do with your promotion, of course? Nothing to do with *your* wants?'

He threw down his striped pyjamas. 'Susannah! We're not going through all that again. Look –' he held out his hands as if about to make two karate chops – 'why are we being like this? Why can't we be friends again? Why do we have to keep hurting each other?'

Susannah went and stood by the window, her arms folded across her chest. She was as miserable as the world outside appeared, cowering under a dark grey sky. She didn't want any of this to be happening. She wanted to slip into Paul's arms and be comforted. She wanted it just to be the two of them again, left to get on with their lives: him to his count-down to retirement; her to her new little career. Was that so selfish?

'This could all be so simple,' he went on, 'if you'd only listen to reason. Us going to Scotland together means all our problems will be solved.'

'Solved to your satisfaction, you mean.'

'Solved for everyone in the family. It's the best thing you could possibly do for them.'

'Best for them if I was out of their way.' She turned to look up at him bleakly. 'Well, if that's what you're all waiting for, I'm sure it could be arranged. I hardly need to go as far as Glasgow, though. I'll find somewhere of my own to live.'

'Oh, now you're just being ridiculous.' Paul fell on to the bed and closed his eyes. And he didn't open them again until she'd gone.

Perhaps she *was* being ridiculous, she thought, running downstairs. But she really couldn't see it. Something had got into her – a stubbornness that urged her on. And if she didn't hang on to what she believed in then she knew she would lose all faith in herself. She would virtually cease to exist.

She went for a walk across the fields behind the cottage, feeling conspicuous and vulnerable without a dog, and finally returned through the village so that she would pass the public phone.

Shutting herself in the booth she got a number from directory enquiries and fed change from her pocket into the slot. Minutes later it was all arranged; she knew what she was going to do.

But she hadn't reckoned with the effect her decision would have on the rest of the family.

The first person she told was Jan, who she found making out a shopping list on a wipe-clean board. Jan had got as far as writing 'bread' beneath the harvest fruits motif when Susannah burst into the kitchen.

'No doubt you'll be delighted to know,' Susannah immediately informed her, 'that I'll be moving out as well.'

Jan paused and looked up, preoccupied, the pen hovering with her thoughts. 'Of course you are, dear.' She smiled. 'You're going to Scotland with Paul.'

'No, I'm not. I'm going to London.' She looked up at the ceiling and waited.

'To London? But . . . I don't understand.' Events were moving too quickly for Jan to keep up.

'I've just phoned Dora Saxby,' Susannah went on. 'That's the woman my uncle left his house to, if you remember. I asked if she would mind me renting the place for a while. I knew she wouldn't have done anything about it yet. And she seemed pleased to have someone to look after it.'

'But you're . . . not . . . leaving Paul!'

'Well . . . I wouldn't put it quite like that. He's insisting on going to Scotland; I'm going to London. It's just a parting of the ways.'

'Oh, Susannah, please don't. There's surely no need for all this.' Jan clutched the onyx pendant at her throat, her eyes flickering about as though she could take nothing in. 'I – when I asked for ideas as to how we could all manage together . . . I didn't mean . . . I didn't think it would all come to this . . .'

'Come to what?' Katy came into the kitchen, her eyes wide and alert, but when neither Jan nor her mother would look at her, she needed no further telling. Her mother and father really were going to split up. They were no different from hundreds of other parents. She fled back upstairs to her bedroom and slammed the door in disgust.

Simon went very quiet at the news. Only Natalie could talk to him. Finding him stretched full-length

286

on the sofa without even the television on, she squeezed in beside him and lay down.

'Perhaps it's the menopause,' she said helpfully, snuggling under his arm. Jan had got her a book of women's ailments from the local library, and she felt well prepared for any eventuality now. 'That's all to do with hormones too, you know.'

'Bit young for all that, isn't she?'

'Well, some women start earlier than others; there aren't any written laws.'

'So what d'you think the solution is?' Simon's tone was cynical. 'You think this is just another problem for the doctors to solve? They can cure a twenty-five-year itch, can they? Or bring Glasgow nearer to Bristol?'

'No, of course not. But perhaps your mum needs pills of some sort, and – and counselling, maybe, like me.'

Simon showed his contempt of the idea with a grunt; there was a limit to what pills and talk could do.

He fell into another silence, then broke it by saying with a scornful laugh, 'D'you know, before all this, I was going to ask you to marry me. What do you think of that? I was thinking: wouldn't it be good to have what my parents have had all these years? Something really good and lasting and strong. Perhaps if we'd been married – properly committed – then we wouldn't have had difficulties either. We would have had more reason to stick at working things out. But now they've bust up like everyone else does. It was all nothing but a sham.'

'That's what I thought when my parents parted,' Natalie said forlornly, forgetting her intention to comfort Simon. 'Marriage is a complete waste of time, really, isn't it? You might as well not bother.'

Paul didn't know what emotion to put on his face when he discovered his wife heaving a suitcase down from the top of a cupboard in their room. Should he show delight that she had decided to come with him – or was she about to carry out her threat of going off on her own?

'I'm going to London,' she told him, putting paid to his last shred of hope, and she briefly explained where she would be staying.

Paul didn't know whether to hit her or throw himself at her feet. He waved his arms about help-lessly for a moment, then put both his hands on his hips. 'Well, if that isn't the daftest thing I've ever heard!' he blustered. 'What the hell's the point of going there? I thought you were desperate to stay in this area – to be nearer to your god-damned clients.'

Susannah snapped back the locks on the case and threw up the lid. 'I'll be within commuting distance,' she told him tightly. 'I'm not working in people's homes at the moment. All I need to be able to do is to deliver completed items when necessary.'

'Sounds to me like you'll be losing all your profits on petrol.'

'Well, it would sound like that to you, wouldn't it?' She put a hand to her forehead, suddenly weary. 'Look, I don't want to start another argument, Paul.'

'You can't expect me to take this lying down like a helpless lamb. God – I haven't even done anything! It's not as though I've played around with another –' He stopped, shocked by his own thoughts – and by their implications. He stared at her, round-mouthed, his eyes bulging with the pictures conjured up in his mind. Then he let out a self-deprecating laugh.

'My God, how naive can one get?' He rubbed the back of his neck and walked a full circle, trying to take it on board. 'So that's what this is all about, is it? Jeez – now it makes sense. Now I see why the family was too much trouble for you all of a sudden. And who's the lucky fella, eh? This Harvey Watchamacallim, I suppose? Him with the smooth talk and the money to fritter away? And nothing better to do?'

'No!' Susannah reddened at the accusation. 'This has nothing to do with him. Or any other man. I – I give you my word on that.'

But Paul almost wished there were another man involved; at least he would know what he was up against. At least there would be something to fight. 'I simply don't understand,' he said, sinking on to the edge of the bed.

He watched her fold jeans and fleece-lined sweat-shirts, and his tone was almost pleading when he spoke again. 'You've still time to change your mind, you know. Oh, come with me to Glasgow, Sue! Just for the two days. I'm sure you'll like it up there. At least it'd be a break for you. You'll be able to sort your thoughts out; get everything in proportion.'

He thought he saw her wavering as she turned with a nightdress over one arm. But after briefly glancing at him she shook her head – hard.

'Susannah.' He sprang from the bed and turned her back to face him. 'Don't break up the family like this. Please, Susannah, please!'

But if there were any magic words he could say to make her change her mind, he didn't know what they were. He had to give up in the end. And pray that she'd soon see sense.

Susannah found Katy in her room. She hadn't appeared for the evening meal.

'Are your hands hurting again?' she asked worriedly.

'A little.' Katy regarded her mother with soulful, accusing eyes. 'I wish you weren't going away. How can you go and leave me like this?' She held up her hands as though they were in iron chains. 'And why do you keep changing everything? Why can't things stay the same?'

'Nothing ever stays the same, Katy. You know that perfectly well.' She shrugged. 'I just feel I must get away for a while. I can't stay here.'

'You'll come back, though, won't you?'

The words were a knife in Susannah's heart; her

290

mother hadn't been able to come back. At least she wasn't exposing Katy to the same gut-wrenching sense of loss that she'd experienced when her mother died.

'I'm not going to the ends of the earth, you know. I'll still be able to pop in. Anyway,' she tried to smile, 'you're a big girl now. You don't need me.'

'But we don't want you to go to London. And we do need you. We want you to stay here with us.'

Susannah looked at the fluff gathering in rolls on top of the pine chest, exasperation welling up through layers of sympathy, helplessness and guilt. 'But it's not the real me that you want,' she said. 'And I can't be the old one any longer.'

She got up from the bed then, muttering something about dinner going cold, and left Katy more confused than ever. But there was no other way she could explain her feelings; no way Katy would ever see.

CHAPTER 24

The Webbs' utility room was a part of the old dairy, the original purpose of which could only now be guessed at. A spacious but gloomy room, it was currently cluttered with an assortment of household items for which neither Harvey nor Julia could find a home. Only a large gleaming white washing machine that loomed out of the shadowy muddle served any real purpose in their lives – along with a battered stainless steel sink and a floor mop.

'You left them on the draining-board, you say?' Harvey flicked the strip light into life and set it humming. 'Let me get them for you then.'

He began picking his way over old shoes, a piece of dented brass curtain rail, an empty plastic petrol can, and a trug containing weeds. He had forgotten he was supposed to have sorted it all out.

'I'm sorry to be a nuisance,' Susannah said, watching him negotiate the mine-field like someone wading through glue. 'It's not so much the value of the things, otherwise I wouldn't have troubled you; it's just the bother of getting replacements . . . Silly me, I should have remembered I'd left them there to dry the last time I was here. It would have saved – oh, thank you. Thank you very much.'

Harvey had retrieved her spatulas, sponges and mixing bowls and thrust them into a Woolworth's carrier bag, and now, dangling the bag by one finger, he held it out to her.

'A pleasure to be of assistance, ma'am. But I know what you really came for,' he added, giving her a comical nod and a wink.

'I – what?' She took the bag from him, not sure what was in his mind.

'Yes –' He was grinning broadly. 'I'll write you out your cheque.'

'Oh no! Good heavens! That wasn't the reason I came.' But of course he'd seen through her excuse. She should have realised he would.

She would rather not have had to come at all, only she was desperately in need of the money. She didn't want to have to touch the account she held jointly with Paul, unless compelled to do so.

'Please don't think that I –' she went on.

'– that you're as avaricious as the rest of us? I know you better than that. All the same, I must pay you some time; it might as well be now. Now where did I put that cheque book?'

Stepping out of the utility room he strode through a coolly tiled inner hall and into the carpeted lounge, leaving Susannah to follow him meekly. When he had found the cheque book among a litter of papers in the bureau and filled one in with a flourish, he grandly ripped it off.

'Your first job complete and paid for,' he said, bowing as he handed it to her. 'Allow me to congratulate you, Mrs Harding, on an accomplished piece of work.'

'Thank you,' she mumbled awkwardly, folding the slip of paper without looking at it. She tucked it into the pocket of her thick-knit cardigan.

'You don't seem very pleased,' he remarked, watching her all the while.

'Of course I'm pleased . . . very.' She forced herself to smile. 'I – I'm sorry but I have to dash now. Lots of things to do.' She was already moving towards the front door as she spoke, but Harvey managed to get there first.

'Susannah, what's the matter?' He had put his hand on the latch – not, it seemed, with the intention of seeing her off the premises but of holding it firmly in place. She was not going to get away, apparently, until he had had an answer.

'Nothing's the matter. Really. I'm perfectly all right.'

'Really,' he echoed flatly, cynicism curving his mouth. 'You drift in here looking like the world's come to a tragic end – but nothing's really the matter?'

She stared at the typically masculine area of his throat revealed by his blue open-neck shirt. 'Well –' she tossed her head dismissively – 'I've a few minor problems at the moment. Nothing for you to worry about, though. I'm sure I shall survive. Would you let me out now, please? I really must be off.'

'But, Susannah, I thought we were friends.' He admonished her with a frown. 'Didn't I give you your first commission? And encourage you all the way?'

'Yes, and I'm eternally grateful to you.' She swallowed as her eyes flickered to his. 'And – yes, of course we're friends . . . only –'

'Then please let me try to help you. You're looking very distraught.'

She allowed him to walk her back to the sitting room. She may have only come for her money but the need to pour out her heart to someone, was suddenly overwhelming. And right now Harvey was the only person in her life who seemed to understand.

'I've a rather nice white wine in the fridge,' he was saying to her from the kitchen, 'or – second thoughts –' he hurried back to where she sat – 'perhaps a brandy would be better right now.'

'No, no. No alcohol for me, thanks. I've . . . got a long drive ahead.'

'Drive?' He paused on his way to a drinks tray. 'And where are you driving off to?'

'London. I'm going to London. I'm . . . leaving the family, you know.'

'Leaving?' A start of surprise seemed to catch him. 'No, I didn't know.' He walked round her so he could face her. 'That's . . . an odd way of putting it, though, isn't it? I mean, I've heard of women leaving their husbands, and of husbands leaving their wives – who hasn't these days? – but . . .' He waited for her explanation.

'Well, you see, Paul's got himself posted to Glasgow, but I've decided I can't go with him. And as for the rest of the family – well, I've just got to get away.'

She began to pace about the room, thoughts of her family making her agitated all over again.

'I really can't take any more.' Her voice wobbled and she choked on the words. 'I've reached the end of my tether.'

She didn't realise she was crying until a clean white handkerchief appeared in front of her nose. And then she gave way to huge, heaving sobs of self-pity.

'Oh, why can't I be what they want me to be?' she wailed, her face buried against Harvey's chest.

'Because you're you, Susannah,' he said gently.

'I don't want to be me! It's too difficult! It was all much simpler before.'

'But wrong. You know it was wrong, now don't you?' His hand fell softly on her hair. 'You've done the right thing, taking charge of your life the way you have.'

'And where the hell's it got me?' She pulled away from him quickly, appalled at the way things were developing. She knew she couldn't cling to him like this a moment longer. A brief hug of comfort might be just permissible, but spin it out a second too long and trouble must surely ensue.

She sniffed and bunched up the handkerchief. 'I've alienated my whole family, following the selfish path, and –'

'Sod it!' Harvey suddenly cursed. 'That sounds like Julia's car.' He grasped Susannah by the shoulders and forced her to look up at him. 'You are *not* being selfish,' he almost shouted at her, 'so stop chastising yourself. Now, where are you staying in London?'

'M-my uncle's old house.'

'The one in Haringey you told me about? Remind me of the address.'

Susannah had never mentioned the address before: the information had been superfluous. But now, finding herself incapable of inventing a reason for not doing so, she breathlessly rattled it off, her teeth clattering together all the while.

Harvey went over to the bureau and scribbled the details down. 'Just in case there's more interest in the mural,' he was saying loudly by the time Julia opened the door, 'so that I can pass more customers on to you.'

Julia glanced up in surprise as she stepped over the threshold in high-heeled boots and trousers that moulded her bottom. She was clutching a carton of semi-skimmed milk and a small paper bag from the chemist's, and had looked preoccupied on opening the door.

'More make-up, I suppose,' Harvey commented, the scathing remark being aimed at the pink-striped paper bag.

Julia flushed, obviously aware that they had a visitor and that he was being less than polite, and tried to make as small a package as possible of her purchase.

'Oh –' Harvey remembered better manners – 'you haven't met Susannah yet, have you? Susannah's the lady who did the mural. I've talked about her a lot.'

'Oh, yes. Yes, of course.' Julia smiled, her lips sliding apart over perfect teeth. 'I wish I was clever like you,' she added wistfully. 'It must be nice to be really, really good at something.'

'You're very kind,' Susannah murmured, touched by her heart-felt words. Julia was not as she had imagined her; she was much more likeable than she'd thought. But Harvey hadn't treated her with much respect, and the thought disturbed her a little. She rallied herself with difficulty. 'I'm afraid I have to be going. I – er – just came to collect some of my things.'

'I wish you good luck for London,' Harvey said, formally seeing Susannah off the premises. His face revealed little as he waved and shut the door.

As she hurried away Susannah couldn't help wondering what might have happened had Julia not turned up.

'So, how was bonny Scotland?' Jan asked, attempting to lighten the atmosphere. The cottage hadn't seemed the same since Susannah left. Funny how one person could make such a difference . . . but she didn't want Paul to feel it too much.

'Scotland,' he said slowly, like someone coming out of an anaesthetic, 'was – well – bonny, as you said. At least, once you get out of the city it is . . .'

'And?' Jan prompted. But Paul was miles away. He seemed incapable of concentrating on anything for long. His eyes kept roving the kitchen, his ears listening out for the right sounds.

'I suppose . . . she's actually gone?' he forced out.

Jan sought silent opinion from the rest of the family as to how she ought to proceed. They were squashed round the pine table at the moment, waiting for the evening meal. But one after another they glanced away from her; she would get no help from them.

Jan went over to the cooker, her hands padded in big mitts with a hen design on each. She took out a large pot of chicken fricassee, lifted the lid with difficulty and stirred the contents around. Jan's meals were irresistible, and even Simon and Natalie now succumbed to them daily – no matter what they contained.

Dumping the dish in the middle of the table Jan said with conviction she did not feel: 'She'll be back before long, I'm sure she will. You'll see, Paul, if I'm not right.'

But everyone knew it was unlikely in the extreme. Why, even Frank had had a good go at his daughter, just before she'd left. Not that that had really helped much; in fact it might have even made things worse. But at least he had done his bit.

Paul let Jan ladle the mixture on to his plate and took rice as it was passed around. Then he got up from the table. 'Sorry, but I'm not very hungry. I'll just . . .' But whatever he intended to do, he was keeping it to himself.

'Oh dear, he's taking it badly,' Jan said. 'And I always thought he was so strong.'

'I don't think I'm hungry, either.' Katy sat back in her seat.

'Nor am I,' Jan had to admit.

And yet the food managed to disappear somewhere; not a scrap was left after a quarter of an hour.

'Life,' Jan said to herself as she stacked the empties, 'goes on regardless.' But she was deeply concerned about Paul.

Dora Saxby wanted none of Bert's personal effects. 'Just his old pullover, pipe rack, and foot stool,' she said, having given the matter careful thought.

Susannah gathered the items together, thinking how appropriate Dora's choices were. Nothing else could have brought the man's presence back to earth more assuredly than those shabby possessions.

She glanced out of the window, as she often had done at home when lost in thought, and encountered a row of red chimneys. They gave her a shock, used as she had been to seeing fields, and she was smitten with painful awareness – with the enormity of what she had done.

Had she really walked out of her previous life, her beloved cottage, for this? She glanced around. There was no need to look further than Bert's threadbare curtains to experience the vast differences in her environment.

Whereas the cottage had been pleasantly antiquated, Bert's two up, two down was decrepitly old; whereas signs of maturity had there been welcomed – and even manufactured at times for the sake of consistency – here they were causes for concern. Here, if surfaces looked stressed and parched of paint, it wasn't the result of expertise and expense; it meant something had to be done – and very quickly – if the place wasn't to fall apart.

Susannah sighed at the amount of work ahead of her.

'I only want to empty one or two rooms,' she had told Dora the day she arrived, 'so that I have space to do my work.'

'Clear the lot,' the woman told her grandly, making a drastic decision. 'I think, after all, that when you've finished with the place I'll sell it; and that will be much simpler when it's empty, I believe. I only wish I could help you with sorting it all out.'

But help from her was out of the question. Her husband still clung to life – if such it could be called, for he was in a very bad way – and he needed her full attention. Uncle Bert's old neighbour, however, claimed to have plenty of time to spare.

'I'll give you a hand, Susannah,' she said, wrinkling her nose with a sniff. She didn't quite approve of Dora Saxby, who was standing close by at the time.

'That's ... very kind of you, Mrs Wardle,' Susannah managed to say. She hadn't bargained on having to clear the whole house, and something told her that Mrs Wardle wouldn't prove to be the biggest help she could have wished for.

She was right. Mrs Wardle wore Susannah out with her constant chatter as she emptied cupboards and drawers. She had no method of dealing with the contents and constantly consulted Susannah as to whether things should be saved.

'You never know,' she would say, peering into a tobacco tin containing what looked like fossilised worms – and probably was, 'you never know whether something is valuable or not.'

'Junk sack', Susannah would tell her. Or 'Boot sale', if that were the case. She might as well have tackled the whole job herself.

And when it came to cleaning the place afterwards, the woman was no more effectual. It appeared that Mrs Wardle didn't approve of Hoovers – or anything with a conveniently long handle. Floors had to be scrubbed on hands and knees with an old wooden brush and polished up afterwards with a tin of wax. Spray polishes and cleaning liquids were anathema to her, and windows had to be rubbed with wads of newspaper.

Later, she would complain of chronic back pain,

and stiffness in all her joints. Mrs Wardle was soon laid up, and Susannah's sanity preserved. She got on much more quickly from then on and the mini-skip she'd had delivered to the roadside began to fill.

After three more days of hard work, Harvey Webb turned up.

CHAPTER 25

Susannah was emptying a sack of old paint tins into the skip when she saw Harvey's car pull up at the kerb. And the clatter of the tins as they hit the metal sides was no louder than the sudden thumping of her heart. She hadn't imagined he would come here – and yet had wondered if he might. She found to her disgust that she began babbling at him, out of nervousness, the minute he stepped from the car.

'Not a good place to leave it – lucky to find a space – kids around here are little terrors, you know. You'd better lock the – that's right – and does that bonnet thing come off?' And all the time she was trying to pull her sweater down over her stretch trousers to eliminate any unsightly bulges, and straighten her gypsy-style scarf.

Harvey looked her over and grinned, then glanced up and down the road. His keen eyes took in the shabby, hemmed-in houses with their filthy paintwork; the numerous boarded-up windows; the piles of scattered litter and damaged property. There was even a half-wrecked car opposite them, its wheels long since spirited away. Harvey's immaculate model shone smugly from under its soft-top hood.

'What have you done to deserve this?' he wanted to know. 'You must feel like a fallen angel.'

Pain passed over her face. 'Long way from Upper Heyford, isn't it?' she agreed. Sometimes over the past few days she'd had the feeling she was being punished for her defection from the family, and Harvey's words didn't help. This could hardly be seen as a step up in the world. And there were times, too, when she thought she must have taken leave of her senses.

'You OK?' He looked at her uncertainly as a gleam of sun struggled through the morning's clouds.

'Rushed off my feet,' she told him, leading the way indoors.

'Tea or coffee?' she offered him, once they were in Bert's old front room. She took a surreptitious breath, but the place still smelled damp and unused in spite of all her scrubbing. 'I'm afraid that's all I've got in at the moment.'

She watched Harvey step over her mosaic stuff, immaculate in a Harris tweed jacket and light wool trousers, his shoes as polished as his car. She had dumped things all over the floor while she cleaned up the back room for a studio. There was nowhere to sit: all the furniture had been taken to the auction room, except for two tub chairs that were at present stacked under a pile of household articles, and the carpets had been taken up.

'I'm afraid I haven't had much time to organise anything much in the refreshment line,' she apologised, 'I really wasn't expecting –'

'Me?'

'– any visitors yet.' Her mouth had become clumsy and dry again, because of the way he was looking at her. What, she thought, scurrying out to the kitchen, had he come here for?

Once out of sight she snatched off the gypsy scarf and ran her fingers through her hair. She wished she could put a hand on her lipstick, but unfortunately it was up in the bedroom. She checked her face in a small square of speckled mirror that her uncle had wedged behind some pipework – for some reason best known to himself – and let out a groan of despair. Pasty-faced and hollow-eyed, this was not one of her better days.

When she came back into the lounge with a small tin tray on which she had balanced two blue-striped mugs and some Hobnobs, she found Harvey pacing about in the confined space and running a finger round his collar. He was hardly likely to be too warm, she thought; the house wasn't centrally heated and all the grate had in it was an empty ash pan and a cleaned out grid.

'I was wondering whether you could do with some company,' he said, taking a mug of coffee from her. 'Better still, a helping hand? I mean, you shouldn't be wasting your time cleaning and sorting stuff out, should you? You're supposed to be establishing your business.'

'Don't I know it.' She looked at him over the rim of her mug and tilted her head to one side in a wistful attitude. 'It would be wonderful if you could help. But really, I can hardly expect you to do so. You aren't even suitably dressed. Apart from which it would be a huge imposition.'

But Harvey correctly deduced that some of her uncle's clothes might still be hanging around in the black sacks he'd just passed. They were currently lined up in the hall, waiting to be taken to the nearest textile bank. And he said he wouldn't at all object to wearing old trousers and a sweater, so long as she didn't mind.

'Great!' She shrugged and smiled her consent; then her smile faded. 'But . . . er, what about – well – Julia?'

Harvey's face froze as he looked across at her. 'What about Julia?' he grunted, before taking a gulp from his mug.

'Well . . . what would she think of you doing this? I mean . . . well, *you* know.'

He set the mug down on the mantelpiece. 'Julia,' he said, as though the name was a bad taste in his mouth, 'has no idea that I'm here, and it wouldn't make any difference if she did. She's supposed to be visiting her mother right now – if you can believe a word of that.'

Susannah eyed him shrewdly. She had thought when he first walked in that he wasn't quite

307

his usual ebullient self. Now, seeing him leaning dejectedly against the fireplace, she knew for certain that something was up.

'You sound as though *you* don't believe she's at her mother's.'

'Too right. I don't. Not a word.'

Susannah, a little embarrassed at being told things that were surely private between husband and wife, shook her head. 'I – I'm sure Julia doesn't tell lies. I mean, she just doesn't look the sort.'

'Shows how wrong you can be.' Propping an elbow on the mantelshelf he picked at a flake of paint with one of his nails. It was several seconds before he went on. 'My dear sweet Julia has been lying through her teeth for weeks on end. I've only recently got to know about it.'

He told Susannah how Julia had been attending college without telling him a word about it and that then he had quite by chance seen her with another man.

'Oh, but surely that doesn't mean a thing,' Susannah said, when she had considered his detailed description of the event. 'Two people meeting on their way into a building and having a bit of a laugh? It's hardly anything to go on, is it?' He was surely making a mountain out of a molehill. 'Take that as evidence to a solicitor,' she said, 'and I think they'd laugh in your face.'

Harvey swivelled his jaw. He seemed intent on believing the worst. 'She's been lying all this time about college,' he pointed out.

'And perhaps there's a very good reason.'

'She seemed shifty when she told me she was going to her mother's,' he added.

Susannah closed her eyes. 'In your present state of mind, Harvey, you could convince yourself that the tower of Pisa doesn't lean.'

'Well, I just happen to know that I'm right.' He rubbed his chin, hesitated, and plunged on. 'There are other matters to take into consideration too. Since I became redundant, things haven't been going all that well between us. Our marriage is – not what it was.' He held her eyes with his. 'So you see, that makes two of us, doesn't it? You and me both. And if you can consider yourself a free agent, then so can I.'

'Yes . . . I see . . . but –' Susannah felt for firm support among the largest cardboard boxes and gingerly sat on the edge of one. 'I still see myself as married, actually . . .'

'I suppose I do too, come to that. But I don't feel particularly bound by my vows. Do you? And I don't see why I shouldn't come and go as I please. If I want to spend my time helping you, and you have no objection, then what's to stop me? Anyway, enough of this talk, let's get down to work.'

'Yes. Work.' Susannah looked round the room, her thoughts awry. She wondered why it was, if Harvey was so sure of his facts, that he didn't challenge his wife on the matter? And why bring the tale here to her? What – exactly – was she supposed to make of it all?

But there was only one answer to that, really, and she thought she could guess what it was.

They were sitting by the fire that Harvey had laid that afternoon, eating kebabs from a takeaway. A candle flickered from the top of a wine bottle balanced on a stool, revealing them in their rag-bag clothes, and they ate in reflective silence. They could have been hard-up newly-weds, Susannah decided, except for the obvious signs of marching time stamped on their lived-in faces.

Harvey had been a real godsend. Her new studio was virtually ready and the front room had been straightened out furniture-wise. They were still clattering about on draughty floorboards but there was little they could do about that.

'I'm not going to lash out on new carpets,' she told him. 'Not when it isn't even my place.'

'Perhaps just an ethnic rug of some sort? Shouldn't cost too much.' He looked down at the floor at the space between them where such an item might go. He seemed to be imagining things to himself.

'Hmm.' She looked at him from under her lashes, chewing contemplatively on her food. It was half-past nine and he had made no move whatsoever in a homeward direction – hadn't said a word on the subject.

He shifted his knees and sent cutlery sliding to the floor. She picked up her glass and spilt wine. Meat turned to rubber in her throat.

When they had finished with the food and Harvey had declined anything more to drink – although he had taken only half a small glass of not-bad-at-all Chablis – she took the debris out to the kitchen. She was scraping rubbish into a flip-top bin when he came and stood behind her.

He'd brought the lighted candle with him and he placed it carefully on top of the fridge.

'Susannah . . .'

She started, missed the bin, turned and put a hand to her hair, conscious of how bedraggled she must look. She had hardly had time that day to draw breath, let alone attend to her appearance.

'You look fine,' he assured her, reading her mind, and he slipped an arm round her waist. They stood for some time, surveying each other, as the fridge started up a noisy hum. 'Are you glad I came?' he asked her after a while.

'Yes. Yes, of course I'm glad. I was feeling . . . a little bit lonely.' She could feel his hand on her hip, warm and full of promise. Imagining what that hand might be capable of, she fought to keep calm, to play it cool; act like the mature woman of the world that she was far from feeling.

'It's getting rather late to drive back tonight,' he told her. 'And what's there to go back for in any case?'

'N-not a lot, from what you've been telling me.' She put a hand against his chest. 'I do think you may have got it wrong, though. About Julia, I mean.

311

She seems so – I don't know – really nice. Oh, I know I scarcely know her but –'

'No, you don't. You know nothing. You'll just have to let me be the judge, won't you?'

'And what if it turns out you're wrong?'

He merely looked at her, his eyes glittering. His hand went out to the light-switch. 'Will you let me stay the night?' he wanted to know in the sudden darkness.

'There's only one bed, you know. One tiny little single bed.'

'I know.' His Adam's apple moved twice, up and down as she watched it.

She swallowed hard, full of doubts. 'I don't know . . .'

But he allowed her no time for indecision. He picked up the candle, took her hand in his free one, and led her slowly towards the stairs. They walked up the thirteen steps, jostling side by side. And she could swear his fingers were crossed as they clung to hers. Every step of the way.

Harvey cried when it was over. Susannah didn't know what to say.

'Was – was I that disappointing?' she forced herself to ask him. She stared at the window with its skimpy curtain. She thought she had acquitted herself reasonably well. What had she done wrong?

He reached for Uncle Bert's trousers, dug about in the pockets for a handkerchief, then loudly blew his nose. 'Don't be so damned ridiculous.' His

voice was muffled and cracked. 'Don't you ever
cry?'

'Oh . . . you mean with a climax? Um, once or
twice I have. Yes. I didn't think men did too,
though.'

'Big boys don't cry? Well, I've never done it
before. Cried like that – over anything.'

'So why did you do it just now?'

He turned to face her again, his eyes still wet,
but beautiful. 'Because you just made me so happy,
Sue. You'll never know how much.'

CHAPTER 26

Beneath a grey, ominous sky an endless flow of people traipsed to and from their cars. Paul watched them through the window of the motorway service station for a while, slouched over a cup of coffee in an attitude of total despair. How had it all come to this, he was wondering for what must be the hundredth time.

He drew his eyes to Katy on the opposite side of the table. At least he had her. But since agreeing to let her accompany him permanently to Scotland he had had many second thoughts. Was it fair to take her with him, even though she'd wanted to come? The job situation was even more dire in Scotland than where they had been living before – supposing her hands improved sufficiently for her to look for one. And how would she amuse herself, all the time he was at work?

But she had insisted that it was what she wanted to do, which was understandable: new horizons had their attractions, after all. He would need someone to look after him, was what she'd said to persuade him.

But he'd much rather that person was Sue.

Katy tore a Danish pastry apart and poked a piece into her mouth. She chewed on it mechanically for a while, gazing at the same drab scene as her father.

'Where are we now?' she asked, washing the cake down with cold milk.

'You've got a milk moustache,' he grunted, passing her a paper napkin. 'We're nearly through the Lake District. Didn't you notice the lovely scenery?'

'Yes.' She ignored the tissue and licked her lips. When would Dad notice she was no longer a little girl? 'So we're nearly there, then?'

But Paul dashed her hopes with the most withering look he could muster. He knew he was being mean to his daughter, but she was the only person around on whom he could vent his ill feelings.

'Didn't you ever do geography?' he chided with a despairing shake of his head. 'The Lakes are not in Scotland, dear girl. We've still got a long way to go.'

'But we've done hundreds of miles already! We started way before dawn. I didn't know it was this far. We should really have flown instead.'

'And leave the car in Wiltshire, I suppose? Fat lot of use that would have been. I told you; the place I found to rent's some way out of Glasgow — a fair bit beyond, in fact, because although I don't mind working in the city, I didn't fancy living there. I'll need the car to commute.'

Actually, he had chosen the pretty little bunga-low on Loch Long with Susannah mainly in mind. She would surely have loved it. He had honestly believed at the time that she would come with him, when it came to the crunch. He still couldn't believe she hadn't.

Katy could see precisely why her father hadn't wanted to live in Glasgow as soon as they hit the M8.

'Da-ad,' she said with growing trepidation as the car plunged on regardless, 'is this really it?'

'Yes,' he answered shortly, daring her to say any more, so she curled up in her seat, her feet pressed up against the glove box, and fell into a silent gloom.

But eventually the monstrous causeway ceased its march through the hell of modern living and began to follow the Clyde. Once Dumbarton was behind them things began to improve.

'We've been stuck in this car all day,' Katy said, yawning her widest yawn. They were passing a village called Rhu at the time, but she couldn't see much of it.

'I had noticed,' Paul growled. His head was beginning to ache. It was dark already again, and he was growing a little concerned. In his initial delight with the bungalow he hadn't realised just how far he had committed himself to commuting.

'We're nearly there now,' he said at last, making tedious progress along a serpentine stretch of road.

'That's Loch Long on your left; the bungalow's just round the bend, I think, if my memory serves me correctly.'

Paul had remembered wrongly. They negotiated a dozen more bends before the bungalow came into sight. But by then Katy had fallen asleep.

After a morning of being all politeness to Harvey, Mrs Wardle discovered that, charming though he undeniably was, he was not Susannah's husband. Much to Susannah's relief she withdrew her services immediately. From then on she was only glimpsed over the garden fence on the odd occasion, pegging out voluminous stockinette knickers on her washing line.

'I feel like a scarlet woman,' Susannah told Harvey, having already suffered many pangs of doubt and gnawing guilt. She had never been unfaithful to Paul in her life and had not intended to be now, even though they were estranged. Romance had never been on her agenda; Harvey was a hidden extra. And she knew she wasn't in love with him – well, maybe she was a little – so why had she gone to bed with him? To feel wanted and comforted, she supposed. He was a good provider of both those things, as well as having obvious physical attractions.

But if Harvey had any qualms about what he was doing, he didn't let on to her; and whenever she got too serious about the situation he would smooth-talk her out of the mood.

'Susu,' he announced on the Saturday morning when they were lounging in bed with a stack of toast, 'we're out of luck.' He had been thumbing through a free local rag he'd found on the doormat, in search of a car-boot sale. 'There are only – let me see – twelve boot sales to choose from today. And a jumble sale or five.'

'That all?' Susannah smiled as she sipped at an orange juice.

'There's one that can't be far away from here,' he went on, 'judging by its name; it's on a school playing-field.' He glanced up at her, licking a blob of marmalade from the corner of his mouth. 'You know, people will buy anything at these sales. Have you ever been to one before? Julia –' he checked himself – 'well, you wouldn't believe the junk they sell. You ought to take along some of your own stuff, you know, not just your Uncle Bert's.'

'My mosaic junk, you mean? Thanks for your vote of confidence.' And thanks for the mention of Julia, she silently reproved him; Julia often sneaked into his conversation. Did he realise just how often? On several occasions Susannah had suspected she might be being used by Harvey somehow to teach Julia a lesson.

'Oh, I didn't mean your stuff was . . . well, you know what I really mean. It's certainly worth a try. In which case perhaps we should go up market a bit; pick a more salubrious venue?'

'It's a wonderful idea,' Susannah said, kissing him on the chin. 'Whatever would I do without you?'

Harvey beamed like a young boy scout who's earned his bob for a job. There seemed nothing he liked more than to be useful.

Perhaps they were both being used.

Rain sheeted across the windscreen of Paul's BMW. His tired eyes pierced the night. He might have been in a car-wash for all he could see of the road ahead. It certainly felt that way; the vehicle was constantly buffeted by a wind blowing up the Clyde, as if by huge invisible brushes. Water streamed from every direction. It scudded up under the wheel arches, hammered a tattoo on the roof; and the wipers were going berserk.

But he was almost used to such conditions now; it had rained like this the whole week.

'Doesn't it ever stop?' Katy had wanted to know after her first three days' experience of it. She was kneeling on the lumpily cushioned window-seat at the time, her mouth turned down at the corners and her head propped up on one hand as she stared out across the loch. At least, she stared as far as she could see, which was the garden gate. Thick mist and driving rain hid everything else from view.

'It can't rain for ever,' Paul had told her. But tonight he believed it could.

Arriving at last at the bungalow, he scurried indoors to be greeted by the smell of . . . he sniffed extra hard . . . he couldn't make anything out.

'Oh, are you very hungry?' Katy dragged her head from her book.

'Well of course I'm very hungry. In fact I could eat a horse. What have you done for dinner tonight?'

'I haven't done anything yet. There's nothing much to cook.'

'Of course there is. There's plenty.' Paul held his temper in check with iron control. He'd had a long day catching up on a pile of paperwork inherited from his predecessor, attended a draggy management board meeting in the morning, and dealt with a tricky staff problem in the afternoon. The last thing he wanted was to have driven all this way home to find no meal ready on the table, no word of welcome, and Katy two inches into a Jackie Collins.

He threw off his wet mac, kicked away his shoes and strode through to the kitchen. 'Look at all this!' he said, flinging open the fridge. 'Loads and loads of stuff. We only went to the supermarket a few days ago.'

'I know.' Katy glared at him through the serving hatch. 'But I didn't fancy cooking any of that.'

'You didn't –?' Paul began to lose control of himself. 'Eggs.' He picked up the box and slapped it down again. 'We could have had an omelette at least. Chicken breasts: you could have done something with those. Cheese. Vegetables. Salmon steaks.' He planted his hands on his hips and waited, but Katy had nothing to say.

Paul crossed to his bedroom, then, to discover that his bed had not been made. And the bathroom was still warm and wet with recent steam. Katy's mattress, when on an impulse he thrust a hand under the knotted covers to test it, was faintly warm too. No doubt about it: she had not been up very long.

Like a bloodhound tracking a scent he loped back to the lounge, his attention now fixed on the carpet.

'Those,' he said, pointing downwards, 'are crumbs from your lemon cream puffs. And you polished those off the day we bought them.'

'So?'

'So why are the crumbs still there?'

'Why shouldn't they still be there?'

'Because they should have been Hoovered up, that's why. You do know what a Hoover is? That grey thing under the kitchen work top. Now is it too much to ask that you become acquainted with it?'

'Oh, stuff it, Dad. What's the point? Who's going to see this place but us? We're stuck in the middle of nowhere, miles from civilisation. Who gives a toss about a few measly crumbs?'

'I do, as it happens. And I care about my empty stomach. And you told me you were going to keep house for me; not slum around all day doing nothing.'

'Oh, stop nagging, will you? I can't stand it! I'm not your wife, you know. God, no wonder Mum didn't want to come with you. I hate you when you're like this!'

She flounced off to her bedroom, wailing, 'I hate this house, I hate this weather, I hate Scotland. And I wish I'd never come!'

'Katy? Katy, I'm sorry.' Paul sat on her bed with a twang. 'Am I really so awful to live with?'

Katy dropped her book and kneeled up to hug him, relieved that he wasn't still cross. 'Of course you're not horrible, Dad. You're the bestest father in the world.' She grinned. 'Except when you're tired and hungry.'

'And . . . I wasn't like that to your mother, was I? Do you really think that's why she went?'

'Don't be daft, Dad, I didn't mean that.' She punched his chest playfully. 'That's not why she went off on her own.'

Katy sounded confident she had all the answers, and Paul studied her with surprise.

'Why then? Why did she? Do *you* know why she went?'

A glow swept over Katy. Her father was asking her opinion? For once he was treating her as an equal? Wonders would never cease.

'It's really very simple, you know. Women these days want more. More than the family and house-work – and not just some mindless little job, either. We want big things for ourselves.'

'Well, I know all about that. I'm not stupid. But it doesn't apply to your mother.'

'It does! That's what I'm trying to say. Being liberated means being free to do . . . whatever you want to do. And Mum wants to do her own thing, for once – something rewarding and interesting and for herself. I can't say I really blame her.'

Paul stared at his daughter in amazement. 'How come you know all about this?'

Katy looked up at the ceiling. 'Well, of course I know all about it. I've never known anything else. My generation takes it for granted.'

'Do they?'

'Oh –' she tucked her feet under the old-fashioned eiderdown, looking a little shame-faced – 'I know I've not shown Mum much sympathy. Not given her much support. I suppose you could say I've been a bit of a pain. I've been just a wee bit jealous, you see.'

'You, jealous of your mother?'

'Yes! Because she'd got it all, hadn't she? Or nearly did have. Somehow she lost you in the process . . . But me – well, I've got nothing. I'm stuck in some kind of warp. No job, no money, no life.'

'Poor Katy.' He patted her shoulder. 'Life's not being very kind to you, is it? What are we going to do about you?'

'I don't know, Dad.' She sniffed hard. 'And you? What are you going to do about Mum?'

'D'you think she'll ever come back to me? Fearful ogre of a man that I am?'

'Not unless things are changed.'

'No. No, I can see that. It would have to be different, wouldn't it?' He sighed. If the world changed, you had to go along with it, it seemed. No use kicking against it. And if your wife wasn't happy with the way things were, then you had to do your best to accommodate her. That was what love was all about, wasn't it? Making sacrifices for others.

Rain splattered on the window as they sat in silence, holding each other's hands.

'You do want her back, Dad, don't you?' He hadn't said anything for so long, Katy was getting worried that he actually might not. But when she looked into his eyes, she knew.

'Of course I do,' he managed thickly. 'I miss her every minute of the day.'

'Christmas should be abolished,' Harvey complained, staggering from the car under a weight of mosaic materials. They had been stuck in traffic on their way back from a supplier in Fulham for well over an hour and a half.

'All in a good cause,' Susannah was quick to remind him. 'Have to keep the customers happy.'

'We certainly do.' Harvey waited for her to find the door key, and when she had located it and was putting it up to the keyhole he put a hand on her arm. 'Are *you* happy?' he asked her in a suddenly serious tone.

'O-of course!' She fumbled with the lock. 'Haven't I good reason to be? I've got an order list as long as my arm, thanks to you.' She smiled up at him, forcing the doubts about what she was doing to the perimeters of consciousness. 'And I've got the best possible assistant into the bargain.'

Certainly, on the surface, everything was going well. The car-boot sale had gone better than either of them had expected. They had sold all Uncle Bert's household items except for an old-fashioned electric iron with a frayed flex and no thermostat, and there had been a lot of interest in the few pieces of mosaic work that Susannah had managed to complete, over and above her Upper Heyford orders. Harvey had been able to slap a SOLD notice on each piece within the first hour of their arrival, and while the items waited for their purchasers to take them to their cars, new orders had come in in a steady flow. By the time they had packed up their trestle table for the day, Susannah had begun to wonder how she could get through all the work involved.

'I'm going to have to find someone to do some of the carpentry for me,' she now said absently, pushing open the front door. She stopped suddenly on the doormat, reminded of how she had once turned down Paul's unwanted assistance. *Perverse and foolish*, she silently chided herself; she had wanted to do things her way and on her own, or not at all. Why had she been so stubborn? And why couldn't she put Paul out of her mind? The enormity of what she had done, and was doing, kept coming home to her in great waves of incredulity, almost knocking her off her feet.

'Let the dog see the rabbit,' Harvey said behind

her. He was carrying a box of tesserae. 'You look as if you were miles away.'

'Oh . . . just feeling a little snowed under. I need to work a lot faster, you know.'

'Hmm. And I suppose I'm not helping a lot, am I?' He gave her a mischievous grin. Having rediscovered his sexual powers he was keen to keep her in bed with him when she should really have been working.

'Look,' he added quickly, 'I'll leave you alone for a couple of days – take the finished stuff down to Upper Heyford. Mrs Tittle-Tattle will be hankering for her plant stands, you know. I think she wanted one of them to take down to her daughter in Cornwall soon. Can't disappoint our clientèle.'

'No . . . can't do that, can we?' While he was busying himself with the rest of the parcels Susannah studied his face. Was there a hidden agenda here? Did he really want to get back to Julia, before she grew suspicious? Because, for all his laid-back attitude, she hadn't totally believed him when he claimed to be a free agent. How could he be when he hadn't even discussed things with his wife?

She didn't know what to make of him. After years of living with the dependable, if a little dull, Paul, she was finding the experience of Harvey – exciting but unpredictable as he was – somewhat mystifying, not to say unnerving.

'Well,' she said eventually, 'it would certainly save me a trip.'

'Unless, of course, you want to drop in on your folks? Those of them that are left, I mean?'

'No – er – well, I'm not sure. I don't think I can face them just yet.'

Harvey glanced at her, frowning. 'You've no reason to feel ashamed, you know. You're not doing anything wrong.'

'No,' she agreed readily, but there was a question mark in her tone. What, she wondered, would Harvey consider wrong behaviour, if what they were doing was not?

She said no more on that subject, though, because she had discovered that Harvey could argue his way round anything; and later that day, having fed her a large helping of what he claimed to be his speciality – chicken tetrazzini – he took her Upper Heyford consignment out to his car and screeched off down the road, breezily waving through the window until he was gone from her sight.

But turning back into the house she discovered that one of the plant stands was still there, languishing behind the front door.

CHAPTER 27

Harvey didn't know what to expect when he got home. Cruising in the outside lane of the motorway at a steady eighty miles an hour he pondered his arrival. Would Julia be there? He still wasn't sure whether she had been telling him the truth about going to see her mother. He had wanted to believe she was lying to him – and yet it was also the last thing he really wanted to believe. Talk about confused; he was as mixed up as the bag of string-ends his mother used to keep on a nail in the cupboard under the stairs.

Once, when bundled by sisters grown weary of his antics into that cobwebby cave full of dusters, floor polish and brushes, he had tried to untangle the string and make a decent length of it. It had been his tearful intention to hang himself from the light fitting – an act designed to serve the girls right for their gross ill-treatment of him. Fortunately he had not succeeded.

And he was no more successful now in untangling his mixed emotions. He no longer felt the need to punish Julia, and could hardly recall the feelings that had seemed to make it necessary for him to do so. Of course this sex thing had had a lot to do with it, but now that he was well and truly over all that he could see things for what they were. It had never been Julia's fault that he'd lost his sex-drive, any more than it had been anybody else's – unless you could blame the prime minister, which would be stretching things a bit far – and yet in his mind he'd put the blame on her. But now he could no longer do so; nor could he blame her for looking for comfort elsewhere. If, indeed, she had. As Susannah had been quick to point out, he had nothing substantial to go on where Julia's behaviour was concerned; he had been all too quick to jump to conclusions – ones that suited him.

And now there was Susannah to consider. He didn't want to hurt Susannah and he didn't want to hurt Julia either. His trouble was, that in spite of his upbringing – or maybe because of it, because his sisters, on the whole, had showered him with love – he simply adored all women.

When he finally arrived home Julia was there. She was getting up from the tapestry pouffe on which she'd been sitting, stuffing a man-size tissue up her sleeve.

Harvey stopped, appalled; he so rarely saw Julia cry. She had always kept tears from him, knowing how difficult he found it to handle them. Even during those years when they'd hoped for children and been disappointed month after interminable month, she had concealed the wet part of her grief from his sight.

For a moment it crossed his mind that her lover had jilted her, but then he spotted a gigantic cake sitting on the breakfast bar and knew at once that she'd genuinely been to see her mother. No one else made fourteen-inch slabs of dense, impossibly yellow sponge cake, filled with a whole pot of home-made jam and lavishly trowelled all over in pink frosting with blobby rosettes on top. They'd probably be shot if they did.

'Well, what happened?' Julia asked him, snorting the thickness from her voice. 'Did you get it?'

'Get . . . ?' Harvey was at a loss.

'The paper-boy said you'd gone to London. For an interview, I assumed he meant. Not that he said anything about an interview, but I couldn't think what else you could have gone for.'

'Oh –' Harvey thought quickly; he recalled bumping into the paper-boy and asking him to stop shoving things through the door until further notice. 'Oh, the job you mean. Well, I don't know if I got it yet. My, but they put you through it on those assessment-type interviews these days. I'm absolutely shattered, believe me.' He slumped into an armchair and contrived to look suitably stressed.

'At least you get interviews,' Julia said. She took a letter from behind the bronze horse on top of the bureau where such things were usually kept. 'Here, you've got another one.'

Harvey stared at the long white envelope she

was holding out to him; this was the first real reply he'd had. Was someone actually prepared to consider him? But Julia had already opened the letter; presumably she knew what she was talking about. And he wanted to whoop and dance and twirl her off the floor, but he checked himself just in time: it wouldn't do to appear too ecstatic about an interview when he was supposed to have just come from one.

He scanned the letter three times and contented himself with a grin. 'Things are looking up, aren't they? This is for a consultancy – did you see? – just what I was looking for. The money should be good.'

It seemed the wrong thing to say. Julia's face had crumpled as he spoke and now she was turning away. Out came the tissue again and she began to mop at her nose.

Harvey scratched the back of his head, disconcerted again. She couldn't possibly know what he'd really been doing these past few days. Could she? But no, if she did then she wouldn't be snivelling; by now he would be drenched in vitriol. Julia, in a paddy, could breathe fire. No, it had to be something else. Not him; not her lover. So what?

Then he suddenly twigged, or thought he did.

'Oh,' he said solemnly, crouching down beside her. 'I think I understand after all.'

'What?' Julia blinked through her tears at him. 'What do you think you know? I don't think you've got a clue.'

'Oh yes, I have.' He gently put his arm round

her shoulders, feeling her sorrow as his own. She had tried so hard to keep it a secret from him, no doubt wanting to spring her achievement as a surprise. Only now she couldn't. 'I suppose you've failed your exams, haven't you? Well, it isn't the end of the world. You can always take them again sometime. Lots of people do.'

Julia stared at him from behind her tissue with something akin to contempt. 'I'm not due to take any exams until June next year. And what do you know about it anyway? I never let on what I was doing. Oh, you –' she threw his arm off her shoulders – 'you're such a little know-all, aren't you? Why didn't you tell me you knew?'

'Well, why didn't you tell me what you were up to? I only found out by chance. I discovered one of your books lying around; it was tucked inside something else.'

'I didn't want you to know about it,' she sniffed, 'not till there was something to tell.' She slid off the pouffe on to her knees and began to poke the stove, jabbing ferociously at the charred wood and sending sparks all over the hearth.

'I still don't understand why,' Harvey said, watching her. He seemed to be seeing her properly for the first time in many years, and was finding her more mature, more sensible than the inner picture of her that he was used to carrying around. And the idea of her having an affair with the man he'd seen her with at the college had somehow become remote. 'I mean, were you doing it because

I'd lost my job? Did you think you might have to be the breadwinner and get more qualified work? Or what?'

'I started long before you were made redundant,' she scoffed at him. 'I've been doing it for over a year.' Then, her cheeks glowing red from the fire, she looked up and flung at him, 'I did it because of you, Harvey! You think I'm so stupid, don't you? Well, I wanted to prove I wasn't. I got fed up with you treating me like some kind of pet poodle. Like some spoilt little kid!'

'Julia! I didn't. Did I?'

'Can't you see I'm a grown woman now? And that I do have a brain in my head? How do you think I manage to do hairdressing and yoga and all the other things I teach? I've had to learn how to do them, that's how. Oh, I know they don't count for much in your book – only brainy things count with you. Only degrees and diplomas and certificates. Well, that's what I've been trying to –' she gulped hard – 'get!' But the gulp didn't help her struggle for composure, and she broke down in tears once more.

Harvey ventured to put his arm back. He was more touched than he could say – and riddled with barrow-loads of guilt. Julia had been doing something to bridge the gulf that the years had widened between them, whereas he – well, what had he done? Not a lot. Worse, when things had gone really wrong he had turned to another woman, led her astray and probably mucked up *her* marriage for ever and a day, instead of facing up to things at home. God, what a mess.

'But,' he said, stroking Julia's hair while she sobbed into his shoulder, 'if you haven't even taken the exams yet, what are you crying about? Have they asked you to drop out of the course, or something?'

Julia broke away and thumped him on the chest with her fists. 'There you go. What did I say? You think I'm useless, don't you? You don't think I can do it at all.'

'No, of course not. Sorry. That's not – well, what then?'

Julia adopted a prim expression. 'As a matter of fact, my tutors say I'm doing very well. They think I'll get through the exams OK. They don't see why I shouldn't even start a foundation course next year. But –' her composure broke down once more – 'I can't. I ca-a-a-an't!' She fell against Harvey then, sobbing over the frustration of it all.

'But *why* not?' Harvey was growing exasperated. He almost shook her as he prised her from him, wanting to get some sense out of her. He held her firmly at arm's length. 'Get a hold of yourself, Julia. This is ridiculous. You're not telling me anything at all. How can I help you if I don't know what the matter is?'

Julia gulped and swallowed twice. She was making a desperate effort. 'I can't carry on,' she wailed, 'because I've gone and got pregnant!'

Harvey let her go as though she'd contracted

bubonic plague. So he'd been right about that bloke after all. They *must* have been having an affair. He stood up and began to back away. 'You cow!' he said in a shaky, shocked voice. 'You dirty... little ... cow!' He collided with the wall when he reached it.

'What?' Julia's eyes flew wide open.

'It's no use trying to look innocent. I know what you've been up to.' He jerked his head, set his jaw and admitted it. 'I followed you to college one day.' He sank down the wall clutching his stomach as he went. He actually felt physically sick. Sick with such a seething jealousy – because some other man had been able to impregnate his wife so easily where he had abysmally failed – that it was enough of a blow to wind him.

'So you followed me to college.' Julia shrugged. 'I really don't see ... oh, wait a minute; perhaps I do. You think I've done this with someone else?' She spluttered in feigned amusement, so preposterous did it all seem.

'I saw you there with a man.'

'Harvey, this is ridiculous. The baby's yours and mine!'

'Oh, please –' he rolled his eyes. 'Do me a favour! I'm sorry, Julia, but that simply will not wash.' He laughed a harsh, humourless laugh, shaking his head in disbelief. 'It may have escaped your notice but we've not been able to get you pregnant when we've been going at it like rabbits. So how the hell you expect me to believe all this when we've not even –'

'It happened on August the thirtieth. I'm just over three months gone.'

Now she had his attention. The day in question had been the day before he was made redundant. And he wasn't likely to forget it.

'I did a test the other day,' Julia went on in a matter-of-fact, unexcited tone. 'I got a thingy from the chemist. I didn't really expect anything to come of it. Well, imagine when it came out positive! I couldn't believe my eyes. I went straight out and bought a different one – just to see if it was a mistake. But that one was positive too. I nearly fainted on the floor, I can tell you. And then I went to the doctor. And then –' she suddenly looked away from Harvey – 'I went to see Mum.'

Harvey fought the mounting swell of excitement that was rising up inside him, telling himself he didn't believe a word of it, it was all lies. But supposing – lord, supposing – she was telling the absolute truth?

'You went to see your mother?' he repeated and, alerted by the sudden shame in her eyes, his blood began to run cold.

'I . . . needed to talk it over.' She shrank back a little from him as he took a step towards her.

'Julia . . . you weren't thinking – you couldn't have thought – of not actually having it?'

But it was clear that she had been prepared to at least consider the possibility.

'I'm sorry, Harvey, I know it was wicked of me, and Mum was furious that I hadn't discussed it with you, but I couldn't think straight. All I wanted was to get my certificates. I knew I couldn't get certificates with a baby; I wouldn't have been able to cope. I'm finding it hard enough as it is. Actually –' she took a little breath to boost herself, but apparently it had to be said – 'I'm still not sure I want the baby. Not after all this time. Not now you're old, and out of work, and – everything. And if you don't want it either . . . Harvey?'

Harvey had grabbed her round the waist and was laughing and sobbing and whirling her round the room. Soon she, too, was laughing and crying all over again, but with happiness this time, because he was so happy. She'd never realised before just how much having a child meant to him. And everything was going to be all right.

It was only a tiny advertisement; Katy almost missed it.

'Crap newspaper,' she muttered to herself, and was about to toss it aside when the word 'staff' caught her eye. She brought the print up to within inches of her nose, her heart beginning to thump. This might just be the answer.

Paul fell over a pair of drenched shoes when he came home that evening. Katy's coat was drying on top of a radiator.

'You've been out,' he said in the surprised tone of a warden finding an escaped prisoner back in his cell. Although irritated by her lack of activity, in his heart he could hardly blame her. Without a car, where could she go? There was scarcely anywhere within walking distance that could be of any interest to her, and the weather was utterly foul.

'Yes,' Katy told him, 'I went for a walk. And,' she added quickly, 'I've made you a cheese and red pepper omelette.'

'Good.' Paul smiled. 'Good,' he said again, his smile fading; he was half an hour later than he'd said he would be. The omelette could now be the consistency of leather. But he'd better not say anything about that.

The omelette turned out to be reasonably edible and he managed to clear his plate, with Katy leaning against the boiler watching every mouthful. As soon as he put down his knife and fork, she drew out the only other chair that the small kitchen possessed and sat opposite him.

'Dad,' she said in the tone of one intending to ask a favour, 'I've been thinking.'

'Uh-huh?' He met her eyes.

'Well, I saw this advert,' she began, pulling a piece of crumpled paper from her jeans. Her eyes bright with excitement, she went on to tell him how she'd remembered seeing the place called Arrochar on the map and how she'd wondered whether she could walk that far, and reckoned she could. She had phoned the hotel and the manager suggested an immediate interview. 'And would you believe it, Dad? They offered me the job on the spot!'

'Receptionist in a hotel . . .' Paul mused. It was

hardly what he would have chosen for his daughter. Better than nothing, though. And Katy looked happier than she'd done in a long time, so who was he to put a damper on it? 'I think it's a great idea. How clever of you to get it! Oh – but your hands. What about your hands?'

'That's the best part of all. I won't have to do any typing. Well, maybe the odd menu and so on. Mostly the manager's wife likes to do it. All I have to do is hand out keys and do a bit of bar work. I think I could just about pull a pint. The down side, of course, is that I'll have to do shifts.'

'Ah.' Paul sat back; there had to be a flaw. 'So that means long walks in the dark late at night, doesn't it?' And surely she didn't expect him to wait up all hours with the car?

'Well, that's just it.' Katy hesitated. 'I thought it would be best to live in. Most of the other staff do – and I've been given the option.' She looked at her father worriedly. 'But if you don't want me to leave you on your own . . .'

It struck Paul as she spoke that, for all her faults, he was going to miss her. She had helped to mask the emptiness left by Susannah. From now on he would have to come home to an empty house and a solitary meal, as well as a lonely bed. But it was better for her this way; she had her own life to live.

Katy was chewing her lip. 'I could pop in to see you all the time . . . I'll only be up the road . . . so . . . you don't mind if I take the job – do you, Dad?'

'Of course not. I'll manage all right – I expect.'

'Great! I'm going to ring Mum and tell her. Oh –' she stopped half-way out of the room and looked guilty – 'you don't mind if I phone her, do you?'

She had been running up a big bill phoning her mother lately – much to Paul's surprise. Absence certainly did seem to make the heart grow fonder.

'Of course I don't mind,' he told her. Anything to help keep the family together.

'Would – would you like to speak to her, Dad?' Katy crossed her fingers. When was he going to do something about getting her back?

'Er – not right now, Katy. Not right now.' He wanted to. But he couldn't.

CHAPTER 28

Susannah clucked over the plant stand, mildly cursing Harvey. Trust him to go dashing off to Upper Heyford without the most important item: this plant stand was the very one Mrs Titchmarsh wanted to take down to Cornwall.

Well, there was only one thing for it: she would have to deliver it herself. She would go right now, stay the night at the cottage, and come straight back in the morning. The only snag was that she had doubts about staying at the cottage. Of course, it was her home and she had more right than anyone to stay in it, but she had left it in such unhappy circumstances, she wasn't sure she could face it just yet. But where else was she to go ... unless she went to the Old Dairy? A bit risky, that would be, even with Julia at her mother's.

She was still undecided when she turned off the motorway. Her home or Harvey's? Eeny meeny...

Well, she had better call in on Harvey and let him know where she was, and why she had had to come. Then she would take it from there.

Night had fallen when Susannah drew up

outside the Old Dairy. Julia's car was not in evidence and neither was Harvey's. But a light shone in the porch and the curtained windows glowed from unseen lamps inside.

Susannah sat and looked at the place, still unsure what to do. Supposing Julia came to the door? What should she say to her? A few more minutes ticked by while she rehearsed a suitable excuse to cover that eventuality, then she let herself out of the car.

Nevertheless, it was still a shock when Julia actually answered her knock.

'Oh!' Julia almost squealed with pleased surprise. 'How nice to see you. Do come in. I suppose you wanted to see Harvey, really, didn't you? Harvey, look who's here!' She ushered her visitor into the cottage, drawing the edges of a long silk robe over her large round breasts as she did so, and tightening the sash to secure it. 'You'll have to excuse the mess, I'm afraid.' She giggled into her hand. 'We aren't usually quite this bad – are we, Harvey, love?'

Seeing Julia's state of undress Susannah felt compelled to step inside and shut out the wintry wind, but her instinct was really to run away. One swift glance around the place had told her more than she wanted to know. Clothes were scattered about the floor – which Harvey, looking alternately startled and sheepish in a short striped bathrobe, was frantically trying to scoop up – along with cushions, a fringed throw, and a bottle of

342

champagne. Two champagne flutes were balanced on the hearth, and a sickly looking partly cut cake sat beside them.

Julia giggled again. 'We've been celebrating,' she confided, then added, as though Susannah might disapprove, 'Oh, but I only had a drop.'

'C-celebrating?' Susannah's eyes travelled across to Harvey, but he only got as far as opening his mouth.

'Yes,' Julia answered for him, her face growing pink and coy. She darted a look at Harvey. 'We haven't told anyone yet, but everyone will know soon.' She almost did a little jump of triumph. She actually clapped her hands. 'We're going to have a baby! A baby after all this time. Neither of us can believe it.'

'A baby!' Susannah blurted out. She looked to Harvey for confirmation. 'But – but that's really marvellous,' she managed to say. She thought quickly. She was no actress but clearly she was going to have to give the performance of her life. She couldn't possibly cast any kind of shadow over Julia's obvious joy.

And Harvey's? Yes, he too was patently thrilled beneath his embarrassment, and trying not to look too smug. God, but this was a lot to take on board. Julia, however, saved her from having to do much more than nod and smile and give the odd polite laugh.

'Yes, I know I shouldn't be drinking in my condition –' more giggles – 'but you can't really blame me, can you? Not that I was all that thrilled at first, mind you, because I was up to my ears in exams. But Harvey's going to help me with all that, even when the baby arrives.' She nudged Susannah's arm. 'I doubt whether I'll get a look-in with the baby, actually. Loves little kiddies, does Harvey.'

'Yes – well –' Susannah forced her biggest grin; he'd never shown much interest in Justin. 'I can't say how pleased I am. F-for you both. But I must let you get on with . . . your celebrations. Must dash. I – er – only popped in to ask you, Harvey, if you would deliver the plant stand I've got in the boot of my car. For Mrs Titchmarsh, it is. I'm only here for the night, you see, and Mrs Titchmarsh appears to be out.' She nodded hard as she spoke, hoping Harvey would understand. He probably hadn't the remotest idea that he'd left the plant stand behind.

Harvey stood looking at her, a bundle of clothes in his arms, a bra dangling over one wrist. 'Plant stand? Yes, of course.' But he was plainly mystified.

Susannah made for the door. 'I'll see myself out. And – and congratulations again to you. I hope it all goes well.'

'Susannah! You're back!' Jan's greeting was so warm and genuine that Susannah felt like the prodigal son. She wouldn't have blamed Jan if she had given her the cold shoulder. 'But you're looking a bit peaky. And what a time to turn up.'

344

Susannah glanced at the kitchen clock before slipping off her boots. Had she been driving around for that long? Since Harvey and Julia's news, time had had no meaning. She had simply sat in the car, letting it take her wherever it went while she sorted out her mind.

'I just want a bed for the night,' she told Jan. 'I don't want to put you all out.'

'Nonsense, Susannah, good heavens. This is your home, you know.' Jan had taken Susannah's coat off her back and now she put a hand on her arm, eager to give her good news. 'What do you think? We're selling the farmhouse! And you'll never guess who to.'

'To whom,' Frank corrected her, shambling into the room. He leaned over Susannah and pecked her on the cheek. 'Looking pooped, my girl. What've you been getting up to?'

'I expect she's been working hard – haven't you, dear? Business been going well? But you can tell us all about that in a minute. Let me get you a hot drink.'

Susannah slumped down at the table, afraid she was going to cry. She had been too incredulous up till now to feel anything else about Harvey. But now Jan's and her father's kind concern broke through her frail defences; hurt feelings began to overwhelm her.

'As I was saying before Frank interrupted, we've got rid of the farmhouse at last. Those friends of ours in Poole – you know the ones with the catamaran? Well, their son and daughter-in-law. They're not put off at all by our little tale of woe. They're a bit like that, you know: anything you can do, we can do better, sort of thing. And they've got stacks of money, more to the point. So –' she put a mug of Ovaltine in front of Susannah – 'as soon as it's all settled we'll be able to buy ourselves a modest little place somewhere, won't we, Frank?'

'That's right.' He pulled out a chair and sat down next to Susannah. Years seemed to have dropped from his shoulders since last she'd seen him. 'And we're going to do some private coaching to get a bit of extra money.'

'Yes!' Jan joined them at the table, bringing two more mugs and some biscuits. 'It'll be much more interesting than lolling around in the sun for the rest of our lives.'

'If you say so.' Susannah pulled a disbelieving face, but had to admit they were probably right; if they didn't know what they wanted out of life by now then they never would.

'And how's the world been treating you, Sue? Are you –?' But the phone began to ring then and they all looked at each other, unsure as to who should answer it.

Susannah didn't want to take it, but it was she who ended up doing so.

'It's me,' Harvey whispered down the line. 'I thought you'd be there by now. Julia's gone to sleep.'

So what, was Susannah's reaction, but she was too wound up to say anything.

346

'Look,' he went on and then foundered.

'There's no need to explain,' she told him. She was suddenly tired of it all. There would be no question of his leaving Julia now – if there ever had been. She wasn't even sure she wanted him on a permanent basis anyway. Oh, she was grateful for all that he'd done for her – he'd walked into her life when she needed someone who understood. But his usefulness had surely run out. If he'd stayed around any longer he might well have become a liability eventually. And if that all sounded callous – well, OK, it was. But that made two of them, didn't it?

'I feel I owe you an explanation . . .' he went on.

'I think I can fill in for myself.' She sighed. 'Let's just call it a day, shall we? I'm tired and I'm going to bed.'

'But I feel so bloody –'

'Goodnight, Mr Webb. And goodbye. And good luck with your bundle of joy.'

Jan and Frank gazed at her when she joined them again in the kitchen.

'Paul?' Jan asked hopefully.

Susannah just shook her head. She was saved from having to say any more by the arrival of Simon and Natalie. They had been to the cinema in Bath.

'Mum!' Simon's face lit up – if that were possible; he looked happy enough already. Natalie was blooming too, her eyes bright and alert, her cheeks red from the cold. Susannah had been away from them little over a week, yet she found the change quite remarkable. 'Mum, we tried to phone you earlier on. In London, I mean. We didn't know you were coming here. We wanted to tell you our news.'

'More news? Good heavens.'

'Well, it was Jan's idea, really, though I suppose it's been going through my mind too.' He grinned, a shade embarrassed. 'I've told Dad already, and he's cock-a-hoop.'

'You see,' Natalie burst in, 'Si's going to apply to be a mature student. We've been finding out all about it and we think it can be done.'

'But – but how? What will you live on?' Susannah wanted to know.

'I'm going to support him! When I'm completely well, of course. Oh, I'm sure we'll be able to do it. I'm sure we'll manage somehow.'

'That's wonderful news.' Susannah hugged them both delightedly. All sorts of problems crammed themselves into her doubting mind. They had a hard road ahead of them; Simon's future was by no means assured. For surely never before in history had so many people been so well qualified for so few jobs. But their happiness was infectious, and as Susannah knew all too well, if you believed you could succeed, you would.

'Jan,' she said next day when her step-mother was packing up sandwiches and insisting that Susannah take them back to London with her because she obviously wasn't bothering to feed herself properly. 'Jan, I –' She stopped. She had been about to refuse the sandwiches, even though they were making her mouth water. But then she was struck – forcefully – by the older woman's innate kindness. She couldn't think why it should have come to her at that precise moment, but it did. And she knew that her stupid bitterness had finally burnt itself out.

'What, dear?' Jan went on with her buttering.

Susannah was hanging her head now, scuffing her shoe against the kitchen cupboard like a two-year-old. This wasn't going to be easy. In fact she would sooner put her hand on the chopping board and have Jan lop off her fingers. 'I . . . wanted to apologise. For all the trouble I've been. I know I've been such a pain. Always. Ever since . . . and oh, Jan, I wish I hadn't been. You simply never deserved it.'

'Susannah, don't . . .'

'But I must. I don't know what we'd all have done without you. You've sorted out the kids, and tried to help me, and never said a word about me being horrible to Paul. You've been an absolute saint. And what have I ever done for you? Nothing but get in your hair.'

Jan merely slipped her arm around her, too overcome to speak. They clasped each other in silence, grieving for all the wasted years. And Frank, putting his head round the door just then to find his wife and daughter in an embrace, thought his eyes were playing tricks on him. Closing the door, he crept away, blowing noisily into his handkerchief.

*

'Won't you come home soon?' Jan asked Susannah tearfully, seeing her off in her car. 'I mean, what's to keep you in London? Surely you can do your work here just as easily?'

Susannah reeled out her seat belt and spent a while clicking the fastener. Jan had a point: why couldn't she come home now? Why had she felt so compelled to leave it in the first place? It was hard to see why now, difficult to recapture those feelings of desperation, of needing to be left alone to get on with her work, to succeed. Perhaps it was because she had done just that: she had proved her point. A warm glow began inside her; to think that she was being asked to return. The conquering hero! They wanted her!

But Jan's next words quickly scotched that fond notion. Seeing Susannah's hesitation she added, 'We'll all be gone from here before long.'

She smiled wryly up at Jan. How could she expect any of them to want her now? She had not been there for them when they needed her. 'I'll think about it. I don't know. Am I . . . welcome to come for Christmas?'

To her surprise Jan firmed her lips. 'There's only one place I'd be happy for you to be at Christmastime, and I think you know where that is. It's where you ought to be. With Paul. Oh, Susannah, I wish you'd get back together again.'

Susannah turned on the ignition and selected reverse gear, shaking her head a little. 'I don't know that Paul would want that. I don't think he likes the new me. Go indoors now, Jan, it's getting cold. You'll catch your death out here.'

When she got back to the London house it seemed strangely silent. Huddled inside her coat against the bitter cold she strolled from room to room. In her new work room materials were stacked high. She could no longer count her orders on the fingers of one hand and had had to buy a book in which to keep track of them. She flicked through it: enough work to keep her busy for several months, and a whole world out there for the taking. She ought to be over the moon. Instead she felt dull, and listless, and lonely. 'Doing your own thing' seemed suddenly pointless, if in the process you lost all those you ever cared for. Molly had been right. You had to have someone to share it with: to rejoice in your triumphs and commiserate with your failures. And now she didn't even have Harvey.

Harvey would have snapped her out of this mood. No, that wasn't right: he would never have allowed her to slip into it. He wasn't much of a one for introspection, she didn't think. Though how well had she actually known him? Traits, it had to be said, had already begun to surface after only a few days together: traits that could be amusing or annoying to live with, depending on your mood. At first she had laughed at his happy-go-lucky attitude, finding it a refreshing change after Paul's, but sometimes . . .

Susannah suddenly jumped as though someone

had poked her in the back. She rushed out into the hall, leaped the stairs two at a time and ran to the back bedroom. No!

She clattered back down the stairs, threw open the front door and hurtled down the path. But she knew it wasn't there. The skip. It had been collected. And in it must have been her Uncle Bert's card-table.

She had told Harvey ten times over that it wasn't part of the junk, but junk it had now become. He must have tossed it in without a thought. With as much ease as he had now ditched her. Slowly she went back indoors, put a match to the fire, and gave herself up to a good long howl.

'So what are you doing now, Mum?' Katy asked over the phone. She was showing a keen interest in the mosaic business, which Susannah found a little puzzling; she hadn't cared less about it when she had the opportunity.

Still, Susannah thought, it was nice to be asked. And at least Katy was keeping in touch. She struggled to her feet. She had fallen asleep after her fit of weeping; now she was stiff and cold because the fire had died down to nothing. 'Well –' she raked a hand through her hair – 'I'm about to start on a wall panel. For someone over in Highgate . . .'

'But you're not going to be working over Christmas?'

'Christmas? Well . . . I might be.' Nothing had really been settled.

'You can't spend Christmas alone!' Katy was clearly horrified. 'Look, why don't you come up here? There are things going on in the hotel; it should be quite a hoot.'

A shudder ran through Susannah. For carefree youth, perhaps. 'Oh, I don't think it's quite my scene . . .'

'Well, there are a lot of old dears here, too.'

'Thanks.'

'They come up by the coach load, you know. Oh, please come and stay here for Christmas. I'll book you a room right now. Whatever you do don't drive, though. Get a seat on a plane before they're all gone.'

'Katy, I'm really not sure . . .' It was easy to see through Katy's ploy: there was no doubt some sort of scheme afoot for getting her together with Paul, and she wasn't sure she was ready for that. It would be useless going back to their old ways, and even if he admitted the need for change she didn't feel strong enough at the moment to hammer out a new set of rules with him.

And yet to be alone at Christmas . . . well, that seemed like the end of the world.

CHAPTER 29

The girl on the reception desk was a stranger; Susannah had expected to find Katy there. Then she realised, as the girl looked up, that it *was* Katy. She was wearing a smart white blouse and a navy pencil-slim skirt. And her hair had been neatly cut, although it was still unnaturally blonde.

'Mum!' Katy shrieked, and flung herself across the counter for a hug. Then she walked round the desk properly and grabbed her mother by the hand. 'Look at the tree, isn't it lovely? And I helped put up those decorations. Did you hire a car from the airport? I've fiddled you a room with a view. Can you stay until New Year's over? That's going to be the best part of all.'

Up in her chilly room overlooking the loch, Susannah wished she had not come. It was good to see Katy happy again, but the girl's ebullience and renewed joy in life only emphasised Susannah's own loneliness. It wasn't much help, either, that when Katy wasn't rushed off her feet doing her job, she was busy socialising. It was a big hotel and there were a number of room maids, waiters and waitresses all roughly Katy's age, who were obviously much better company for her than her mother. Not that Susannah minded that, of course – she was pleased for Katy – but she herself felt like a spare part, an oddball, an intruder. Nobody needed her.

Why was it, Susannah wondered as she gazed across the loch with unseeing eyes, that it was hell to be needed when you didn't want to be needed, and hell not to be needed when you did?

She needed someone. She ached for someone. Every guest at the hotel had someone, or so it seemed. Someone to walk and talk with. Someone to sit at the dinner table with. How conspicuous you could feel on your own! Mealtimes were so painful that she would have preferred to stay in her room, and only made an effort to go down to the cavernous, draughty dining room for Katy's sake. Not that Katy could eat with her, but she would have worried had her mother pined away upstairs.

Sometimes a kind, well-meaning soul would spot Susannah making for her lonely table by the window (Katy's influence again) and draw her into their group. Susannah couldn't decide which was worse: having to pretend she enjoyed her own company or having to exert herself to converse with total strangers. It was at the end of evenings like those that thoughts of her pretty little cottage in Upper Heyford flooded her mind; of Justin's first Christmas, raucous laughter, and family jokes round the log fire. She would crawl into bed, her heart breaking, furious because she had only herself to blame.

But on Christmas Eve it appeared that she would be forced into sharing her own table. It had been set for two, instead of the usual one, and she nearly bolted away. If it hadn't been for the young waiter on her heels, escorting her to her seat, she would have done. Perhaps, she thought, sinking hopefully on to the hard seat, Katy was going to be allowed to eat with her for once, instead of having to go to the cubby-hole off the kitchens where staff usually snatched what they could. She had almost relaxed, having convinced herself she was right and that Katy would be with her soon, when a pair of dark trousers came to her attention out of the corner of her eye. Then she nearly knocked over her jug of water.

'Mind if I join you?' It was Paul, and he didn't wait for her answer. He pulled out the other chair and planted himself down on it. But he avoided meeting her eyes.

Susannah slumped with her head in her hands. Since he hadn't shown up so far, she had decided that nothing had been further from Katy's mind than an attempt at reuniting her parents. Susannah had been on tenterhooks at first, knowing that he was only a few miles down the road and could appear at any moment. And now he had, when she least expected it.

'This was Katy's idea,' she said, when the shock

of his arrival had ebbed. 'I guessed she might try something like this.'

'Actually, it was mine.' His voice was quiet and reasonable; the harsh tones of the previous weeks, she was relieved to note, had gone. 'I thought it was time we talked.'

She made her tone matter-of-fact too. 'About our bank account and so on, I suppose.' They had both been dipping into their joint account – Uncle Bert's estate was still being sorted and the five hundred pounds hadn't yet materialised – but it was a convenience that couldn't go on for ever. If Paul wanted a proper separation there were all sorts of things to go into. If. But surely he wasn't going to broach such a subject on Christmas Eve?

In the background a recording of 'Once in Royal David's City' had started up. Susannah hoped she would be able to clear the lump it always brought to her throat before she next had to speak.

'No,' Paul said firmly, snapping the big red menu shut, 'I didn't want to talk to you about money.'

'Well . . . what then?' She took a sip of water.

'I think we should talk about us. Don't you? It's what we should have done in the first place. Then perhaps we wouldn't be where we are.' He made a window-wiping gesture in the air. 'And I'm not blaming you for that, Susannah. I know I'm very much at fault.'

The waiter came for their order, and while Paul was giving it Susannah stared at him over the single candle. There were hollows in his cheeks and under his eyes. He looked as though he had really suffered over their split. She drew her gaze away. And that was without him knowing anything about the Harvey business. Pray God he would never know about it. *She* would never tell him; he'd been hurt badly enough.

'I know I wouldn't discuss things in the past,' he went on, seeing that Susannah seemed incapable of speech, 'for the simple reason I didn't want to. I didn't want things to have to change, you see. Selfish, I suppose you'd say.'

'No, Paul –'

'Of course, they had changed, anyway,' he hurried on. 'With the children leaving the nest they had to change. But I wasn't ready to accept it. It's funny –' he attempted a little laugh – 'I always thought it was women who were supposed to suffer from the empty nest syndrome, and men who got the mid-life crisis. In our case it seems to have happened the other way round. You know, I really missed Katy and Simon when they left. Life seemed so flat all of a sudden, and sort of – I don't know – finished, without them. I was thrilled when they had to come back.'

He took her hand. 'Does that sound really awful of me? I suppose it does. And I couldn't understand why you didn't feel the same.'

'You thought me a wicked mother.'

'I did. Heaven help me, I did. But I'm the one who's not such a good parent. I should have been able to let them go, not try to over-protect them.'

'Don't be so hard on yourself.' She placed her other hand over his. It was breaking her up, seeing him castigate himself like this. 'You've been a wonderful dad, and don't let anyone tell you differently. Anyway, they're both doing fine now, aren't they? I suppose you've heard about Simon and Natalie? Oh, I don't suppose we've heard the last of any of them, not by a long chalk. And that's just the way I want it, in spite of what you might think.'

'Really?' Paul's face lit up with a smile.

'Yes! I don't wish them right out of my life; I never did. All I ever wanted was to be treated as an individual again, and not just somebody's mum. Somebody with needs and desires of her own, and to be allowed the chance to fulfil them.'

Paul was nodding his head. 'I should have listened more to you. You were right to want to do your own thing. But that was the very reason why I behaved like a prize pillock. I didn't know why at that time; it was Katy who brought it all home to me.'

'Katy?'

'Yes, Katy. Perhaps she's more in touch with her emotions, as current jargon would have it. She had the insight to realise that she was rather jealous of you, which was why she adopted that sullen attitude of hers. And that made me see it was just the same with me. Don't look so surprised. I was jealous too. Because you'd found something interesting to fill the rest of your life, whereas I had

359

nothing in particular to look forward to. I didn't think I would even have a job for much longer at that stage, and the thought half scared me to death.'

'Poor Paul.' He looked so guilty. But wasn't she guiltier than he? At least he hadn't gone off with another woman. 'Retirement's going to come to you one day, you know. You have to prepare for it.'

'I know, I know, I'll be working on it.' He smiled. 'I've been given a couple of years' grace.'

Susannah shook her head, trying to sort out her thoughts. 'I feel I've only just started in life. I can't seem to think of all this as the final years of our lives.'

'And that's the way it should be.' He studied her as she took a sip of wine. 'Sue . . . couldn't you . . . wouldn't you like to have a craft shop one day – one that was attached to your studio, perhaps? I've seen potteries and places like that all over the place up here. But it wouldn't really matter where it was. And when I finally retire I could run it for you. Couldn't I? While you got on with –'

Their eyes met across the table, suddenly wary, suddenly shy. 'O Come All Ye Faithful' started softly above their heads. Not that one, Susannah thought desperately, getting choked all over again.

'Sorry,' Paul muttered eventually, loosening his collar a little, 'I can't seem to get used to the idea of . . .'

'Of not being together for ever? Me neither.'

'Seems a waste, somehow, chucking it all away.'

'Is there something the matter, Sir – Madam?'

The waiter had sidled up. He indicated the untouched plates; they hadn't even noticed them. 'I – er – couldn't help hearing you talking of throwing it away. If you'd like to order something else?'

'Oh –' Susannah managed to giggle past the constriction in her throat. 'I don't think we want to do that.' She looked Paul straight in the eye with a message only for him. 'What do you say, Paul? Shall we hang on to what we've got? It really hasn't been all that bad.'

Paul smiled broadly and raised his glass to hers. 'No, not at all bad, really. Let's give it another try.'

'To us,' they murmured together, leaving a confused waiter to scratch his head and silently drift away.

If you enjoyed this book, you might also enjoy *The Company of Strangers* by Eileen Campbell.

The Company of Strangers

It's the summer of 1959 and eleven-year-old Ellie Fairbairn is exiled to the tiny Highland village of Inchbrae, to stay with a grandmother she hardly knows, after her mother's nervous breakdown. Her grandmother Dot is decidedly eccentric: partial to more than the odd dram of whisky, she's a passionate fan of Billie Holiday and none too keen on housework. Worst of all, she's never been married – and once Ellie discovers this shameful secret she's determined to find her missing grandfather and make her family complete.

Ellie is drawn into Inchbrae; its lifelong friendships, its half-buried secrets and its larger-than-life characters. There's Rita, torn between her love for Pat the local butcher and her dreams of a more glamorous lifestyle; Pat's son Joseph, who plans to run away to find his real mother; Dreep the cultured wino; and Hooligan, the battered old mongrel stray who captures Ellie's heart. And when Johnny Starling comes to stay, it seems he holds the key to Dot's past and Ellie's future.

Eileen Campbell brilliantly evokes a young girl's awakening to the mysteries of adulthood in a heart-warming novel about the power of friendship, the pain of loss and the indomitable spirit of a Highland community.

If you would like to order a copy of *The Company of Strangers*, please turn the page for details.

If you would like to be put on a mailing list to receive regular updates on further new books from Fourth Estate, please send your name and address on a postcard to Puppies Are For Life, Press Office, Fourth Estate, 6 Salem Road, London W2 4BU.

To order a copy of *The Company of Strangers*, price £5.99, please complete the form below. Post and packing is free in the UK. Overseas customers please allow £1.00 per book for post and packing.

Please send me ... copy/copies (insert number required) of *The Company of Strangers* by Eileen Campbell.

Name ....

Address ....

....

....

You may also use this form to order any other books published by Fourth Estate. Please indicate the number of copies required and quote the author and title.

Send this page with a cheque/eurocheque/postal order (sterling only), made payable to Book Service by Post, to:

    Fourth Estate Books,
    Book Service By Post,
    PO Box 29, Douglas
    I-O-M, IM99 1BQ

Alternatively you can pay by Access, Visa, or Mastercard: please complete the following details and return this page to the address above.

Card number ....

Expiry date ....

Signature ....

You can also order by phone, tel: 01624 675137; by fax: 01624 670923; or by e-mail: bookshop@enterprise.net

Please allow 28 days for delivery. Please tick box if you do not wish to receive any additional information. ❑

Prices and availability subject to change without notice.